Redemption

by

Katja Desjarlais

The Haunt Vault, Book 3

Redemption

Cover Art by *Diana Carlile*

The Wild Rose Press, Inc.
PO Box 708
Adams Basin, NY 14410-0708
Visit us at www.thewildrosepress.com

Publishing History
First Edition, 2021
Trade Paperback ISBN 978-1-5092-3491-2
Digital ISBN 978-1-5092-3492-9

The Haunt Vault, Book 3
Published in the United States of America

Her jaw set, Bianca completed the unpacking of her bags and reverently spread the contents of her boxes on the bed.

"Those edges need work."

With a sigh, she turned toward the small balcony off her bedroom. Jagger stood against the rail, his arms crossed nonchalantly over his chest despite the impending rise of the sun.

"Where are the others?" she asked through the glass, unlatching the sliding door.

"I doubled back and dropped them off in Lincoln," he replied, fixing his ice-blue eyes on hers. "We're working under the assumption you plan to deal with the mob yourself."

"You assume correctly," she said, motioning for him to enter. He strode past her, his normally full lips taut and his lilting hum replaced with a staccato tune. He continued into the living room, assessing the large windows disdainfully.

"That'll hurt in ten minutes," he stated, reclining on the burgundy sofa.

She stood over him, blue eyes narrowing. "Then you should probably seek shelter."

"I've been ordered by Nichol to ensure you do nothing stupid until we've reached an agreement," he said casually. "Nine minutes."

She stood her ground. "Nothing good will come from you igniting my Queen Anne."

Dedication

Dedicated to my Uncle Otto

Chapter One

"Absolutely stunning."

Jagger took his time to examine the beauty in his hands, knowing he would be gone from the haunt for at least two weeks and the masterpiece before him would be tarnished by his brethren before his return. Pouring a small drop of wax on the spine, he watched it slide unimpeded toward the belly, pooling at the tip.

Dominic leaned back in his chair, tapped him on the shoulder, and crossed his arms impatiently. "How long do you intend to drool over those? Because moonlight's a-wasting and I have a date."

He selected a microfiber cloth from his arsenal and slowly rubbed the renaissance wax into the carbon blade. "The last batch I left in your care was rusted to shit, blunt, and nicked all to hell," he stated with exasperation. "If you use that abomination of a sharpener on my blades again, I will test their efficacy on your ass. Understand? The wax protects the steel when exposed to liquid. I want it applied after every usage. The same goes with the sharpening stone. Wet it first."

He pulled the cover off a stack of magazines on his workbench. "If the blade cannot do this," he said, slicing a clean ribbon effortlessly from the glossy paper, "it isn't sharp enough."

Dom ran his hand through his hair and groaned. "Fine, I'll do it. But there was nothing wrong with the last set of blades."

Fixing a hard stare on his youngest brother, he reached to the bottom drawer of his workbench. "This," he growled, tossing a butterfly knife onto the table, "looks like it's been chewed on by a garbage disposal and left in the rain for a month."

Picking up the offending weapon, Dom flipped the blade over in his hands. "I can't see anything wrong with it."

"And that's why you're here now. Because you're a moron."

As the rusted butterfly knife flew past his shoulder and lodged into the mounted wood blocks on the far wall, he flashed his fangs at Dom's challenge. He collected the rest of the damaged weaponry from the drawer and passed the pile to Dominic. "Good luck with your new practice blades," he said, neatly assembling the newest arrivals. "Deepest, truest hit wins."

Dom eyed the casualties of his sloppy handiwork. One by one they tossed their blades at the wall, heckling each other's skills until the final blade embedded in the wood.

"Fuck," Dom moaned as they went in for assessment. "Fine. I'll wax. And buff. And use the wet stone. I may even sing to them like you do."

He grinned, removing the assorted knives from the wall. "You can start tonight. I have to leave within the hour or risk getting caught in the sun before I reach Lincoln."

"Did Nichol decide who your ride mate is yet?" Dom asked as he settled himself into Jagger's chair.

"Boy. Apparently he's still clinging to Audra, and

Mick's patience has run out," he replied, packing a small tote of various weapons and cleaning supplies.

"I can understand why Mickey's on edge," Dominic mused. "That old fucker could snap at any time and go caveman on Audra. If he was sniffing around Moll, I'd fucking move across the country with her."

He nodded distractedly, actively repressing his own experience as a connected vamp. "The break may be good for both Mickey and Boy. A territorial dispute over a woman isn't something we need to be adding to our plates right now. No sex in my workroom. Remember to wet the stone before you use it."

With the tote bag on his shoulder, he left Dominic alone to hone his weapon care skills. Despite the inattention to detail the young vamp had exhibited on his first foray into his position, he was confident Dom would put forth more effort during this round.

If he didn't, he would be sparring with nothing but his own ill-maintained weapons for a year.

He moved swiftly through the stairwell into the topside garage. The haunt's *de facto* haunt leader, Nichol, was lying awkwardly across the driver's side of one of the new vehicles, his legs sprawled out the door. After much discussion, Nichol had made the executive decision to purchase a fleet of new four-by-fours for the haunt, enough to outfit each vampire, with two additional units for Molly and Audra. Despite Molly's pleas for cherry red, Nichol's choice to stick with a flat black had won out.

"Am I good to load up?" he asked, accepting a small screwdriver from Nichol's hand.

The eldest brother twisted himself out of his

position, a scowl on his face. "All serial numbers have been removed. Insurance and licensing are in the glove box. The GPS and tracker are functional, but I'm having an issue with the Bluetooth mount. It's on, but loose. If you need to be incognito, running lights can be deactivated here." Nic demonstrated, his hand twitching as it neared the improperly installed mount before he knelt down to pat the underside of the vehicle, keeping his face angled toward him. "I affixed a spare key here. The antennae should be good but notify me immediately if one snaps. They manage the global positioning and amp cell service. Their signals are scrambled and feed directly to the com room, so if you run into any problems, we'll know your precise location. I also left a few burner phones in the front seat for you. Questions?"

He held out his hand.

"Right," Nichol muttered, passing over the keys.

He assessed the neatly stacked baggage in the hatch before adding his own. Boy arrived soon after, the small leather backpack looking strange against his large form. The mute vampire was not of their bloodline, his presence in the periphery of the Kaius haunt both a bone of contention and a mystery their leader had refused to address over the centuries.

Jagger didn't mind him. Intimidating as the old vamp was, Boy's muteness was a reluctant complement to his own deafness, and both understood silence in a way the other hauntmates couldn't.

As he and Boy settled into the front seats, Audra tore up the stairs, her cheeks pink with the exertion. She halted at the passenger door, her hands on her hips.

"You don't have to go," she said to Boy, her eyes

flashing with anger. "Mick doesn't get to dictate where you do or do not go."

Boy avoided her gaze, choosing instead to lock his blank stare on her hips. Mickey appeared at Audra's side, his muscles tensed. "Audra. Leave it."

Jagger sat back, knowing the argument would likely continue until Justine finally arrived. Boy, the source of several disagreements between the haunt's newest couple, refused to look at either one.

"No, Mick," Audra barked, "I will NOT leave it. You and Nichol made the decision for him without once asking if he was okay with it. How do you know this isn't a huge inconvenience for him?"

Mick met his eyes. "Sorry, man. She's on a bit of a rampage about this," he grumbled.

"Of course I am," the woman seethed, cat eyes narrowing. "Boy isn't your servant, and it's about time everybody stopped treating him like one."

"Maybe I'd be more open to the idea if he wasn't currently staring at my woman's tits," Mick yelled, his temper flaring.

"My. Woman's. Tits," Audra echoed, a brow cocked.

Nichol flicked a hand in his view to pull his attention, mouthing his opinion silently. *He needs to learn when to keep his trap shut.*

Grinning at his eldest brother, he closed his door, put the key in the ignition, and started the vehicle up. Boy eased his own door closed, leaving Audra and Mickey to their quarrel. As the garage door lifted, a frazzled Justine hopped into the back seat with a small bag.

"Is that all you're bringing?" he asked, unable to

recollect seeing any feminine luggage in the hatch.

She sat a little higher, ensuring her lips were visible in the rearview mirror. "Rhys said my new master is extremely wealthy." She smirked. "I need a new wardrobe."

He shook his head and pulled out of the garage, giving a quick wave to Nichol, and stifling a laugh as he watched Mick's slouched form look suitably abashed while Audra gestured angrily at the departing car. He estimated her ire would last no longer than dawn, at which point Mickey would reap what he happily referred to as "make-up sex."

The uneventful drive passed quickly, the night void of traffic as he pushed the new four-by-four's abilities on the open road. With Boy's silence, he was able to relax and focus on the feel of the vehicle, adapting to the unique handling and sensitivities without keeping one eye on the lips of his hauntmate.

Justine sat behind him in the back seat, her fingers grazing his neck, caressing his hair softly as she relaxed. Coached by his older brother Rhys, Justine was a trained Tender, a courtesan in vampire society. She, like hundreds before her, was molded and educated to survive and thrive as companions for haunts across the globe.

It was a lucrative trade in both wealth and reputation over the centuries, but the tides of human and vampire politics were shifting, and Justine was likely one of the last Tenders who would pass through Rhys's rooms.

Her hands soothed him now as they had numerous times over the past year, her manicured nails scratching lightly across his spine before flitting along his shoulders.

"*I can hold on to her for another few months if you want,*" Rhys offered, monitoring the bidding war erupting over Justine. "*It will only drive her price up.*"

He studied the edge of the stiletto blade he was sharpening. "*Whatever you need to do is fine. All I ask is you make sure she goes to someone worthy. Justine is too sweet to be wasted on some young fucker with a rich daddy.*"

Rhys pursed his lips. "*That eliminates two of these bastards.*" He scanned through his texts. "*I'll toss the final bid to William Conall.*"

With the blade meeting his intense scrutiny, he closed it up and set it back on his workbench. "*What do you know of him?*"

"*Just over two hundred. Made a killing in oil and chose to hole up in Minnesota for what he calls his 'retirement.' Justine would be his first Tender, if he mans up and ponies up. He has the reputation of being quiet, and he lacks the aggression of the coastal vamps,*" Rhys said. "*Justine would be cold as fuck in Minnesota but would want for nothing for the rest of her life.*"

He nodded. "*If you can make that work, I'd appreciate it.*"

The vehicle cruised into Lincoln and into the driveway of the Former Tender's house, the porch light illuminating both the entrance and the petite blonde smiling from the stoop. Boy was quick to exit, unloading the contents of the hatch on the ground as Justine bounced over to greet Bianca.

Throwing the baggage onto their broad shoulders, Jagger and Boy joined the women in the opulent house, bypassing the tour Justine was receiving in favor of depositing the luggage into the basement dwelling. They arrived topside just as Bee was placing heated carafes and glasses on the table.

"Jagger, honey," she said, placing a hand on his arm to hold his attention, "Justine is going to shower and meet you downstairs. Poor girl is exhausted!" Bianca smiled fondly. "It's so exciting for her, knowing she's only hours away from reentering the big, bright world." With expert movements, the stunning blonde poured two glasses of blood from the carafes. Boy received his hesitantly, pulling it close to his body with a nod.

Bee held a glass to him. "I spoke with Nichol tonight, and he told me you three could spare an extra night here to help me with a few things I need done. I do so despise having unknown workmen stomping through here at all hours of the day whenever I need assistance. Would you oblige?"

He accepted the offered glass of A negative. "Of course. I'll text Nichol before dawn and let him know it works. What do you need done?"

Jumping to her feet, Bianca motioned for him and Boy to follow her through the house and into the manicured yard. Her airy pink shift dress fluttered between her thighs as she walked, making the small blonde appear more like a fairy than a human. "The placement of the gazebo is blocking my view of the gardens from the deck. I want it moved four feet to the left so I can see my wisteria when I take tea outside."

He smiled wryly. "You want that monstrosity disassembled, moved, and reassembled in one night?"

Bee's hands flew to her slim hips. "It is NOT a

monstrosity. And I know you strapping brutes will be able to move it without tearing it apart. Boy, honey, you could do it, right? It will need a coat or two of paint as well. Though I suppose it can wait until spring. And sod laid so I don't have to look at a horrific barren patch in my sanctuary."

He watched in amusement as Bianca turned her charms on the mute vampire, her five-foot-two stature appearing positively diminutive next to the hulking vamp. Boy inched past her to assess the structure, shaking the posts, and running his hands along the base. Bee disappeared into the house, returning quickly with a damp towel.

"Let me wash the dirt off, honey," she crooned to Boy, who stood awkwardly before her as she carefully cleaned his hands. Bianca took her time, seemingly oblivious to the discomfort she was causing him. When she finished, Boy shoved his hands into his pockets and angled his body toward the expanse of the yard. Bee winked at Jagg. "Okay, you two. Bedtime. You have a busy night tomorrow. I'll have the paint and replacement sod delivered this afternoon. Now chop chop!"

Chapter Two

Bianca closed the bedroom door, leaving Jagger alone in his suite, his constant humming growing quieter as she collected her guests' laundry and padded up the stairs into her living quarters to rush through her daily chores. Once she was satisfied with the shine of her crystal, the sheen of the hardwood, and the fresh scent of the dryer sheets, she taped a quick note on the front door for the delivery men, scanned the streets for unwanted visitors, and hopped into the shower. She was anxious to get to bed, her underused body deliciously aching from her early morning romp.

She rinsed the last of the shampoo from her hair and turned off the shower. Wrapping herself in a large towel, she walked quickly to her bedroom, checking her phone before she crawled into bed. Her sensitized skin felt every wrinkle in the sheets, her body exhausted and pleasantly relaxed.

The door to his suite was unlocked, its occupant either feeling very secure in his strength or hopeful for her visit. She slid into the room, staying tight to the wall as her eyes adjusted to the darkness. When he stalked toward her, Bee assumed the customary Tender position of servitude, her hands clasped at her back and head tilted to expose her vein. His fingers danced over her face, caressing her forehead, her cheekbones, and her lips over and over, reacquainting himself with her features. He ran his hands down her arms, pulling her forward slowly to provide him with enough room to circle her, to view her from any angle he desired.

He ghosted his fingertips over every inch of her skin, and she stilled, willingly at the whim of the predator grazing against her. She focused on her breathing, detaching herself from the sensations he was stirring with his attentions. When his deft fingers finally tugged at the zipper of her dress, she felt her body tighten in anticipation. The pink shift fell to the floor, providing him with more skin to tease and tantalize as he circled her, tracing patterns on her spine and rib cage.

Tick. Tick.

The familiarity of the dance was welcoming, her body eagerly recalling the intense experience from decades past. Her breathing hitched slightly when her bra joined her dress, the cool basement air skimming her taut nipples. When his fingers grazed the pebbled peaks, she drew a deep breath, pushing her breasts against the friction she desperately craved. The touch withdrew instantly, earning a huff of both humor and frustration from her.

When he finally resumed the gentle caresses, she doubled her efforts to remain motionless, her body screaming to be touched as her mind sought to provide a brief respite for the melancholy vampire, just as she'd done dozens of years earlier. So she stilled for him, losing herself in his desires.

She stretched forward and rolled onto her back, her muscles aching. "Get some rest, honey," she said softly, standing to dress. The vampire's fangs peeked from behind his lips and she sighed, offering her wrist. "I'd forgotten this part," she whispered. "I offer, you refuse. I insist, you walk away. I have laundry to do, honey, so I'll do the walking away this time."

He approached her hesitantly, zipping her dress for her before fixating his defeated blank stare at the back wall. She planted a quick kiss on his bicep as she opened the door, noting the twitch of the muscle as she did so.

Then, as she had done during her time at the Kaius haunt, she slipped unseen from Boy's room.

****

It was easy for Jagger to forget the immense strength Boy had when he skulked through the haunt, his empty blue eyes boring into the walls or floors. The tilt of the gazebo as they moved it across the lawn was decidedly in Jagg's favor, his hauntmate taking on the brunt of both the weight and the balance of the atrocious structure. With his back to Bianca, he followed Boy's lead while he carefully maneuvered the cedar pavilion into place.

He stepped back, motioning to the handiwork for Bianca and Justine's approval. "Yes?"

Bee frowned, her delicate brows knotting across her tanned forehead. "I would prefer the entrance to be angled more toward the deck."

"Of course you would," he muttered, hefting the heavy beast back up and shuffling its angle over three feet. He glanced over at the women, mittens adorning their hands in the cool night air. "Why don't you head inside? We can toss the sod down and be in shortly."

Justine waved cheerily as Bianca led her inside. He and Boy made quick work of the lawn repair, tossing a few shovels of soil onto the uneven ground, and stomping the edges to create a seamless grass field he was certain wouldn't survive the harsh winter.

With a few hours until dawn, he was anxious to have some time to touch base with his haunt and, more importantly, with the vamp in charge of his weapons room. He scrubbed the dirt from his hands in the kitchen, careful to avoid splashing mud onto the pristine counters. Bee was quick to his side, offering a towel.

"How is Mikhail doing?" she asked, glancing toward the back door.

"Good," he said with a grin. "Audra is keeping him in line."

She laughed, her eyes continuing to dart toward the exit. "Would I be right in assuming Boy's unexpected presence here was a deliberate decision?"

Leaning against the counter, he crossed his arms. Unlike his brethren, he had not been living at the haunt during her training and had no personal history with the Tender. He cocked a brow, refusing to answer. She was undeterred as she began collecting carafes and glasses from the hutch.

"Boy is quite taken with Audra," she chattered. "It was obvious when you came through a few weeks ago. I can't imagine it's going over well with Mikhail. Perhaps an extended break would be good for Boy. And you. My home is always open." She motioned toward a set of scissors on the counter behind him. He passed them over, his expression blank. Haunt business was precisely that. Regardless of the accuracy of her meanderings.

"Will you two be coming through here on your way back?" she inquired as she expertly snipped the corner of a bag of O positive and poured it into a crystal decanter. "Rhys had initially mentioned he would spend a few nights here."

He plugged in the warmer, impressed with the fluttery woman's steady hand. "We may take a night on the way back if it works for you. Until Justine is settled, I don't know the timeline."

She gently gripped his forearm, her large blue eyes meeting his. "If you could spare it, a few nights would be greatly appreciated."

"More home improvement work?" he asked, his expression flat.

She gave his arm a squeeze and smiled. "Some. Nothing major. I could just use a little help…" Her eyes flicked to the door as Boy slinked in, and she flittered over to the vamp, guiding him to the sink to wash up and professing her gratitude for his hard work. Boy accepted the pampering with resignation, his broad shoulders slumped as warm water and soap was lathered onto his hands. "We should move into the living room." Bee smiled cheerfully. "I'll set us up. You two must be starving."

Justine was quick to curl up beside Jagg, nuzzling against his pectorals as he wrapped an arm over her shoulders. The Tender had become weepy when she woke in his bed, her blonde hair tangled on his pillow as she wallowed in her fears of her new master.

"What if I'm a disappointment?" she whimpered, her dark blue eyes wide. "What if he realizes I'm not worth what he paid?"

He chuckled, putting his arms behind his head. "You'll be fine. Rhys assured me William Conall is kind, wealthy, and very eager to possess you. He's been preparing for your arrival since his bid was accepted, and he's been texting Rhys almost hourly with questions regarding your likes and dislikes. I think he's more afraid of not measuring up to you than you should be of not measuring up to him."

Justine leaned over him, her ample bosom grazing his bare chest. "What if I'm not ready? Amy was in the rotation so much longer than me. What if I screw this up? What if he's violent or mean?"

With the roll of his eyes, he reached up to brush a stray strand from her damp cheeks. "Amy was around longer than she should have been. You're ready. Conall will take one look at you, and anything you could possibly screw up will be forgiven. Just give him your wide-eyed pout, and he'll be as indulgent with you as I have been. Boy has a link to you and will know if anything is wrong. If it makes you feel better, I'll upload my number into your phone, and should you ever feel in danger, you can call me."

With a nod, Justine settled on to him, her warm heartbeat pounding against him. He reached out for Justine's phone and quickly entered his direct number before checking his own phone and firing off a few messages to Dominic and Rhys.

It was going to be a shame to lose Justine.

She was highly intuitive and adapted easily to the different hauntmate dispositions without missing a beat. Once he was made aware of her pending sale, he had watched her closely, studying her interactions with his brethren. The cantankerous Nichol was never offered more than a wrist as she snuck silently into the communication room at dusk. Mick was no longer more than a polite smile as she collected his laundry during Audra's absence, subtly cleaning his room as she did so to save Mick from his lover's chastisements.

Rhys was flirted with incessantly, his ego stroked through her over-the-top compliments as she fussed over his hair and made pouty requests for assistance she assured him only he could fulfill. Her respect for Dominic's connected mate, Molly, kept her far from him, their passing interactions little more than good-natured ribbing.

Justine switched to a sex kitten with Louis, her whispered innuendos eliciting knowing smirks from the vamp as he led her toward his bunk. According to Rhys, Kaius was met with reverence and quiet awe, his mere presence bringing out the refined Tender Rhys had created. She would stop her tasks when he passed, tilting her neck in offering and avoiding his unblinking gaze unless directed otherwise.

Boy was, understandably, avoided at all costs. He had yet to see a Tender pass through the haunt who did not actively elude the sullen vampire, his physical presence often raising their heartbeats in fear and uncertainty.

Audra didn't count.

Apparently Bianca didn't either.

A chameleon, he mused as her soft fingers began trailing across his bare hips.

With him, Justine was quietly attentive. Her face was consistently turned toward his, so he was able to read her lips with ease. She knew when to talk, when he required silence, and when he needed little more than the warmth of her body pressed against him. She would spend hours in the weapons room, watching him as he honed the blades and ogling him when he practiced with them.

The first time he had brought his hand to her throat during sex, she had embraced it, placing his fingers along her vocal cords so he could feel the vibrations as she moaned under him. All other Tenders instinctively tensed. Although he could comprehend their hesitation, it always threw him off. Their distrust dredged up thoughts and regrets he despised and deserved.

Justine had sheltered him from his memories as much as she could, easing him away from his self-loathing with the warmth of her hands and beating of her heart. Conall was a lucky bastard.

He was almost sad to see her go.

****

Boy stood at the front window, peering into the darkness while the women chattered about movies Bee was insisting Justine had to watch once she settled in her new home.

"Make sure to add an Internet streaming service to your requests," Bianca advised. "With a limited household staff, you could find yourself with a lot of downtime. There's nothing wrong with indulging in a little series binge-watching, providing you maintain your top effort on your duties."

Justine listened in rapture, her admiration for the seasoned Tender apparent in both her attention and her expressions. "I don't think I should be making demands of him," she said, biting her lower lip. "He may not take to it well."

"Nonsense!" Bianca laughed. "William is an absolute gentleman. My Johan and I spent much time with him over the years. He's a pussycat with women. Indulgent to a fault, I dare say." She leaned forward with a conspiratorial gleam in her eye. "I once complimented him on a rare Masaccio he had squirreled away in a back hall. It now hangs in my bedroom."

Justine grinned, her fears over her new master quickly dissipating. Jagger squeezed her shoulder softly, grateful for Bianca's reassurances for both himself and Justine. Bianca continued to expound tales of Conall's lavish purchases, her speech peppered with comments about "those brutish Kaius boys and their barren haunt." He merely smirked, enjoying the relaxed atmosphere Bee created so easily until the tension in Boy's stance caught his eye.

Chapter Three

Rhys lay back on the sofa, his long arm tucked behind his head as he texted with Jagger. His newest trainees stood motionless in the corner of the room, their heads tilted and hands clasped behind their backs in submission.

It was fucking annoying.

"Why don't you ladies join the others in the common room?" he muttered distractedly, his attention on his phone. "We can work on your posture before dawn."

"Yes, master," they chimed simultaneously, obeying without question. He eyed the pair as they strode out of the room. A concert violinist and a nurse. So much intelligence and talent wrapped in beautiful packages. Beautiful, boring packages. With a groan, he fired off another text to Jagg and awaited the ringing of his phone.

"Bee, baby," he purred when the call came in. "How's my favorite girl?"

"Safe and sound with my barbaric protectors, darling," she replied lightly.

"You've been holding out on me, angel," he chastised, adding a disapproving growl for effect. "We agreed you would come to Nichol or me if things began heating up there."

Bianca sighed. "It isn't as big an issue as Boy and Jagger are implying. I've had three, maybe four nights

19

when the group came a little closer, but it truly isn't anything to worry about."

He ran a hand through his hair. "Have they seen Jagger? Had a good look at his face?"

"No, I don't believe so," she said softly. "But it's possible they got a good look at Boy when he was bringing some supplies around the house tonight."

Stretching as he stood, he began his trek to the com room to find Nichol. The online release of Mick, Jagger, and Audra's fugitive photos from their rescue mission in Vansburg last month had spurred groups of underground bounty hunters into action. Two registered young vampires were captured the previous week in Oregon. Their hunters gained Internet notoriety as they brought the newly created vamps to their knees using the same UV flashlights Detective Whitman had turned on Jagg. With the capture on film and uploaded online, sales of the devices soared, with reports pouring in of vampires being outed through broad light sweeps across crowded streets in urban centers.

Alongside the vampire hunt came the vampire companion hunt, and that one had taken a far more unnerving tone. Blood whores, as the online chatter called them, were being stalked to their homes by unscrupulous groups led mostly by men hell-bent on "cleansing the streets."

Photos of the women began appearing online, their addresses and routines posted for all to see. Many of the women outed as lovers of vampires had no ties to the vampire community, their neighbors often targeting them based on unrelated vendettas. To date, the Kaius haunt was informed of only one Tender caught in the mobs, a former Rhys-trainee from years earlier who was followed to her home, beaten, and left on the doorstep.

A message to her, as well as to her master, Charleston.

Charles was quick to vacate the country, contacting Nichol once he crossed the border into Mexico with his Tender at his side. Rhys had forwarded Audra's personal phone line to Charles, urging him to seek out the haunt psychologist's help for the woman as they dealt with the aftermath. Although Audra's phone had yet to ring, he knew it would eventually. Charleston was tightly tethered to his Tender, his voice warming fractionally whenever he spoke of her.

Once news of the bounty hunters hit the Kaius haunt, they had begun contacting all haunts and Masters on their lists. Former Tenders were first to be called, their lack of protection leaving them amongst the most vulnerable population. He gave each woman one instruction.

Call.

Call and report anything unusual

Call and report anything concerning.

Call for anything at all.

"Bee," he snarled, "am I right in assuming you requested my extended stay because of this?"

She went silent for a moment. "Perhaps."

Rounding the doorway into the com room, he waved to Nichol and covered the phone mic. "Bounty hunters have been circling Bee's neighborhood for the past week, maybe longer," he growled to his eldest brother. "She's only reporting it now because Boy caught their movements."

Nichol glared at him, holding out his hand and

snatching the phone away. "You've put two haunt members at risk with your decision to withhold," he barked. "List your security measures."

Rhys swung a chair around to listen in as Bianca rattled off the various alarms and coded exterior doors outfitting her home, as well as the specs for the fire-resistant basement suites doubling as a bolt hole.

"Johan was thorough," Nichol grumbled. "You will join Boy and Jagger on their mission to Minnesota. I'll text Jagger with the change of plans."

Bee's laugh rang through the speaker. "Oh, honey, I'm not leaving my home because a few men have a rage-on for me. I'll be fine. I promise to remain indoors until the boys return. Yes?"

Nichol tossed the phone over. "I won't waste my time debating. I'll have Audra call Bianca and talk some sense into her. Fucking Tenders."

With a grin, Rhys returned to his conversation with Bee. "Hear that, sweetheart? Nichol is going to sic Audra on you. Go with the guys. For me. Maybe consider coming back here for a few weeks afterward until the worst of this dies down or the law steps in."

With assurances to consider it, Bianca hung up.

"She's bullheaded," Nichol stated. "Unwisely so."

"I didn't think she had it in her during her time here," he mused fondly. "She was such a compliant little pixie. A supple, compliant little pixie. Am I right?"

Nichol grunted, refusing to acknowledge the nights he had spent with the petite blonde prior to his self-imposed chastity over three decades earlier. Rhys typed up a long text to Jagger, copying it for Boy.

****

"Get packing," Jagger called out to Bianca as he read over Rhys's message. Bianca appeared from the kitchen, hands on her hips and brow cocked. "Please," he added with a smirk.

Justine's shoulders shook with giggles beside him as Bee huffed down the hall toward her bedroom. Justine followed suit, moving swiftly to the basement to prepare for the following evening's travel.

He strode over to Boy, following his gaze into the darkness. "Those are no bounty hunters," he said softly. "That's a fucking mob."

The vampires stood guard until dawn broke, the women hastily preparing the house for a quick vacancy come nightfall. Though her lips remained still, he was certain Bianca was cursing his name creatively in hushed whispers, judging from the intermittent outbursts of laughter from Justine. Despite the apparent levity of the household, the severity of Rhys's message was not lost on him.

Bianca Schumann was an integral part of the Kaius underground. More importantly, she was a preferred Tender, one known throughout North America for her kindness, her warmth, and her bravery. Her decades with Johan were volatile, the Nebraskan vampires fighting a war amongst themselves for dominance over the area. The state's central location made it a prime hub for trade and information, and Johan sat staunchly at the gateway.

Bianca had accompanied her mate to numerous meetings, her small stature and quiet disposition hiding a fierce hellcat until Johan was threatened. The woman was proficient in various weapons, her strongest skill set centered on throwing stars. Johan had spent years training her, determined his mate would be able to protect herself in his absence, and betting on her good heart he would not be on the receiving end of her talents. The ambush resulting in the death of her mate had also seen Bianca walking calmly from the fray, his murderer's sludgy remains covering the decapitating stars thrown by her hand.

Bee was, in a word, badass.

Tenders as far as Europe and Asia were told tales of Bianca, her revenge, her subsequent hunting of the offspring of her mate's murderer, and the eventual establishment of a tentative peace in the region, with Bee as the mediating entity of the region. An invitation to her home was held in high regard, as was the sound of her beguiling laugh. Although he himself had not been able to indulge in the auditory thrill of her voice, he had to admit the woman was far more perceptive and disarming than most Tenders he had encountered.

Bianca's safety was paramount, and it was currently sitting squarely on the shoulders of Boy and Jagger.

As the sun rose higher, the house became quiet, the mob having disintegrated in the early hours. He watched as Bee checked her alarms, testing each door before unexpectedly kissing his cheek, patting his backside, and sashaying to her room. Unwilling to wake Justine, he slid into the bed beside her, pulling her warm body to his and scenting her hair before he fell into a light rest.

****

"This is much better than that contraption you arrived in last time." Bianca smiled as she watched Boy pack the vehicle's hatch. "It's been so long since I've been on a road trip! Well, one not involving bloody negotiations and excessive male posturing."

Jagger tossed Boy the keys, climbing into the back with Justine. "I promise nothing."

With a playful swat at his chest, Justine settled in at his side, her legs curled under her as she relaxed against him. He scanned the area for movement, for any sign of the mob inching closer to Bee's house the previous night. Flicking her sun visor mirror open, Bianca met his eyes and winked. "This work?" she asked, ensuring her lips were visible in the small reflection.

He nodded, adjusting his position slightly for a better view. "Nichol says Conall is expecting us at dawn today. He's anxious to see you again. I think your presence may alleviate some of the pressure of meeting Justine for the first time."

"Oh, William." She laughed. "So much nervous energy for such a sophisticated vamp. He actually sent me pictures of Justine's sleeping quarters, requesting I make any suggestions to improve them before her arrival."

Justine sat up, eyes wide. "I have my own quarters?"

"Of course," Bee replied. "Rhys places it as a stipulation for every sale. He's well aware of how strange these boys can get about their personal space and wants to ensure we have a place dedicated solely to us, should we need the respite."

"We aren't weird about our space," he argued. "We're…protective."

Justine hid a smile, schooling her face before addressing him. "You once threw a fit because I moved your boots from the right side of the door to the left."

He frowned. "Boots always go on the right. Everyone knows that. And it wasn't a fit. It was a rational, calm explanation of my preferences."

"You tossed the boots in the hall, yelled, 'Is that better?' and locked yourself in the bathroom for ten minutes."

Rhys had mentioned over the past few weeks he could take on Audra, and he could take on Molly, but when they combined forces, no male could escape with his ego and his sanity intact after more than an hour in their presence.

The drive to Bemidji, Minnesota, took exactly nine hours, eighteen minutes, with Bianca and Justine at the top of their game.

The short reprieve at a fuel station had ended as the women climbed back into the vehicle and filled the small space with the odor of a chemical they referred to as dill pickle chips.

Boy rolled his window down, his eyes straight ahead as he ignored the women's chatter, their jibes at Jagg, and Bee's constant pats on his taut forearm. Jagger sought his own shelter from the onslaught, turning away from their lips as the women discussed vampire peculiarities and temperaments.

He eventually gave in when the constant tapping on his shoulder became more annoying than the musings of women who knew far more about him and his brothers than they should.

When they finally pulled up the long drive of the Conall estate, Justine began squeezing his knee, her eyes shining with excitement and apprehension. He grasped her hand, intertwining her fingers with his and escorting her out of the vehicle to the pacing vampire on the veranda.

William Conall halted his steps, his eyes locking on Justine as she unlatched her fingers, clasping her hands behind her back and assuming the standard Tender pose for his appraisal. Jagg stepped to the side, Bianca sliding up to him as they watched the vampire circle his newest purchase, his expression feigning disinterest despite the anticipation in his eyes.

"Perhaps we should move the valuation indoors to a more secure, less bright setting," Bianca suggested, noting the inevitable signs of sunrise. "Rhys has instructed me to witness the assessment, with your permission, of course."

Conall nodded, motioning for the group to enter his home. Boy brought up the rear, his shoulders and arms loaded with bags and coolers. "I have separate guest quarters on the main floor, down the hall," William gestured. "Ms. Schumann, I prepared several rooms for you to view in different wings."

Bianca gave a curt nod, her shift from endearing hostess to visiting royalty unnerving.

Boy handed him a folder and skulked down the hall toward the guest rooms, his role in Justine's delivery complete. Jagg followed the others into an elaborate sitting room, scanning for all possible exits and scenting the air for unknown vampires while Justine resumed her stance in the middle of the room, patiently waiting for her new master to examine his expensive acquisition.

Conall's gaze flicked to Bianca. "May I?"

"Flat palm only," she instructed as William moved closer to Justine.

Jagger had never witnessed a sale before, with

Rhys preferring to bring Boy along should the need arise for backup. Watching Conall physically inspect Justine placed an unease in his shoulders. His own eyes studied every movement, ensuring the vampire was being both gentle and respectful in his ministrations. Justine, for her part, appeared unaffected by the manhandling.

He was aware Rhys thoroughly reviewed the process with purchased Tenders but witnessing the clinical nature of the event was unsettling. He stepped forward to speak, his intention to vouch for the beautiful woman being patted down as one might a show dog.

A small hand on his lower back stopped his momentum, Bianca's blonde hair shaking slightly.

"Time is up," Bianca said coolly. "Her price increases with each touch from here on out. Will you sign?"

Conall reluctantly dropped his hands from Justine's waist, his lips taut as he extended his hand in Jagger's direction. Bianca plucked the folder from him, passing it to their host and closely monitoring his signature on the official documents.

William passed her the pen and folder, a smirk on his lips. "Are we done this charade?" he asked, humor in his voice.

She flashed a dazzling smile. "Only if you bribe me with some of the Belgian chocolate you promised."

Chapter Four

Bee was delighted with Conall, his formal demeanor evaporating as he escorted Justine on a tour through the house. Jagger remained behind them, his ice eyes scouring the property for danger and boogeymen while his quiet hum filled the halls. Upon seeing her room, Justine had squealed in excitement, all training washing away as she perused the opulent boudoir.

William had taken it upon himself to stock his new Tender with a variety of electronics from a television to a computer to an array of music-playing devices straight out of the future. On either side of the canopied bed were bookshelves filled with classics, romances, thrillers, and magazines spanning the numerous interests she had suggested during their phone call the previous evening.

The cream and gold color palette was punctuated with a deep blood red, creating a warm, sensual space. When she remembered her place, Justine approached her new master sheepishly, attempting to hide her enthusiasm behind her practiced thank-yous and curtsies.

If Conall could blush, his pale cheeks would be flaming.

Jagger stood in the doorway, quietly observing the din of activity as William began explaining how to work the complicated devices peppering the room, a laminated instruction sheet in hand. She tilted her head toward the hall, a subtle suggestion they leave the new pairing alone as early dawn gave way to morning. With his lips tight, Jagg followed her lead toward the guest quarters.

"Conall mentioned you had a few choices of rooms," he finally spoke, his eyes turning to her lips. "Where will you spend the day?"

She considered her options, reflecting on Conall's traditional boarding offerings. "I'll join you and Boy in the guest rooms," she said with finality. "The main wing has activity during the day from the grounds staff. And the basement, while artfully decorated, tends to feel quite suffocating regardless of the ceiling height."

As she passed down the hall, she pushed each slightly ajar door wide open, assessing the rooms with a stern eye. She avoided the one closed door, knowing Boy was likely holing up, hiding from her as he had consistently done so long ago. When she found the room with a basket of Belgian chocolates on the bed, she grinned. "I'll be in this room," she stated. "Should you require anything during the day, my door remains unlocked in Conall's home."

Jagger frowned. "That's a risky move in the home of a vampire."

She brushed off his concern with the flick of her wrist. "Nonsense. William will be occupied all day, making lists of anything Justine has said this morning and comparing them to the books and movies he accumulated for her entertainment. He's anxious for her to be happy and comfortable, and that will keep him engrossed for the next few months." Leaning in to kiss him on the cheek, she took the opportunity to brush his dark hair from his forehead. "She will be well cared for, honey. I promise."

He huffed. "My duty to Justine has been completed. Now I hold the responsibility of keeping you safe. Which is made infinitely more difficult if you refuse to follow basic self-protection."

"Perhaps I should bunk with you for the day, then," she replied with a grin.

****

"You cannot truly believe this last election has nothing to do with the increased persecution vampires have been facing," Bianca said, her arms crossing in defiance. "His promise to institute a registration system is what made him a front-runner!"

Jagger grinned, internally agreeing with Bee's position on the human political leader's role in the vampire database implementation but outwardly playing the devil's advocate to extend her exasperated indignation. "The tide was already turning," he replied, enjoying the verbal sparring with the tiny blonde beside him. "He merely organized the hate movement. Brought it from grassroots to policy."

She huffed, angling from his view as her lips moved quickly. Her slim shoulders rose as she drew a deep breath and faced him again. "That's my point," she stated tersely. "Had a cooler, more levelheaded candidate been elected, perhaps he or she would have been able to promote positive human-vamp relations instead of this unwarranted hate mongering."

"Hardly unwarranted," he scoffed. "There are enough wild cards out there to give us a bad name regardless of any sunshine media campaign some hypothetically tolerant president could conceive. The hatred is global and growing. Considering our unveiling, I'm amazed we had a decade of calm before the mobs and torches hit the streets."

She pulled her legs up under herself, turning fully in her seat to argue. He glanced down at his speedometer to ensure he hadn't sped up during the heated discussion. While vamps viewed the world at four times the speed humans did and could maintain focus on both the road and their companions, he suffered from a lead foot on the best of nights. "It was two vampires and one human. Hardly a bloodbath."

"It was one vampire, his Deviant creation, and a mother of two at a county fair. We were lucky the vamp was smart enough to end the Deviant before it was captured as well." Deviants were a scourge among vampires, misturnings who functioned solely within the id. They were mindless eating machines, unable to form coherent thoughts. It created an unstable link to their creators, who inevitably went mad if they didn't put the creatures down.

He slowed the vehicle down, pulling off the empty highway and into a fuel station. "I'll fill up. You head on in and pick up what you need," he said as he opened his wallet and handed her a wad of bills.

Her wide blue eyes narrowed. "We are not done with this discussion," she stated before looking to the back seat. "Boy agrees with me. Right?"

Without waiting for the answer she wouldn't receive, she hopped out and strode into the small convenience store, her tall boots clomping across the empty lot. He filled the tank, noting Boy's exit from the vehicle and his silent stalking into the shadows of the store's eaves to watch over Bee.

The petite woman was strolling casually through the store, her purple high-waisted shorts and elegant pink satin shirt at odds with the neon signs and cigarette ads adorning the windows. He fired off a quick text to Rhys, letting him know they were on schedule and expected to arrive back in Lincoln well before sunrise.

—Rhys: Louis meeting you there. —

He frowned for a moment, replaced the fuel nozzle, and prepared himself to antagonize his entertaining companion a little longer.

****

Rhys maintained his position on the sofa, his long arms folded behind his head as he stared at the ceiling. "You two are being unreasonably emotional."

He didn't have to look over to know Audra's cat eyes had become angry slits as she inhaled and exhaled methodically. "This," she growled, "is not about emotion. It's about respect for us and respect for our relationships."

"This," he echoed, running a hand through his black hair, "is about me having a job to do, and you two standing in the way of both work and profit." He lifted his legs, maneuvering them out of the way of Molly's foot as she kicked at him. "Jagg and Kai are gone. Louis left at dusk. Nichol is fucking no one anytime soon, and they are already well adapted to me. Which leaves Mick and Dom."

"Go fuck yourself!" Molly yelled, her pale cheeks flushed with revulsion.

Audra placed a staying hand on her fellow complainant. "You can't truly expect us to be okay with this," she spat. "It's bad enough they walk around in their underwear all night, trying to seduce our guys.

This needs to end."

He closed his eyes. "But it isn't ending. Therefore, I need the guys for one, maybe two nights a week until I can confidently gain a sale. I'm trying to be reasonable here," he posited. "A few hours a week, and they're yours the rest of the time."

Audra pulled out her phone, her manicured nails clicking as she typed. "I'm getting Mickey in here," she stated. "He'll refuse. As will Dom. You cannot do this to Molly."

Pinching the bridge of his nose, he sat forward and stared at the women hard. "Audra. As a connected vamp, Dominic is likely already out of the equation due to performance issues. Which leaves Mick, who is both unconnected and more than capable of performing as needed. Two hours a week is all I require. I'm willing to do group lessons to speed up the process. Once the sales are complete, perhaps we can all have a sit down and establish a schedule—"

"Schedule?" Audra hissed angrily. "There will be no schedule. This is barbaric! If the haunt is so desperately in need of money, Molly and I are more than capable of working in the human world. I can take on clients again—"

He frowned. "We aren't in need of money," he corrected.

A rap on the door preceded Mick's entrance to the Tender training room. Audra strode to him, her hands on her hips as she stood toe to toe against her slouching, perplexed mate. "You are not fucking those women," she spat out.

Mick's eyes widened. "I was just training with Nichol in the forest." He lifted his booted foot, clumps of snow and mud falling onto the pristine hardwood. "What the hell is going on?"

"I require your expertise for a few nights to retrain the Tenders," he explained as he rose and sandwiched Audra between Mick and himself. "Audra takes issue with your duties."

A hand ran through his long blond hair. "Damn," he muttered. "I never thought about it. I guess with the others gone—"

"No. Fucking. Way," Audra barked. "You are not considering this. It's not an option. I've already said I would return to working outside the haunt if money is an issue."

Mickey glanced over her head to him. "We need money? And I never said I was considering it. Just that I hadn't thought about it."

He shook his head, fantasizing briefly about breaking Audra's delicate neck and putting an end to the evening's escalating debate. "Impossible. But you know I need these women cycled if I aim to get a good price."

As realization dawned on Audra, she turned slowly to face him. "You don't sell them out of financial need."

"Not at all!" Mick exclaimed, eager to offer what he gauged to be appeasing input. "We're sitting on centuries of wealth and land acquisition. The quality of the Rhys-trained Tenders is purely for reputation. The higher the price, the more valuable the Kaius name becomes, the more clout we hold amongst other haunts."

It was fascinating to observe Audra's cat eyes as they morphed from indignant to aghast to a hardened disgust. He momentarily lamented the loss of opportunity to train such an alpha. Bianca was the last true alpha he had had the pleasure of molding. Audra would have fetched a prime rate.

"And the bloodslave quarters?" she gritted out, refusing to turn back toward Mickey.

"Public service, sweetheart," he replied, ignoring Mickey's growl at the flippant endearment.

Audra squared her shoulders, swatting away Mick's hand as he brushed her hip. "You run a human trafficking ring and an enslavement camp for the purpose of maintaining a reputation," she clarified in a disturbingly flat voice.

"Technically, we rescue them from haunts who can't, or won't, provide the humans with basic needs. Like an animal shelter."

Mick's blue eyes flinched at his lover's tone, recognizing too late his futile attempt at an explanation had only further stoked Audra's ire. "Reputation is survival," Mick said quietly. "The Kaius name has saved our asses countless times over the centuries through the fostering of favors and alliances. Maintaining the status of our haunt is a matter of continued existence."

"My Tender sales to the DeChamplain line provided a safe haven during Jagger's extrication in Vansburg," Rhys added, observing the woman's reactions closely. "And blood sales to the Zorias' haunt in Washington gave your boyfriend an escape when the full force of Dominic's connection to Molly hit and pushed them both over the sanity cliff."

Mickey scoffed at the colloquial term "boyfriend" as Audra's eyes softened slightly at the mention of the difficulties Mick had faced with his empathic abilities. Her hand reached back, fingers clasping the rough fabric of Mick's cargo pants. "You both know this needs to end," she said slowly. "Neither I nor Molly will give approval for your women to train under our males."

Molly emitted an annoyed sound of agreement over his shoulder as Audra breathed steadily. "The others will return within the week. If the training is so important, the unattached hauntmates should remain on site until the final sales are complete. One week will not deter your future buyers, nor will it be detrimental to the prices you set. But make no mistake"—Audra rose on her toes, her finger pushed into his chest—"the Kaius haunt is getting out of Tender sales and blood deals."

****

Boy was out of the vehicle and stalking toward Bianca's house before the vehicle slowed in the snow-covered driveway. Jagger skimmed his hand over his thighs, ensuring his blades were secure and accessible as he shifted into park and assessed the perimeter. He leaned over Bee, unlatching the glove box, and slipping a small knife into her lap.

"Get in the driver's side when I exit," he instructed. "Doors locked, weapons ready."

Bianca's bright blue eyes narrowed as she took in the destruction pouring from her home, and she nodded tersely.

Boy moved silently across the yard, skulking behind the treed pathway leading into the back gardens. He climbed out of the car and crept into the open front door, nimbly avoiding the smashed trinkets adorning the walkway. The lingering scents of over a dozen humans permeated his senses as he entered the dark house and began examining the extensive damage.

Moving through the main rooms, he noted not a single surface had gone untouched, every carefully displayed artifact and memento laying in ruins on the scuffed floors. A flash of movement outside caught his eye, and he sprinted from the house, blades and fangs extended for battle.

The vehicle lurched forward, pinning the runner between the grill and Bianca's splintered garage door. Boy appeared alongside him and they advanced on the male. Boy's hand was around the intruder's throat before freezing midgrasp.

Louis's scent hit them simultaneously. Boy removed the black hat from the guy, tossing it into the snow when the telltale red hair sprang free.

"You are one stupid bastard," Jagger growled.

"I'm also one stuck bastard," Louis stated, his teeth clenching and distorting his words.

He motioned for Bianca to back the vehicle up. "It's Louis. Feel free to accidentally lurch forward before you release him."

Bianca rolled her eyes and reversed. She hopped out of the car, ignoring her destroyed home. "What in almighty Hades are you doing here?" she demanded, hands on her slim hips. "Jagger, get him inside while I warm up some blood."

He offered a hand to his injured hauntmate. "My fault," he apologized. "Rhys informed me Louis was meeting us here. I was too distracted by your faulty political dialogue to pass on the information."

Louis rose from the ground, brushing mud and

snow from his legs with his unbroken arm. "We can't spend the night here," he mumbled. "The place is completely trashed. It's been targeted. Even if we hole up in the basement, we run the risk of a daytime attack."

Bianca's eyes hardened. "There's less than an hour until daybreak. The closest ally is three hundred miles away." She turned on her heel and strode toward the front door. Louis limped after her, shaking his head as his lips moved quickly. Jagg left Boy to monitor the landscape as he caught up to the arguing duo, attempting to catch their rapid discussion despite the poor angle.

Bee flipped on the lights as she moved swiftly through the house, stepping over her shattered collectables on her trek to the fridge. She yanked the door open, swaying backward against Louis when the sight of the fridge contents met her eyes.

"That's a rat," she gasped. "Many. Jagger. That's a lot of rats."

He shoved the door closed, removing the visual of dozens of disemboweled rodents. "Louis, book a motel room for the day. Something close. Bee and I will load up with blankets and tinfoil to block light until dusk."

Louis pulled his phone from his pocket, his broken arm dangling awkwardly at his side.

Her jaw set, Bianca walked across the kitchen, pulling a roll of foil from a drawer, and tucking it under her arm. "I need to pack a few items," she said tightly before walking toward her bedroom.

Jagger passed her in the hall, his eyes and nose assessing the quarters as he entered Bee's room.

The ornate boudoir decor was shredded, textiles

torn, strewn across the floor, and reeking of human urine. He gently nudged Bianca back into the hallway. "Tell me what you want, and I'll grab it."

Bee pushed past him, her small hands digging into his waist as she forced her way into her desecrated room. She flung the door wide open, covering her nose when the smell hit her, and she entered the room, scanning every soiled surface. "Blood whore." She chuckled mirthlessly, pointing at her headboard. His fangs pierced his lip as he took in the bloodied writing adorning the crafted wood. "How many scents?" Bianca murmured.

"Fourteen."

"All human?"

He nodded.

"In my closet, top right shelf, are two boxes and a backpack. Could you please grab them for me?"

Chapter Five

Bianca ignored the lecherous stare of the night clerk as she handed him her credit card. The sun would rise in fifteen minutes, and she was unwilling to waste valuable time schooling the balding middle-aged troll on appropriate behavior. Taking the keys in her manicured fingers, she made her way back to the Kaius hauntmates and led them to the rickety exterior door of their room. Boy and Jagger backed the matching vehicles up tight to their location, popping the hatches and unloading their bags into the room as Louis hobbled toward the small desk chair.

She arranged their possessions, staying clear of Boy and Jagg as they fastened blankets and tinfoil to the frosty window. Once they were satisfied with their work, Boy wedged a towel under the door and took up his sentry position. Jagger pulled out his phone and began texting rapidly.

"Louis," she whispered as she took off her coat and exposed her wrist. "Your arm is going to heal incorrectly if Jagger doesn't place it. After he does, you need to feed to ensure it sets properly."

Louis glanced over at Jagger, waving his good arm to get the deaf vampire's attention. "Could you snap this into place?"

Jagg nodded, putting his phone on the shared bedside table, and kneeling beside Louis. "Don't fucking bite me," he warned as he gripped the broken appendage. Louis grinned, gritting his molars as Jagger aligned the bone in place with a twist. She approached Louis from behind, wrapping her arm around him and bringing her wrist to his lips. The piercing crunch of his fangs penetrating her flesh held a flash of pain before the rhythmic suckling took over, soothing the discomfort and embracing her in the security of her ingrained caregiver role.

"At dusk, we'll travel home," Jagger said quietly, his eyes fastened on his feeding hauntmate. "Nichol and Mick are investigating the online chatter around here in hopes of identifying the culprits."

She ran a soothing hand through Louis's fire-engine hair. "There has been little retaliation against human perpetrators of anti-vampire violence. What precisely will the Kaius haunt do?"

He sat back on his haunches, his dark brows furrowing over his ice-blue eyes. "Honestly, Bee, we'll continue to collect names and monitor their online accounts. Follow post trails. That's about it."

She skimmed a finger down Louis's cheek, indicating he had taken enough. His fangs released immediately, and he vacated the weathered chair, bowing in appreciation for her gift before reclining on the threadbare bed. She sat primly, crossing her legs, and angling her body toward Jagg as he knelt beside her. "As long as these acts go unanswered by the vampire community, they will only increase in frequency and level of violence. Kaius can no longer sit back and observe."

"We're spinning a lot of plates," he stated slowly, choosing his words with effort. "The past year has brought many issues to our door, and our haunt is comparatively small. Tracking and eliminating Dovidas is our top priority right now."

"Deepfryers are inevitable," she argued, pulling information from the rumors encircling the Kaius haunt over the past months. Vampire Kaspars Dovidas had aligned himself with human lawmakers pushing the anti-vamp agenda. Whispers of his involvement in the peddling of Deepfryers, glass enclosures outfitted to burn vampires alive publicly through UV ray technology, were spreading like wildfire among vamps. "The removal of Dovidas will only postpone their implementation. Unless, of course, you deem Kaspars a greater threat than he appears to be in his middleman role."

Jagger's silence on the matter confirmed what she had suspected. The Kaius haunt had a reputation for holding their cards close, for revealing little until the ashes were drifting on the wind. She mused wistfully about the haunt she had known during her training, one prior to Internet espionage and frequent flyer miles. The Kaius haunt of the early 1900s was even smaller than it was now, with Jagg living abroad and the youngest hauntmate decades from birth. Yet despite their meager numbers, they were a powerful force amongst the burgeoning North American vampire migration. Newcomers were welcomed with fangs and swords, with territories and boundaries enforced through diplomacy and beheadings. Johan would often regale her with tales of the valor and ferocity of the Kaius haunt he had accumulated over the centuries.

"Modern technology has made you passive," she murmured, leaning back, and crossing her arms. One black brow lifted beneath Jagger's hood. "You, the

Kaius haunt. Nichol and his toys. You've become reliant on easily accessible information while neglecting the application of the immense knowledge at your fingertips. A century ago, the fourteen humans of that mob would have been stalked in the night, eliminated one by one, ghosted from existence and memory." She straightened. "Kaius established himself as a king, a general. The others follow your lead. And they are being led to their crypts, to cower like rabbits as the wolves close in."

****

Jagger woke with a start, a soft floral scent engulfing him as his skin burned from the heat of the tiny woman curled at his side. His eyes scanned the room, noting Louis resting on the second bed as Boy stood guard at the door, his lifeless blue eyes unseeing while he held position. He untangled himself from Bianca, taking care to avoid waking her.

"Boy," he whispered. "I'm up. Take a few minutes."

Without acknowledgment, Boy disappeared into the bathroom and turned on the shower. Bee stirred, stretching her small form across the mattress. With a tired smile, she rose and followed Boy.

He cocked a brow.

Her obvious comfort with the mute, sullen vampire intrigued him. Aside from haunt psychologist Audra's insistence the Kaius hauntmates treat Boy as "an equal contributor to the success of their cohesive unit," women instinctually avoided Boy. His vampiric qualities had overtaken his former human mannerisms long before Jagger was brought into the haunt. Tenders recoiled intuitively, the breadth of their services ending at the hulking form of the bloodslave caretaker.

The bathroom door opened, steam pouring through the opening as Bianca emerged, donning a small, threadbare towel. Boy followed on her heels, fully clothed with his long blond hair hanging in wet tangles over his face.

"Sit," Bee instructed as she reached into her luggage. Jagger looked on with amusement and curiosity as Boy awkwardly folded his large body onto the chair. Armed with a brush, the petite blonde stood behind him, delicately easing the bristles through his hair and chattering contentedly. "Once I arrange for contractors to clean and repair my home, you should consider taking an extended vacation in Lincoln," Bianca offered, arching her body across Boy's shoulders to meet his gaze. "Or perhaps you could join me overseas for a month or two. I could use a handsome guardian as I visit Stonehenge." She righted herself and winked at Jagger. "And frankly, it would be nice to surround myself with males who don't argue with me when I'm right."

"You're hitching your wagon to the correct horse, then," Louis mumbled from the bed, standing to assess his injuries. Pleased with the results, he strode to the shower.

Bianca swatted the red-haired vamp with her hairbrush as he passed. "Be quick," she said. "The sun set five minutes ago."

Jagger began pulling down the blankets and foil from the windows, taking care to fold them neatly while Bianca busied herself packing their bags and checking the two boxes she had insisted join them in the room.

"All good?" he asked as Bee laid out her clothes on

the bed.

"All good." She smiled, shimmying into her panties under the precariously held towel. He averted his eyes, turning his back to provide the woman with a semblance of privacy. Boy joined him at his side, pretending to be enthralled with the dark paisley curtains adorning the window. When his hauntmate finally turned around, he peered quickly at a fully dressed Bianca before filling his arms to load the vehicle.

Although she had appeared eager to hit the road, they ended up sitting on the two lumpy beds, observing her as she applied lipstick and wove her hair into an intricately looped ponytail at the base of her neck. Louis was fascinated, leaning forward as nimble fingers flipped and maneuvered strands of blonde hair until Bee finally stood, satisfied with the result. She spun quickly, the blue ruffles of her short sheath dress fluttering around her thighs.

"You're going to freeze," Jagger said, grinning when Bee glared at him. "Those boots won't help you much in this weather."

"I don't intend to leave the warmth of the front seat," she said, her lips pursing. "I'm not walking into the Kaius haunt for the first time in decades looking like a scrub. I've texted an order to a restaurant a few blocks away. One of you will need to go in to pick it up. So I don't get cold."

He bent over to rifle through his sack, pulling out tin snips and the small case containing his colored contacts. "Give me a minute."

Popping in the brown iris-rounding contacts, he leaned closer to the mirror to clip the tips of his fangs.

The harsh lighting of the bathroom gave the severed pieces a darkened silvery glimmer as he pocketed them. Scanning the room one final time, he joined the others outside.

Following Bianca's directions, the two cars arrived at the restaurant quickly. Boy exited Louis's vehicle and kept watch as Jagger collected Bee's order. He returned quickly, a large bag in his hand.

"There is no way you can eat all this," he said as Bianca's blue eyes lit up. She ignored him, carefully pulling tray after tray out of the bag and arranging them in a semicircle around herself. "If I hit the brakes, that's going to be a disaster," he warned, easing slowly onto the highway, and cracking his window slightly as the food odors began to coat his tongue. With one eye on the road, he watched in fascination as the petite woman beside him sampled each dish before selecting one tray to devour. "If you don't slow down, you'll choke."

She barely hesitated as she emptied the first container of slimy-looking noodles and started on the second.

For thirty minutes, he remained silent while Bianca indulged in the large meal on her lap. When she was finally sated, she sat back in the seat with a smile.

"Sorry you had to witness that." She laughed. "I wanted one last greasy meal before I walk back into Rhys's healthy kitchen. I swear, that vampire purposely keeps boring food around. I'm afraid I will need to stop and grab a drink, though."

He nodded, signaling to pull into a fuel station. "What shall I get you, m'lady?" he inquired as he put the car into park at the back of the store.

"Water would be fine," she answered, carefully

handing him the bag full of empty food containers.

Boy and Louis hopped out, scenting the air, and scanning the premises as Jagger walked around the building to the front doors. He took his time reading over the multitudes of labels in the store cooler, annoyed with the plethora of choices existing for such a simple request. As he selected three bottles appearing more water-like, Louis appeared at his elbow.

"She's gone, man."

Chapter Six

Bianca glanced at her rearview mirror again, ensuring the deserted highway behind her remained so. She pushed the speed limits on the secondary road, betting on the state troopers staying close to the main arteries where the bulk of tickets could be issued. What should have taken an hour on the main road was closing in on three as she did her best to zigzag toward Omaha and the small downtown apartment Johan had secured months before his death as a quick escape for her should she ever require it.

Her confidence grew as she maneuvered her way through the quiet downtown core, the Old Market boutiques having closed their doors hours earlier. Slowing as she entered the small parking garage, she took a final look back and breathed with relief as the heavy metal door closed behind her.

Arms laden with her luggage and boxes, she carefully eased herself down the long hallway, noting the exposed brick and beams with approval. It was years since she had returned to the bustling location to oversee the renovations she had impulsively begun during an extended time of peace among the Nebraska vampires. Placing her load on the floor, she lifted the lid of one box, turned the lock on her door, and replaced the key with the others. She used her foot to push her boxes and bags through the door and flicked on a light to assess her new accommodations.

Trailing her fingers along the ornate tapestries she had pulled from Johan's collection a decade earlier, she carried her suitcase down the hall and into her bedroom. The king-sized bed overtook the room, dwarfing the redwood dresser and obscuring the matching vanity. She opened her case and slowly placed her assortment of shift dresses in the closet, ignoring the large suits and dress pants hanging in the corner. Returning to the entranceway, she double-checked the lock and carried her remaining boxes and backpack to her boudoir. Placing her makeup alongside the jeweled hairbrush on her vanity, she hesitated, stroking the silver handle.

"It isn't a choice, bunny," Johan said, his deep baritone rumbling in his chest. "There's too big a target on my back to leave you without options."

She huffed and crossed her arms, looking up at her lover. "We have a home," she argued back. "A beautiful home. I will not run from it if something happens to you. You've turned it into a safe haven, and I won't abandon our memories out of misplaced fear."

"There's nothing misplaced about the desire to survive," he countered, bringing his large hands to her face. "I'll rest better during the day knowing you have options. Bring some of our memories here. I task you with making each escape into a home where you can rebuild."

She nuzzled into the strong palms of the vampire she fought with and alongside. "Where we can rebuild," she corrected.

He smiled, the faint silvering of his fangs shimmering in the dim light. "You, we, semantics, my sweet bun. I've petitioned Rhys Kaius for your freedom in the event of my death. You are to contact him immediately. He will protect you."

"I can protect myself," she stated through gritted teeth.

With a dark chuckle, he shook his head. "I am well aware. However, the Kaius haunt has the strength of name and the resources to keep you safe. You WILL notify the haunt immediately, and you WILL NOT seek your revenge."

She turned away, storming angrily across the small living room. "There'll be no seeking," she seethed. "My retribution will come before your bod...instantly." She closed her eyes, refusing to visualize her greatest fear.

"You are a vengeful woman, bunny. I fear it will mean your death."

Her jaw set, she completed the unpacking of her bags and reverently spread the contents of her boxes on the bed.

"Those edges need work."

With a sigh, she turned toward the small balcony off her bedroom. Jagger stood against the rail, his arms crossed nonchalantly over his chest despite the impending rise of the sun.

"Where are the others?" she asked through the glass, unlatching the sliding door.

"I doubled back and dropped them off in Lincoln," he replied, fixing his ice-blue eyes on hers. "We're working under the assumption you plan to deal with the mob yourself."

"You assume correctly," she said, motioning for him to enter. He strode past her, his normally full lips taut and his lilting hum replaced with a staccato tune. He continued into the living room, assessing the large windows disdainfully.

"That'll hurt in ten minutes," he stated, reclining on the burgundy sofa.

She stood over him, blue eyes narrowing. "Then you should probably seek shelter."

"I've been ordered by Nichol to ensure you do nothing stupid until we've reached an agreement," he said casually. "Nine minutes."

She stood her ground. "Nothing good will come from you igniting my Queen Anne."

He placed his arms behind his head, tugging his hood off as he settled deeper into the cushions. "Nothing good will come from a tiny blonde going in half-cocked and guns a-blazing on an organized group of bigoted assholes. You're thinking with your emotions, not your head. Eight minutes."

Cheeks flushing with anger, she turned her back on him and walked into the kitchen to pour a glass of water, whispering curses toward him as she did.

"You can curse me all you want," he called at her back. "You know I'm right. And yes, I can be a self-righteous bastard when the mood strikes me."

She slammed her glass on the counter and turned toward the vampire. "I thought you were deaf."

"I am," he replied, his Cheshire-cat grin showing off his slowly regenerating fangs. "I also know enough about women to know you couldn't bite your tongue. And I saw your lips moving in your reflection. Stainless steel fridge. Five minutes."

She bit back a brief smile before refocusing her anger. "I have no need for your agreement or your assistance. Tell Nichol thanks, but no thanks." She opened the door to her apartment. "If you're lucky, you can make the storage facility in the basement before dawn. How did you even find me?"

Jagger made no move to leave. He closed his pale eyes and crossed his ankles. "Nichol has a list of Johan's real estate holdings left over from your status change. You're irrationally furious about 'things.' There was no life lost. Your Johan has been gone for fourteen years, according to Rhys. This is a suicide mission."

"Those were not things," she hissed. "Those were MY things. Johan's things. Our things. Our life. Our memories. They're all I have left after I was denied centuries with my lover. And those animals had no right to soil them because of their misguided hate."

He unlocked his ankles, unhooked his arms, and sat up slowly. "All right. Close the shutters. We have work to do."

****

"No."

Rhys ran a hand through his black hair. "Nichol. I wouldn't ask if things weren't getting tight."

"Do it yourself."

"I have been," he growled. "I also have three trainees becoming uncomfortably attached, two women who are going to stake me in my sleep, and an AWOL Former Tender with revenge issues."

"Kai will arrive in a day or two."

"Not soon enough," he grumbled, leaning back to peer out the com room door. "Mick is hiding out in his room. Dominic keeps giving me his fucking apologetic sneer. Louis, Boy, and Jagg are driving all over winter's bitch looking for Bianca."

"Not looking," Nichol corrected. "With. Jagg is

with her now. Louis and Boy returned to Lincoln to start following scents."

He frowned and glanced at Nichol's laptop. "What for? Get her ass here, and I'll deal with her."

"Deal with who?" Audra's voice inquired from behind him. He grimaced and hunched forward onto his knees. "Rhys. Deal with who?"

"Bianca's gone rogue," Nichol commented, turning the laptop to show Audra the images of Bee's home circulating on Lincoln's anti-vampire web page.

She pulled up a chair between them and began flipping through the photos, her cat eyes narrowing as she took in the destruction. "Was anyone hurt?"

"All safe," said Nichol, tapping a few keys and bringing up another series of photos. "These are the men identified in the photos. We have links to nine of them. According to Jagger and Louis, there are five scents we haven't accounted for yet. Boy and Louis are staying in Lincoln to connect the missing scents before they return."

Audra sat back in contemplation. "What's she planning to do?"

"Johan trained her as an assassin. What do you think?" Rhys grumbled. "Took my beautiful flower and poisoned her."

She scoffed. "Armed her, you mean. Nichol, keep me posted. Mick asked me to come check if you've opened his last email."

"I did. Serial killers aren't our problem."

She took a deep breath and exhaled slowly. "Did you at least read his notes? One body going missing every three days starting in Miami, traveling up into Alabama as of this morning. Just keep an eye on it, okay?"

Nichol grunted as she rubbed his back quickly and left the room without a glance at Rhys. Nic continued to tap away on his computer, his fingers flying over the keys as his auburn brows knotted. Knowing harassing the older vampire more would only result in injury, he left the com room to wander the halls.

"It's time, Rhys," Audra's voice said softly behind him.

He turned to her, hooking his thumbs in the belt loops of his cargo pants. "I'm ready. Are you?"

One manicured brow cocked. "I'm ready to work with you," she posited. "You know it, I know it. The Tender game is over. As are the bloodslave quarters. There aren't enough males around to keep them functional, and the tide is turning."

"The guys will be back within the week," he replied, unaffected.

"For how long?" she pushed. "This haunt is so far from battle ready right now. And the battles are coming, Rhys. How long can you hide here with your precious Tenders while your brethren go topside against the ever-increasing numbers of enemies?"

He rose to his full height, towering over the brunette. "I hide from no one," he roared, baring his fangs. "To abandon the Tender training and blood running sends a message to the others we are combusting."

"Abandoning them in favor of war preparation sends the message you are ready to lead," she snarled back, lifting herself high on her stiletto heels. "Whether I like it or not, my safety is dependent on the vamps of this haunt. As is Molly's. And Simone's. And even that of the two retrainees. If Dovidas finds us, or the humans find us AS THEY HAVE OTHERS, which of us will you push behind you as bait while you retreat?"

He could feel his eyes ovaling, reacting to the truths and rage she was laying at his feet.

She was right.

Even at full capacity, the Kaius haunt couldn't afford to spread their resources across the Tender front, the bloodslave ring, the emboldened human mobs, and the unknowns Dovidas carried on his back. He crossed his arms defiantly, staring down the astute brunette.

Fuck, she would have fetched a high price.

"How?" he finally asked, voice clipped as he reined back his elongated fangs.

Audra blinked slowly, tilting her head. "I have a few ideas," she said, speaking slowly and gathering her thoughts. "It would be intensive. And we would need Boy and Louis. Nichol, too." She paused, cat eyes narrowing. "You're sure you have a few hundred thousand in the banks to cushion this?"

He smirked. "Add a few zeros to your estimate, sweetheart."

She cocked a brow. "Millions."

"More zeros, honey."

Drawing a deep breath, she pursed her lips. "Don't call me honey," she said, turning to walk away. He strode alongside, keeping his pace slightly ahead of her and reveling in the quickening clicks of her shoes as she struggled to surpass him.

Chapter Seven

Jagger stretched awkwardly on the old sofa in Bianca's suite. The sun wouldn't set for three more hours, and the tingling of his regenerating fangs was keeping him alert and agitated. With the realization rest wouldn't come that day, he allowed himself to sink into the memories Bianca had inadvertently triggered.

"If we do not hurry our pace, we will be forging paths through the snow," Rhys grumbled, his dark eyes fixated on the clouded night sky. "Berlin is still sixty nights away."

Jagger lifted his head from the soft earth. "Maybe the next time you anger an ancient, you'll do so on a closer continent."

Rhys grinned, removing his filthy pants and pulling his heavy coat off his shoulders. "Alexandria was far more temperate in the winter season than Berlin will be," he replied before striding into the cold water. "The sunlight was particularly warm."

Rising to join his older brother, he began stripping his clothes off, folding them neatly on the rocky shore as he looked over Rhys's bare form. "Not a mark remains," he stated, pleased. "Aside from those abominations on your arms."

Flexing his biceps for inspection, Rhys angled himself toward him, showing off the intricate designs crawling across his muscles. "Works of art, brother," he said proudly. "Once we settle in Berlin, you can watch me add another loop."

He shook his head, chuckling mirthlessly as he dove under the water. The pair had traded much of their travel money for the vial of liquid mercury now wrapped securely in the bottom of Rhys's worn satchel. Upon their arrival in Berlin, Rhys would make good on his promise to add another swirling pattern to the multitudes of others adorning his skin, each a tribute to his survival of another cell, another confinement, another punishment meted through sunlight and blades.

Breaking through the surface of the water, he froze at the sound of a woman's surprised laughter. His eyes flashed to the shore where Rhys was already walking slowly toward the shadowed woman.

"Stand back," she warned, raising her hands as the humor disappeared from her voice. "My father and my brother are close enough to hear me."

Rhys paused, his enhanced hearing picking up nothing in the distance. He turned toward Jagger for confirmation.

"She lies," he said softly as he moved to the shore.

The brothers stood side by side in the water, assessing the lone woman on the banks.

"You are far from Turgutlu," Rhys stated loudly in her Greek tongue. "There are no settlements near this water."

They made their way to the shore, moving deliberately to avoid startling the brunette. As they exited the water, he began to make out the exquisitely fine features of the woman in the distance. Her unruly black curls framed her face and body, a temptingly dark halo in the moonlight.

"Stay your progress," she spoke again, retreating

slightly. "There are many who know of my whereabouts. They will come looking soon."

He dressed quickly, his ice eyes locked on the plump lips of their intruder. "They were foolish to allow your departure from their gaze," he called to her. "Were you my sister or my wife, I would hide your beauty from the undeserving eyes of scoundrels such as myself. The protectors you speak of are incompetent fools."

Rhys scoffed, his dark eyes rolling.

"You are not from here," the woman responded, ignoring his words.

"We are not," he answered as he moved closer to the cluster of trees shrouding her features. "We are merely passing through from Egypt. Weary travelers in search of a warm bed and a hot meal."

She moved from the shadows, her dark eyes appraising him and Rhys with wary contemplation. "There are rooms in town," she stated, her feet moving her toward the worn path. "I wish you safe travels."

As her form disappeared over the bluff, Rhys nudged his arm. "Your meal is retreating," he muttered, amused.

Jagger's eyes opened, scanning the dark room for signs of danger before he rose and slipped into the shower. With the sound of Seline's voice echoing in his head, he knew there would be no rest for the day, no reprieve from her lilting speech and boisterous laughter filling his broken ears. The thrum of the water on his back lulled him into a melancholy calm, pulling him swiftly from the panicked agitation he had felt building in his muscles and jaw. The steam of the shower fogged the mirrors, a small mercy when he inadvertently glanced toward one.

Curse.

The Burmese writing stretched across each temple, the gray mercury lines dark and unmistakable. His hoods covered them effectively in short bursts, provided he didn't move much or angle his head in such a way as to reveal the markings. It was an imperfection in a world with little tolerance for such weakness. The tattoos labeled him, not only for humans but amongst his own kind. A symbol of his carelessness and a tangible sign of his failure to move undetected by law enforcement.

Bianca had yet to address them, her blue eyes rarely settling on the marks for more than a moment before she looked away, a glimmer of pity flashing until she schooled her features once again.

He wandered into the kitchen, opening drawers and cabinets aimlessly out of boredom and curiosity. He weighed her cooking knives in his hands, testing their balance and edges, then replacing them in the wooden block. One by one, he entertained himself with the makeshift weapons until Bee appeared at his side.

"I'm afraid I don't keep a blood stock here," she apologized, looking up at him as she lifted her wrist. "Straight from the tap will have to do."

With the flick of his hand, he refused the offering. "I have no need tonight. But I may take you up on it before we head back to Lincoln."

Without another word, Bianca padded to the shower, her small stature more prominent in the absence of her tall heels. He leaned against the counter and pulled out his phone.

—*Louis: What's the deal*—

—Jagg: Any luck—

—Louis: Boy tracked all. Putting together a map now. Being called back—

—Jagg: Be there tonight. ETA 2 hours—

—Louis: Giving you 1. Need to get back to haunt ASAP. K's orders—

He frowned at his phone. If Kaius was ordering Boy and Louis to return to the haunt, he likely knew where Jagg was and why. Having Kai's blessing on his involvement would eliminate much of the pressure surrounding his assistance in Bianca's plans. Opening a new window, he fired off a quick message.

—Jagg: Need me back at the haunt? —

—Kai: No. You have a mission. Complete and return. With the Tender. —

"Bee?" he called toward the bathroom, hoping his voice would carry over the stream of water. "We're moving ahead with permission from Kaius."

The water ran a few seconds more before stopping, and a soaking blonde wrapped in a large towel stuck her head out the door. "Under what conditions?" she asked, skeptical.

"You return with me once we are done. Acceptable?"

Bianca sighed and nodded, closing the door with more force than necessary.

****

Kaius could sense the discomfort of the woman across the table, his position as leader of the haunt unsettling her despite his attempts to appear approachable. His unblinking eyes remaining locked on her as she carefully broke down her ideas, pointing intermittently at a neatly penned list laying between them. He adjusted his position, angling slightly away from her to ease the strain his intense attention was causing, consciously looking at the others in timed bursts.

Mickey stood in the corner, a small smirk on his face as the woman spoke. He watched her intently, completely absorbed with her voice. Since Mick's union with the woman, he had felt a more leveled state from his empathic child, a state of contentment Mickey had never fully achieved before. Despite their short relationship, the woman's effect on Mick was promising. Useful.

Her effect on Nichol was equally intriguing. Her strange eyes often flickered to his oldest child for reassurance and agreement, which Nichol provided in clipped replies. The respect Nichol gave the woman was peculiar, his feelings toward her similar to those he held for Mick and Jagger. She was, in Nichol's mind, his hauntmate.

He assessed his youngest child with pride. Dominic was his only impromptu creation, one many would argue was made in poor judgment. Impulsive and resentful, Dom was the cause of much contemplation for him. Unlike his meticulous scrutiny of the others prior to selection, he'd had no grasp of Dominic's personality and traits prior to the night of the accident.

He was, therefore, ruling blind during Dom's first years. Behaviors met by punishments for the others were overlooked, excused. Dominic's lack of self-control was balanced with the immense control his older brothers had mastered. He was, in Rhys's eloquent language, a spoiled brat.

Until the fidgety woman with the long hair and strange clothing entered their haunt.

Dominic's unexpected connection to the bouncy woman had marked a turning point in the young vampire. He no longer had the luxury of being uncontrolled and passive in his existence. Molly, an impressive survivor of Dovidas's sadistic personality, required strength and stability, and he watched in amazement as her influence morphed Dominic into the vampire he'd hoped he could be.

"I recognize we're on a short timeline," the cat-eyed woman concluded, sitting back in her seat. "But I feel if we concentrate our collective efforts on this issue now, it will benefit us in the long run."

He glanced around the table, noting the wary eyes of his hauntmates and the tension rippling across Rhys's shoulders. Although the eloquently spoken woman understood the importance of the Kaius haunt reputation in the greater sense, she didn't realize the importance of the protection it supplied to Rhys. Though he had settled significantly throughout the recent century, the hedonistic and volatile temperament of his second oldest had created a lengthy docket of enemies prior to the creation of marketable Tenders. His eyes traveled briefly across the once pristine skin of Rhys's arms.

"Rhys," he began, selecting his words with care in the mixed company, "there's much riding on the dissolution of the Tender trade. Have you any reservations?"

The simmering resentment spiked momentarily, retreating as Mikhail used his empathic skills to silently drain the harshest of the anger.

Rhys crossed his long arms over his chest, leveling the woman with a hard stare until he regained control. "It's very noble of Audra." He spoke quietly, voice low. "The offering of her wrist to the service of seven vamps."

Mickey's possessive snarl was cut short with a sharp look from Kai and a cocked brow of the cat-eyed woman.

"I offered nothing of the sort," Audra retorted.

Rhys leaned forward and pointed to the immaculately printed list on the table. "I was willing to entertain this idea, but you're petitioning for the complete removal of Tenders and bloodslaves from our haunt. This removes our accessible nutritional source, leaving you and Molly to fill the void. With Molly being connected to Dominic, that leaves you, Audra."

Kai rose slowly, noting Mikhail was siphoning Rhys quicker than was safe in his own heightened state. Rhys followed suit, rising from his chair, and stretching across the table with a lecherous look filling his dark eyes. "And your blood isn't the only thing we'll need from your body."

Rhys's hulking form hit the ground, the fangs of his blond brother embedded deeply into his throat. In his peripheral, Kai observed Dominic shielding his connected woman with his body as they moved toward the exit. Audra was moving toward the increasingly bloody altercation instead of away from it, her progress stayed by Nichol's grasp. Her barked orders for release caught Mikhail's attention long enough for his fangs to disengage from Rhys's veins, providing an opportunity for Kai to intervene.

Mick's body hit the floor with a thud. He lifted

Rhys from the ground, holding his snapping jaw and using his own weight to secure the snarling vamp against the wall as he growled his orders.

"Nichol. Secure and remove Mikhail. Bring the woman with you. Do. Not. Leave. Them. Alone."

Nichol moved swiftly, positioning himself on top of Mikhail's chest and instructing Audra to wait in the hall. Mickey's aggression spiked as she disappeared through the door.

"Audra!" Nichol yelled. "Get back in here and tell him to calm the fuck down."

Rhys continued to struggle against Kaius's grip, his elongated fangs skimming across his forearm in search of an enemy as he spat out a slew of curses.

The woman's authoritative voice punctured the din of snarls and hissed insults. Her words brought a sharp decline in Mikhail's rage, tempering his emotions enough for Nichol to rise and allow Mickey to exit the room under his own power.

"I'll chain her, starve her, and fuck her to death!" Rhys bellowed after the trio, his ovaled eyes gleaming with triumph at the sounds of Nichol restraining Mick in the hallway.

He tightened his hold, pushing the side of his hand deep into Rhys's mouth to silence him. It would be a long night.

Chapter Eight

Bianca pushed Louis's hastily labeled map toward Jagger and sat back against the vinyl of the cafe bench seat. Jagg glanced up at her before turning his gaze to the paper. Although she understood the need to hide the slight vampiric ovaling of his irises, his brown contact lenses were unnerving for her, removing her ability to read his intense ice-blue eyes.

He brought his coffee cup to his lips, pretending to relish the hot liquid for the benefit of the few night owl customers occupying the restaurant. "I suggest we separate the leaders from the followers," he muttered, lips held tight to cover his regenerated fangs. "Return to your home to identify the most culpable. Of the fourteen, we strike the ringleaders and use those strikes to threaten the henchmen. Nichol can assist in that."

She nodded, her unfocused anger from the night before channeling down a more logical path. The culprits were spread across the city, and she and Jagger couldn't attend to each one quickly enough to avoid alerting law enforcement before they completed their mission. Targeting the masterminds took top priority.

"Is Nichol able to email us stills from the anti-vamp website?" she asked, her mind spinning with potential moves. "And is he able to link names to any social media accounts containing pictures of each perpetrator's family?"

Jagg pursed his lips, a hint of a feral smile

beginning until he schooled his handsome face into a bored expression. "Sending the text off now. I…fuck."

"What?"

Pushing his phone in her direction, he brought his hands to his hood and adjusted it slightly. Her attention was drawn to the gray tattoos framing his face, the marks of the imprisonment he refused to discuss with her. Bringing her gaze back to his phone, she read the clipped texts buzzing in.

—Nic: Will do once Mick calms and Kaius is able to remove Rhys from the com room. —

—Jagg: ?? —

—Nic: Discussion of disassembling Tender sales, bloodslaves. —

—Rhys threatened to drain, fuck, kill Audra. —

—Mick losing his shit. —

—Rhys out of control. —

—Busy. —

—Fuck off until I contact you. —

—Unless you are staked. —

Her brows rose in surprise. Although Johan had told her stories of Rhys's legendary temper, she'd never witnessed it during her time amongst the Kaius vamps. "Why would they consider dissolving the Tender sales?" she wondered aloud.

"I would suspect in a time of conflict, there are thoughts toward tightening the ranks." Jagger pulled his phone away, tapped a quick message, and tucked it into the pocket of his sweater. "Let's head over to the house and try to get a line on each scent based on Louis and Boy's notes."

****

It took three hours for him to properly follow the fourteen scents throughout the property, carefully piecing each trail together as Bee made notes on where each started and where each ended. Three scents were present in the most soiled rooms, indicating the foulest of the humans had created the most intense damage.

The pair argued briefly when he refused to allow Bee passage into her bedroom, threatening to put a halt to the scent identification they so badly required. She didn't need to see it again, didn't need to read the words painted above her soiled bed. She finally relented and waited in the hall, but the quick vibrations across the floors indicated she didn't do so quietly. He'd assessed the room more intensely than he had the others, determined no man who had desecrated her space would go unpunished.

Back at the hotel they'd left less than forty-eight hours ago, the room felt significantly more cramped despite the lack of Louis and Boy's presence in the small space. Jagg tucked the fraying towel under the door, sealing out the last of the anticipated daylight. Bianca was in the shower for almost an hour, having disappeared silently into the room upon their return from her home.

Her weapon boxes lay open on her bed, their contents calling for his attention. He lifted each throwing star, trailing his fingers along their edges.

"I've never seen such a detailed a set of butterflies," he called out to Bee, hoping to lure her from her solitude.

He continued to peruse Bianca's collection, impressed with the craftsmanship of each pair of stars, their varied shapes and contours beautiful and uniquely fatal. Despite his comment the previous night, the edges of her weapons were perfectly sharpened, on par with his own weapons care skills.

She'd be an asset in his armory.

The soft floral scent overtaking his senses alerted him to Bianca's approach prior to her appearance. Sitting opposite him on the bed, she smiled fondly at the collection.

"Once I showed an aptitude for these, Johan ordered sets from craftsmen around the world. Those butterflies came from Egypt. The tri-stars from Thailand." She carefully deposited each pair back into her boxes, layering a soft gray silk between each.

He looked away from the petite blonde, a wave of discomfort overtaking him as he watched her bright eyes light up. "I should shower before dawn," he grumbled before stomping to the bathroom.

"I'm not spending another night in this cesspool," Rhys snarled, fangs bared. "Tonight, I walk. Whether you follow me or not."

Jagger stood on the town's outskirts, arms crossed, and refused to look at his hauntmate. "Safe travels, brother," he gritted out, bringing the large, hooded robe down to further obscure his eyes.

"You choose a whore over your blood," Rhys growled.

He held his position, refusing to be baited by his angry brother. "There's no choice."

He remained outside the city until the sound of Rhys's retreating footsteps disappeared into the night.

Rhys wouldn't turn back.

Despite having not fed in over a week, he ghosted swiftly through the town and arrived unseen at the back window of the tiny home. He clung to the shadows as he observed the woman move gracefully through the rooms, hints of her willowy form visible against the movements of her dress. Unaware of his presence, she hummed an unidentifiable lilting tune while she prepared herself for sleep.

For seven nights, he'd stood at her window, memorizing the woman's movements and expressions. He clung to her songs, bringing them to the forefront of his memory throughout the long daylight hours spent holed up in a damp cave by the water's edge.

"Who's there?"

He froze, the hood of his robe shielding his face from recognition.

"My husband will soon return." She stood at the window, her chocolate eyes scanning the darkness as she spun her lie. "He is expected any moment."

He fought a smile as he recollected the night he realized there was no man in her life, no suitor, no husband. He held steady, watching as she moved away from the window and out of his sight. Her candles remained lit, keeping his attention on the empty room.

"You've been watching me."

He started, reaching up quickly to pull the hood down further to hide his eyes. He focused his gaze on her bare feet and remained silent.

"You're the man from the lake," she stated confidently. "Where's your friend?"

Silence.

"Why have you followed me?"

He pursed his lips. "How did you know I was here?" he asked softly, cursing himself for his inattention to his surroundings while simultaneously reveling in the proximity of the stunning brunette.

"I heard you humming my song."

The cold water held no refreshing qualities, its spray pounding relentlessly on his skin. He exited the shower with care to avoid the crystal-clear mirror of the grungy bathroom as he dressed quickly in his cargos, selecting a black singlet to throw on underneath his trademark hoodie. By the time he reentered the sleeping quarters, Bianca had packed the boxes and was waiting expectantly on her bed.

"Hungry?"

He averted his eyes quickly, pretending he hadn't seen the plump lips speaking. In his current condition, he held little faith in his ability to deny himself should the curvaceous blonde offer twice. Feigning intense interest in his phone, he made himself comfortable on the bed closest to the door and turned his back to Bianca.

"Why do you never come to me in the light?" Seline whispered, her hot breath grazing his neck and sending a shiver down his spine. The warmth of her skin against his eased the incessant thrum of uncontrollable longing he felt during the daylight hours. He lifted a hand to weave through her long black curls.

"Until you agree to wed me, the cover of dark is a protection for you," he replied quietly, nuzzling the soft skin of her throat. "Turgutlu is too small a town to hide big secrets."

Seline's body lifted off him, her dark eyes narrowing in suspicion. "In all these months, not one report of a stranger has passed through the market. Wherever you hide in the day, it's not Turgutlu. You are a ghost."

He ran his tongue over his dulled fangs and grinned. "It's only you who needs to see me," he growled as he nipped at the tanned flesh of her arm. Seline's muffled shriek became a moan as he pushed deeper inside her, effectively ending the conversation for the evening.

Chapter Nine

Rhys's irises betrayed the calm stillness of his body. Kaius remained at his side, staying well within the scope of the heavy chains securing his second oldest child to the wall. The bites marring his arms and throat were healing quickly thanks to the scantily clad Tender trainee Nichol had sent into the cells hours earlier, and his broken forearm was knitting together at an acceptable pace.

Mikhail's woman was right. The number and severity of the conflicts closing in on his haunt were occurring at a rate they were unprepared to face. The past century was relatively peaceful in retrospect, allowing them to focus on building trade partners and cementing their reputations.

However, they'd also become complacent in their preparations for combat. Despite Jagger's collection of weapons and his insistence the hauntmates become familiar with each, Kaius reluctantly recognized none of his haunt had maintained a proficiency on par with battle readiness. Jagger's own capture by law enforcement weeks ago demonstrated the glaring omission in his leadership.

He'd allowed his sons to indulge in the illusion of security.

At nearly eight centuries, Rhys was a truly formidable vampire. He was the embodiment of vampiric strength, seductiveness, intelligence, and ruthlessness. His libido and temper had opened doors as frequently as it slammed dungeon hatches. Throughout the years, Rhys had fought for territory, for wealth, for honor. His prowess on the battlefield rivaled that in the bedroom, and his reputation as both a comrade and an enemy stretched across the globe.

It was he who would feel the loss of the haunt's contrived sanctuary the most. The Tender trade had provided a layer of protection for the haunt's fiercest and boldest vampire. With the safeguard gone, Rhys would no longer have his reputation and favors shielding him from the ramifications of his actions, his enemies no longer having need or desire to play nice in hopes of securing a Rhys-trained Tender. Rhys would once again become targeted, but this time, there would be two species hunting him down.

He leaned against Rhys, noting the slight downward shift in hostility his physical presence created in him.

"Are we well-stocked with mercury?"

The rasping of Rhys's voice sounded hollow in the concrete cell.

"There'll be no need," he responded quietly, remaining tight to his child's side.

Rhys's muscles moved against him as he flexed his tattooed arms and scoffed. "There will be plenty of need, I assure you," he sneered. "Unless the human law enforcement gets to me first. Then I suppose I'll be angling for a little sunblock."

The pair fell silent, knowing Kai could not, and therefore would not, guarantee Rhys would walk out the other side of their conflicts unharmed.

****

Jagger sat back in the leather seat of the vehicle, his ice-blue eyes locked on the tiny figure dressed in black moving silently through the hedges. Her blonde hair was piled high on her head and hidden under a black beret that should look far more out of place than it did on the petite woman. Without her arsenal of high heels, Bianca's slight stature was disarming, so much ferocity contained in the small form appearing innocuous to the untrained eye. Even when adorned in black denim instead of her feminine dresses, she radiated such fragile daintiness he was currently fighting the urge to throw her over his shoulder and lock her in the highest tower he could find.

In true Tender fashion, Bianca had foregone addressing his antisocial behavior the night before and had dove straight into her plans for the evening. Until Nichol was able to send the photos Bee requested, she and Jagg were relegated to recon work.

Bianca was relegated to recon work.

He was the chauffeur.

After much heated discussion, it was decided Bee would be the boots on the ground while he was the lookout on the terrain. Bianca's unreasonable aversion to the colored contacts he wore to conceal his vampiric eyes brought about his final acquiescence to the plan, her insistence he not wear them removing the protection of human irises should he encounter anyone. With his fangs fully regenerated, he was prepared to handle any danger Bee encountered amid the sprawling suburb they found themselves.

The passenger door opened quickly, and a breathless Bianca hopped up onto her seat. "That's definitely the third guy," she said once he maneuvered the vehicle onto the freeway. "From what I could see, he lives alone. This puts him at the top of the list."

He smirked at the offhanded remark, impressed the sweet-tongued blonde could so flippantly adjust the order of her kills without hesitation.

"You're smiling," Bianca noted, her blue eyes bright. "I like it."

Schooling his face and ignoring the comment, he pulled into the parking lot of the run-down motel they were calling home. "Don't open the door unless I text you," he instructed as Bee collected her things. "And stay away from the window."

She frowned. "Where exactly are you going?"

"Out."

"Out where?"

He reached over her small form and opened the passenger door. "Out for a bite to eat. Now get inside before someone recognizes you."

She paused a moment longer before she stormed out of the car and into the motel room. With his hunger too demanding to safely follow the angry woman, he tore out of the lot and went on the hunt.

****

"Full?" Bianca asked, trying unsuccessfully to keep the scorn and hurt from her face.

Jagger looked away from her, choosing to disappear into the bathroom instead of watch her lips. His avoidance technique was effective. Without those incredible eyes locked on her face, she was unable to lash out at the object of her frustration and was therefore pushed back to reviewing the sloppily penned notes he had taken as he scanned the properties of their targets.

His penmanship was atrocious.

In the two hours she'd waited for him to return, her mind had spun through dozens of scenarios, each leaving her angrier or more fearful than the last. After the first hour, her concentration had dissipated, and her thoughts remained on a loop of images. Visions of Jagger captured and chained, injured and fighting, sucking and fucking. Although she stubbornly refused to text him and ask his whereabouts, she'd glanced at her phone a hundred times in anticipation of a message.

When it finally came and she opened the door, he'd strode past her without a word.

She took a moment to relish in the relief she felt at his safe return, wrapping herself in the coarse motel blanket and settling into her bed. The comfort was short-lived, as her mind began to turn toward her anger at his silent dismissal. Many household Tenders were treated as such, their masters placing their worth slightly above a security dog or favorite lamp. As a Former Tender, her value in vampire society was high. She was entrusted with vampire affairs, called upon to negotiate delicate matters, and welcomed in the most influential of haunts as a guest of prominence.

She was not ignored, dismissed as one might a poorly performing maid.

The longer he spent in the shower, the angrier she became. A feeding should have taken no longer than half an hour. An hour, tops. Two hours meant he'd indulged in his feeding with more than his fangs. While she waited and worried.

The stream of water finally stopped. She got out of bed and waited until he emerged.

"You are a bastard," she stated, standing directly in

front of the door and enunciating clearly to ensure there was no mistaking her words.

Jagger's dark brows rose, his damp hair falling across his forehead. "You're angry."

She didn't even try to hide the rolling of her eyes. Goddamn Kaius vamps. "Yes, I'm angry. There's a very active anti-vampire movement in this city. You left with nothing to disguise what you are. And you don't think for a moment to perhaps check in and let me know you haven't been captured or staked?"

He tilted his head slightly, arresting eyes narrowing slightly. "You were worried."

With a huff, she felt her agitation decreasing. "Yes, I was worried. You have a perfectly safe food source right here. Why…" She halted her words, not wanting to push him into giving her an answer she did not want to hear.

A small flicker passed through his ice-blue stare before he pursed his lips. "You're an emergency source," he rationalized. "If I take advantage of your goodwill now, I may regret it in a time of need. Though it may not be an issue anyways. My meal was more than sufficient."

Temper flaring once again, she poked him hard in the solar plexus. "Next time take a moment from your suck and fuck to let me know you aren't disintegrating to ash in the ditch. At least until this mission is completed. Agreed?"

She turned on her heel and stomped to the bed, burrowing under the covers. If he could ignore her, she could do the same. As his footsteps moved across the floor toward his bed, his quiet voice permeated her blanket fortress.

"If I'd fucked, I wouldn't have needed so long in the shower."

****

The man's light brown eyes were the last thing to fade into death. Fitting. They were the same eyes peering through Seline's window earlier that night, daring to stare upon her olive skin as she sank into a heated vat of water. Jagger had arrived just as the filthy degenerate was reaching under his robes to pleasure himself to the vision of her naked and vulnerable.

Seline.

He licked the soiled blood from his lips. She would be wondering where he was. Stripping and hoisting the stinking body over his shoulder, he carried the carcass into the depths of the lake and dove under the water. Holding the body to the ground with his foot, he lifted the heavy stones of the lakebed and deposited them atop the cadaver. When he finally broke through the water's surface, her willowy silhouette stood barefoot at the bank.

"You are late," she called to him, her hair still damp from her bathing.

He swam to shore in a haste, anxious to reassert his claim on the woman. She squealed in feigned shock at his nude form, turning and running from him playfully.

The hunt.

He brought her to the ground in seconds, rolling to cushion her body with his as they fell to the hard earth. His lips sought hers frantically, desperate to taste her and reassure himself she belonged to him. Her delicate fingers ran through his hair, pulling him impossibly closer. When she finally pulled back, she gasped for air.

"Your eyes," she whispered, peering closer.

He stilled.

She lowered her face to his, examining his ovaled irises with awe. "Why... How?" Her fingers came to his temples, turning his head slowly from side to side. He covered her hands with his and gently nudged her off him. The kill, the feed, the hunt.

The connection.

Months of careful cover under the shroud of darkness and candlelight had hidden his secret from her easily, allowing him to maintain a semblance of humanity with the perfect creature watching him warily as he rose. When she didn't run from him, he opened his mouth slowly, baring his unbroken fangs.

"Empusa," she breathed out, stumbling back a step before collecting herself.

He remained still, allowing his connected mate to scrutinize him cautiously, her knees bent slightly in preparation to run at his first twitch. Seconds passed. Minutes. She approached him warily, lifting her fingers to his fangs. She appraised him in silence, grazing his lips, his brows, his hair with her hands and peering inquisitively at his face as though seeing his visage for the first time.

"You are not human," she eventually said softly, pulling her touch from him.

He shook his head slowly. "I was once."

"You drink..." She waved her hand across her throat. Her shoulder rose slightly, subconsciously protecting her jugular from him.

With a nod, he averted his eyes and steeled himself for her rejection.

Chapter Ten

"So what's the deal with you and Boy?" Jagg inquired casually as Bianca attempted to connect the new printer and computer. Since her return to the room at dusk, she'd refused to look his way and had instead spent her time setting up her purchases for use. Although he and Bianca weren't a couple, he was beginning to understand the torment Mickey went through when Audra implemented the silent treatment for a wrongdoing.

He didn't find it enjoyable. And he was definitely not in the mood to be teased about it by a haunt full of unattached vamps.

Their easy banter and heated debates were replaced with an awkward sullenness since he'd walked through the door the previous night. Aside from the brief confrontation after his shower, Bee spoke only to communicate the most necessary of information. She was going to the store. She would be back within the hour. She was opening the door.

At least she warned him instead of frying him in his bed.

Determined to go back to an affable relationship with the huffy blonde hunched over the laptop, he pressed on. "You're more comfortable with him than any woman I've seen. Did you spend much time with him during your training at the haunt?"

He wouldn't admit it out loud, but Bianca's

amiable interactions with the mute vamp had plagued his thoughts for the past week. His curiosity was piqued.

As was his jealousy.

Bianca leveled him with a look, crossing her arms under her breasts and sitting back in the worn chair. "It's my job, correct? To provide services to recalcitrant, ungrateful vampires?" A single brow rose, and she refocused on the screen.

He frowned and pulled his hood forward slightly. "I haven't used your services."

"I am well aware."

"So you and Boy…"

She turned to him, eyes blazing. "Boy receives the same treatment as every other vampire in my sphere requiring attention. He is a job. A task. One of my MANY charges throughout the decades."

He could feel his shoulders tensing as the Former Tender confirmed suspicions he truly didn't want to think about. While his body primed to shut down the conversation, his mouth had other plans. "So you've slept with him? Recently?"

"No."

His shoulders relaxed a fraction. Until she continued.

"We don't sleep when I go to him."

Frustrated and livid with her biting words, he bent down and laced his boots. "I'm heading out. I'll text you if I'm longer than an hour. Or if Nichol makes contact."

Eyes trained on the vehicle, he closed the door forcefully behind him, not knowing if she had called after him and not wanting to care if she hadn't.

****

He didn't go far. He drove to the other side of the motel, parked in an unlit corner, and scaled the balconies to the roof. From his position tight to the large unused air conditioning unit, he could see every access point to the motel. He sent off a text to Bianca an hour into his watch.

—*All good. Will check in at one.* —

When no response came, he sat back on his haunches and scanned the area again half-heartedly. His interest in Bianca was reaching a zone he was unwilling to enter. Especially with a woman trained to want his kind. Manufactured desire.

Jagger hesitated again, pulling back from the sweet flesh, and lifting his body from her.

"You don't have to do this," he whispered. "I don't want…" He trailed off. He didn't want her to feel obligated. He didn't want to cause her pain. He didn't want to solidify what she already knew about him.

"I want," Seline responded, wrapping her arms around his shoulders, and pulling him tight to her. "I need to," she said, resolution in her soft voice.

Reaching between them, he slid his fingers into her folds and through her wetness. Her hips rotated rhythmically against his hand, encouraging him with her sighs and her movements. When her body began to tense under him, he slipped inside her, easing into her tight sheath with painful restraint.

He had fantasized for months about the moment he could possess his connected mate through both body and blood. His days were spent pacing and snarling in the blackness of his cave dwelling, fighting dual urges to hide from the sun and race through it toward her.

83

She occupied his every thought, determined his every move.

Hiding his obsession from her had become torturous, feigning romantic interest in the woman while his every impulse screamed to consume her, to link himself to her for eternity. He stilled inside her, gritting his teeth to regain his slipping control.

Frightening her with his intensity now would end badly for both of them.

Long legs tightened around his hips, and he began to rock inside her at a steadily increasing speed. She arched her back, pushing her breasts against his bare chest as the first flutters of her impending orgasm began. When the first wave hit, his fangs pierced the flawless skin. Her blood pumped into his mouth, forcing him to release into her at a frantic, desperate pace.

Perfection.

As she came down from her moment, she tangled her fingers in his hair to hold him against her throat, whimpering as aftershocks rippled through her body. His core sated, he unhooked his fangs and reared up dubiously, uncertain of her reaction with the reality of him solidified.

The repetitive buzzing of his phone's timer drew him back to the present, ripping him from his thoughts and sharpening his attention onto the tangible. He debated sending Bianca another text, another coward's message of avoidance. Keeping tight to the shingles, he shimmied across the roof, descended to the ground, and drove around the motel. Although he had an eagle's view from the rooftop, leaving Bianca alone for so long wasn't sitting well in his gut. His pace quickened toward the door as he messaged his arrival.

The door opened immediately, revealing a sheepish-looking Bee dressed in a bright yellow shift and knee-high white boots. The vision of her standing safety within the confines of the motel room eased a knot forming in his stomach, a small relief he knew passed across his features. The door clicked closed.

"I apologize," she began, twirling a large silver ring on her hand. "I haven't spent this much time in such close quarters with a vampire since Johan. I forget myself."

He sat on the bed and adjusted his hood. "There's nothing to apologize for," he replied. "Except maybe the silent treatment. It's unpleasant. But after spending five decades surrounded by Tender trainees, I should know the protocol."

She smiled and sidled up close to him, her breasts inches from his face as she spoke. "Take me to dinner," she insisted, placing a finger on his lips when he started to refuse. "The cafe across the street has been virtually deserted every night. I'll order enough for two, and you can keep your head down. No contacts."

"It's too risky. And dressed like that, we'll have trouble evacuating you if trouble arises."

Placing one foot on his thigh, Bianca lifted her skirt up to reveal her butterfly throwing stars. "I'm hungry. Either we eat, or I become very unhappy."

****

Bianca was absolutely delighted with the array of boxed desserts spread before her on the sticky table. While the steak was gritty and tough, the chicken was cooked perfectly and the fries were homemade and seasoned with spices from the gods. Several empty plates sat inconspicuously in front of Jagger, making it appear as though he had devoured two of the three dishes she'd ordered from the pretty server. Only the waitress and a young flirtatious cook inhabited the cafe, allowing her and Jagg to relax a bit in the dark dining room.

"I know most women don't eat this much," Jagg muttered, dirtying a dessert fork with a strawberry cheesecake, and setting it aside. "I don't believe I ate this much when I was human. This is both impressive and disturbing."

She flung a small crumb from her plate at him, huffing when he skillfully batted it midair. "I have a high metabolism and need to keep my energy up," she retorted haughtily, digging into a chocolate cream pie. "Audra told me you were a gentleman. I think she was mistaken."

He chuckled, taking care to cover his mouth and fangs with a napkin. "I can be a gentleman when needed," he insisted. "But this"—he motioned across the table—"is keeping me in a state of awe and fascination. Where does it all go? You're so tiny."

Licking the chocolate off her fork and assessing her next choices, she smirked. "Johan often made that remark. He once said if Rhys was forthcoming about my grocery bill, he wouldn't have bid so high. Besides, Nichol sent me the photos earlier, so everything is a go tomorrow. This is our last night to relax for a few days, and I intend to ensure I'm completely satisfied."

She turned her attention back to the sweet selections calling to her and chose a slice of apple pie slathered in caramel sauce. Making amends with the handsome vampire was quite rewarding. Her stomach was full, her head was clear, and her companion was humming pleasantly.

During his absence earlier in the night, she'd made the decision to return to her roots, to apply Rhys's training to her interactions with Jagger. She was rusty, her decades spent with the indulgent Johan and subsequent years as an acknowledged Former Tender nudging at her psyche as she flirted playfully and meaninglessly.

Tomorrow night, she would morph back into a trained assassin, but for tonight, she was a perfect courtesan. Trailing one booted toe over his calf muscle, she scanned her mind for irrelevant, inane topics of discussion.

"So, Jagger," she said sweetly, leaning forward and pushing a stray blonde lock behind her ear, "how do you like driving the four-by-four?"

****

Jagger's body was thrumming as he and Bianca made their way across the barren parking lot toward their motel room. Once he was able to assuage his concerns over their unprotected location, he spent the remaining two hours of Bianca's meal indulging in the sensory overload her presence had brought to the table. A soft floral scent emanated off her skin and hair with every movement, causing him to inadvertently breathe in every few minutes until the plethora of food arrived at their table.

The waitress was pretty enough, a woman he would have looked at twice had she not been standing beside Bianca, paling in comparison. Bee's long blonde hair hung in loose curls around her face, accentuating the professionally practiced makeup making the blue of her eyes appear surreal but containing no strong odors for his heightened sense of smell to detect.

Her plump lips were painted with a shiny pink gloss she reapplied with painful nonchalance after each plate was consumed. Despite the incredible intake of food, he struggled to look away every time she licked her lips in anticipation of the next bite.

The movement of her tongue across her dessert fork brought forth decidedly ungentlemanly thoughts.

As eating turned to talking and numerous cups of steaming coffee for Bianca, he fell into a heavenly hell. The gentle grazing of her foot against his leg was consistent enough to be intentional, but their proximity at the small table left him questioning the meaning, if any, of the intermittent contact. Apparently unconcerned with his increased shifting in his seat, she engaged him in a constant stream of conversation about everything from his new ride to books to favorite tourist destinations.

Every so often, he would disagree with her and her eyes would light up in annoyance before the topic would change and the cheerful banter would return.

Now, with her small hand wrapped around his forearm, he was struggling between dueling threads of want and need. He and Bianca needed to maintain a working distance from each other, needed to remain focused on their impending mission. They needed to rest, prepare, and plan.

They did not need to indulge in the raging want he was concealing with his long sweater and a slight slouch.

With a final scan of the lot, he followed her into their room and leaned against the door to watch her unzip her tall boots and step out of them with gracefully pointed toes. Setting them aside, she began rifling through her suitcase and tossing her selections across the bed. He looked away as the short yellow dress rode high enough to reveal the throwing stars strapped to her toned thighs.

He debated bolting for the bathroom, hiding under a stream of cold water until she was safely ensconced under the hideous motel blankets. When he glanced toward the shower, she caught his eye, a coquettish smile gracing her features.

"You aren't actually considering spending the rest of our last peaceful evening locked up in there, are you?" she asked innocently as she dropped her thin coat from her shoulders.

He remained motionless, his jaw set as the petite woman made his way over to him. Everything he craved was currently encased in a flimsy golden smock and pressing against his taut form. He kept his hands tucked firmly in his pockets, unwilling to release them and allow free rein.

She wasn't demonstrating the same restraint.

Slim fingers were currently sliding up the back of his arms and ghosting over his collarbones. They caressed his tense jawline and hesitated as she looked up at him, her head tilted in quiet contemplation before she continued her trek to his temples, skimming the offensive tattoos adorning his face.

"What do they mean?" she whispered, her blue eyes trained on the intricate designs.

He felt his muscles tighten instinctively. "It's Burmese," he muttered. "Curse."

When her eyes didn't flicker with disgust or pity, another knot released in his gut and the tension in his shoulders lessened a fraction. She raised up onto her toes, her lips brushing against his momentarily before she turned her attention to his throat. He drew in an unneeded breath and pushed his fisted hands further into his pockets as she continued to tease and test his restraint with her full lips and flicking tongue. A single finger trailed over his lips, tracing the curve of his fang and puncturing her soft flesh on its tip.

Chapter Eleven

Nichol stared unseeing at the printer as it spit out page after page, a litany of graphs, timelines, and detailed tables collecting neatly in the tray. When the whir of the machine ceased, he collected the papers, straightened the pile, and placed a single staple in the top corner.

"I should join you to answer any concerns he may have."

With a grunt of refusal, he turned to Audra and leveled her with a harsh glare. "Return to your mate and keep him under control with whatever witchcraft you possess," he growled. "This is a vampire matter. One you are incapable of comprehending."

Light brown eyes narrowed into slits as she rose to her feet. "Louis's hanging out with Mickey right now. This is a psychological issue, and the last time I checked, I was the only certified psychologist in this haunt."

Pinching the bridge of his nose, he walked past the woman who was both a comrade and a massive pain in his ass. The clicking of her heels as she caught up to his march down the hall rattled in the back of his eyes. "Audra, I'm not bringing you into the same room as Rhys right now and getting his scent on your skin. I need you to work with Louis and create a plan for the bloodslave release. I'll send Kai up shortly to check your progress."

Huffing her discontent, she swatted at his arm and headed toward the bunkers. With one crisis averted, he entered the bloodslave quarters and made his way to the cells where Kaius and Rhys were sitting against the damp wall.

"How'd you manage to shake her?" Rhys asked as he scented the air.

He approached his younger brother cautiously, ensuring the rabid tint of Rhys's irises had dissipated. Although he was older and stronger, he didn't relish the thought of having to rip the tongue out of his temperamental sibling. Rhys's snarling threats to Audra were still ringing in the halls of the haunt, leaving an unspoken rift in the air between the hauntmates.

Ignoring the inquiry, he passed the documents to Kaius. "Once we have Louis's input, we can begin to integrate the strongest of the bloodslaves back into human society. Molly has been making meticulous notes throughout her discussions with them, and I've already begun preparing the necessary identification and paperwork for a smooth transition. After we begin the process, I'll have photo identification added and will create a banking profile for each human."

While Kaius hummed in agreement and flipped through the papers, Rhys leaned forward onto his knees. "What's my job going to be?"

He looked to Kai for confirmation Rhys was fully stabilized. A hesitant nod.

****

Louis's angular face was beginning to show signs of exhaustion, a condition rarely visible on a vampire. He rubbed his temples in frustration and refocused on Mickey's eyes.

"I dunno, man. Cluck like a chicken."

Mick's brows rose slightly. "Cluck, cluck."

Booting the coffee table away, Louis rose from the sofa and walked toward the bunker door. "I'm done. Tell Audra I'll work on two, maybe three humans a night. Any more and I'm going to fry my own fucking brain. I'm heading down to the weapons room to hang out with the Dominic for a bit before I hit the city for a feed."

Mick leaned against the wall and crossed his arms, draining Louis's frustrations slowly. "Will do. Don't take it too hard. I'm just exceptionally intelligent. Hypnosis is harder on geniuses than on your average shmuck."

With a snort, Louis left him alone in his quarters to await Audra's return. He paced the room, an uneasiness settling in the back of his mind. Since Rhys's explosion two nights prior, he hadn't permitted Audra to leave the safety of his bunk, despite Kaius's reassurance Rhys was secured in the bloodslave cells and being monitored continually.

Permitted.

Begged.

He had begged Audra to remain at his side. Rhys's threat played on a loop in his head, reminding him with every tick of the clock how fragile and vulnerable Audra was in a haunt of aggressive vamps. Boy's arrival back at the haunt was also plaguing his thoughts. Images of the mute vampire tracking Audra's every breath interjected themselves into Rhys's voice, creating a viperous collage. When she had finally had enough of his jealous rants and irrational tirades, she'd walked out the door and sent Louis in.

He ran a hand through his long hair and fired off a text to Nichol, probing for information on Audra's whereabouts. Not trusting himself to hold his temper should he run into Boy in the halls, he continued to pace as his phone stayed silent.

"Mikhail."

Opening the door to Kaius, he glanced down the hallway for Audra.

"She's in the com room with Molly compiling the first list of eligible bloodslaves," Kai said, responding to the unasked question. "I'm here to communicate a request. From Rhys."

Fangs bared on instinct. "He's in no position to make requests of me right now," he snarled. "Where is he?"

"Chained under Nichol and Boy's watch. You may refuse, but Rhys would like to speak with you," Kaius said quietly. "I'm under the impression he would like to apologize to you."

He filled the doorway, caught between defiance and deference. Despite his stoic facade, Kai was strongly affected when a rift threatened the unity of his bloodline. And most of those fractures had historically centered on Rhys. He set his jaw and nodded tersely.

"Fine. But get Boy out of there. And I'm not promising anything."

The pair walked in silence to the bloodslave quarters, passing the cells of the humans and descending into the dungeon. The hauntmates had worked tirelessly for eight years to build their intricate underground bunker, a safe haven during a time when vampires were still folklore among humans. The damp concrete prison was an afterthought, a place to secure enemies who breached protocols or posed threats.

Rhys had spent the most time in it.

Boy's scent lingered in the air, bringing out an instinctual possessive growl from Mick.

"Relax," Nichol barked. "He's been sent to the weapons room to assist Dom and Louis."

He grunted in acknowledgment and turned toward his tethered brother. "Speak."

With a side-glance at Nichol and Kai, Rhys hunched over his knees. "This is between us."

"This," he snarled, gesturing between them, "was between us when Audra first moved into the bunkers. This was between us when Amy was still dancing around. This was between us when you wanted to stud me out to your newest acquisitions. But now, this is between all of us. Because whatever you say now is going to decide a lot of fucking things around here."

Although his dark eyes narrowed, Rhys remained still on the cold floor. "I have no intention of harming Audra," he gritted out. "Her ideas aren't wholly unreasonable. There's…" He looked over at Kai briefly. "There's merit in the plan. And I'll go along with it."

He adjusted his stance, looming his height over his older hauntmate. "Chain her," he hissed. "Starve her. Fuck. Her. To. Death. You think I give a fuck about your altered opinion on her IDEAS? I should rip your fangs out of your head and leave you down here for a decade with nothing but rat's blood to sustain you. Maybe offer you up to Stojanovski as a peace offering." He straightened, taking a moment to buffer and drain the spikes of anger encircling him.

"I didn't mean it," Rhys muttered as he rose to his

feet amid the clanking of chains. "Mick. I give you my word. I will never harm her. You know that. I know you know that."

Nichol and Kaius remained in his periphery, their stances adjusted slightly to bring them down if a fight broke out.

He and Rhys squared off, neither looking away as they sized each other up. A pang of sympathy echoed through him as he stared down his shackled brother, a brother who moved within his manacles instead of fighting against them. He stepped toward Rhys, maintaining his unblinking gaze. "The next time you so much as flash a fang at Audra, I will stake you. You know that. I know you know that."

****

Jagger stared at the yellowing stucco of the motel ceiling.

It was a classic Tender move when dealing with a recalcitrant vampire, one who required a feeding but was withholding for whatever reason appeared rational to the hungry vamp. A simple slice, the scent of blood, the residue on the fang. A perfectly calculated move to allow a Tender to complete her duty.

A goddamn assignment.

Bianca feigned sleep at his side, the rise and fall of her breathing too shallow for a state of rest. The warm skin he'd craved earlier now burned along his ribs and hip, a searing reminder of his momentary lapse in judgment. The sun was now high in the winter sky, eliminating any chance of escaping the stifling room for another five hours. He shifted his weight slightly, noting the burst of tension rippling through Bianca's naked form before she relaxed against him again.

To be blunt, he fucked up.

The taste of O positive lingered on his tongue. His body was completely sated, but his mind refused to settle. Everything about the experience had felt wrong, rote, and jaded by a perfect execution. Bianca's every move was calculated to provide maximum pleasure for him, intended to gratify his core yearnings effectively and completely. The angle of her hips, the turn of her head, each pose struck with the perfection he had come to expect from Rhys's Tenders.

The submission he had come to expect from Rhys's Tenders.

His elongated fangs dug deep into his lip as he fought back a snarl. "It's not a symbol of ownership!"

Seline turned her back to him, holding her cascade of black hair high and silently inviting him to fasten the long trail of buttons adorning her gown. "When you speak of it as such, it becomes one," she reasoned, unconcerned with his rising ire. "It's impractical for me to wear it at the bakery. Dough hardens in the crevices and dulls the shine. This was not a problem eight months ago. You're only angry now because I received attention from another man." She arched her head to level him with a glare. "Attention I did not return."

The final button fit snugly into its loop, the craftsmanship of the garment withstanding his frustrated movements. "You are not available to others," he growled.

With a sigh, she turned toward him and placed her hands on her ample hips. "This, I know. As do you. That ring is a trinket of affection, not a spelled amulet to protect me from the wandering eyes of strange men.

And until you recognize it is not a leash, you can take the bauble and bury it in the sand."

Eleven months had passed since he first laid eyes on her. Eight since he placed a ring on her finger in an unwitnessed, unsanctioned marriage ceremony beside the water. He patted his pocket, reassuring himself the band was still safely nestled there. Her refusal to wear it for work was rational, but logic was the farthest thing from his mind when she had casually laughed off an encounter she'd had with a human man the day earlier.

A man who presumed to request a stroll with his connected mate.

The man's scent was faint on her skin, a ghosted presence indicating the encounter was brief.

He would track it once the sun set again.

She rose on her toes and kissed his cheek before slipping out the door and into the market. He stalked across the room, lifted the small hatch, and descended into the tight sleeping quarters beneath her home where he would sit and seethe until he heard her footsteps overhead again. The hard earth was softened by the numerous blankets she had insisted upon, refusing to accept his argument his proximity to her more than made up for the lack of luxury. He piled the blankets into the corner and leaned against them, knowing rest would not come.

Submission. Throughout his time with Seline, he simultaneously yearned for and was repulsed by the thought of her submitting to him, bending to his will, and surrendering herself to him completely. Her very essence balked at capitulating, at bartering her independence in exchange for fleeting security. Her strength drew him in as easily as it pushed him to his knees.

Looking down at the fan of blonde hair spread across his bare chest, he closed his eyes and escaped into the memories of the convictions of a willowy brunette. And the prices paid by both of them.

Chapter Twelve

Bianca slipped the printed photos into the cup of her bra, ignoring the rankled tension vibrating across Jagger's shoulders as she did so. She brushed her blonde hair into a ponytail and secured it under an oversized black beret to hide its honeyed brightness.

"It's a pity to hide that mane," Jagg murmured, trailing a finger across the back of her exposed neck.

She responded with a coy smile, nuzzling into his hand on cue and continuing to apply her makeup. He watched her hungrily, his eyes following her movements and unabashedly appraising her as she prepared for the hunt. Her every pass alongside him was met with the grazing of a hand along her thigh, her ribs, her ass.

Precisely as expected.

The sudden shift from reluctant companion to seductive lover was both unnerving and comfortable, and she found herself responding on demand without thought. It was easy. Known. A familiar dance for both parties. The charted territory of Tender and vampire.

Spreading her throwing stars across the bed, she took a moment to contemplate which set would do the honors of spilling the blood of the deplorable. Jagg stood tight behind her and reached for the tri-stars.

"There's nothing delicate or beautiful in what you are doing tonight," he said softly. "Those bastards do not deserve to lose their lives to the craftsmanship of the butterflies. If I had dulled flea market stars on hand, I would insist upon those."

Her eyes fell on the butterfly stars, their exquisite edges and detail setting them apart from all others. With a brief pause, she wrapped them carefully and placed them back in the box. The other stars were scattered across her body, ensuring she was prepared from any angle. Turning to him, she looked up into his ice-blue eyes.

"These kills are mine and mine alone," she reiterated.

A flash of something she couldn't identify passed over his face before he nodded.

The ride to the first location was silent. She reviewed the house layout in her mind, noting doors and dead ends. The perpetrator, a man by the name of Clayton Jorgensson, lived alone in the run-down home. Along with the photos, Nichol had included links to various anti-vampire sites on which the Lincoln mob was active.

Clayton was a leader in the movement, a bitter, spiteful man who viewed vampires as the root of everything wrong in his life. Vampires ruined good, wholesome women with their perversions. They controlled the global economy and were intentionally sending the world into recession to weaken the population and gain both power and numbers. They were abominations, minions of Satan sent to bring about the end of humanity.

Clayton was the man who positively identified Bianca as a vampire supporter, a traitor to her species and a whore to the devil.

A blood whore.

Jagger remained attentive to the winter roads, humming a melancholy tune as he wound through the back alley toward Clayton Jorgensson's residence. One hand sat on her knee, tracing absentminded circles in beat to his unrecognizable song. As the Jorgensson house came into view, she placed a stilling hand atop Jagg's.

"Should you park here?" she inquired, a sudden flutter of nerves settling in the pit of her stomach. "Will you wait in the car or…?"

"I'll come with you," he offered, as if he sensed her change in confidence. "I would be more comfortable with this idea if I was able to ensure your safety from up close rather than attempting to read the situation from afar."

She bristled in her seat, unwilling to give up her deserved kill but recognizing his presence against a relatively unknown combatant could be beneficial. She nodded with certainty. "Park here. Are you armed?"

He took her hand, patting it along his chest and thighs with a smirk. "Enough?"

She cocked a brow. "Are you always this loaded?" she asked, impressed at the number of blades the muscled vamp had managed to stash on his body while she showered at dusk.

"There are six more in my boots," he replied, pulling the vehicle tight to the curb. "I like to have options."

The duo made their way through the rickety back gate of Clayton Jorgensson's house, staying along the shoveled path to avoid leaving boot prints in the snow. Jagger remained behind her, his hulking presence propping her courage. The realization of what she was about to embark on was slowly resonating in her mind.

After decades of preparing for armed conflicts against hostile vampires alongside Johan, this was her first mission against a human, against a man whose body wouldn't dissolve into sludge before evaporating to ash. His dead eyes would continue to stare. His blood would spill across a body that remained intact, recognizable. Someone would find his corpse, and Clayton Jorgensson would be buried, possibly mourned, unlike vampires who merely ghosted from existence within hours.

She halted her progress at the back door, steeling herself.

"Allow me to do this," Jagger whispered into her ear. "Go back to the car, Bianca."

She swayed back slightly, subconsciously using the large form behind her to solidify her resolve. With the shake of her head, she pulled a lock pick from her back pocket and began to work the doorknob.

****

Jagger watched in fascination as the tiny blonde popped the lock effortlessly, her nimble fingers hitting its target with ease. With calculated movements, Bianca opened the door slowly. He assessed the rusty hinges and wondered briefly if they squeaked and were currently alerting their target to the invasion in progress.

Although he understood his purpose in the mission, to remain observant without involvement, he wanted nothing left to chance. He pulled a blade from the holster strapped across his chest and scanned the dark house, memorizing the layout as they slunk through the back hall. Following her lead, he kept one hand on the walls as they made their way through the main floor of the dilapidated bungalow. She was chasing a sound, pausing, and tilting her head as she zeroed in on the noise.

Wherever Clayton Jorgensson was, he was staying put. He noted no rumbles, no vibrations in the floor or along the walls. She led him through the filthy kitchen and moved to descend the stairwell.

He reached for her, placing his hand on her slim shoulder to stay her progress.

"It's too dark down there," he whispered into her ear. "Let me lead. Your eyes will take too long to adjust to the light change, and those seconds could be valuable."

Her muscles tensed for a moment, likely ruffling at his suggestion she fall back. He gave her a moment to acquiesce, pleased when she stepped back and allowed him to pass. The stairwell was steep and narrow, the wooden planks bowing as his weight smoothly transferred from one to the next. When he reached the bottom landing, he moved to the side to allow her to take her rightful place at the front once again.

The basement was a jumble of ill-planned walls and doors, the hall uncomfortably narrowed by haphazardly stocked boxes. The faint light of a computer screen broke through the frame of a poorly hung door, providing enough light for her human eyes to locate the stumbling blocks in their path.

He maintained his vibration assessment, one hand remaining on a wall while his booted feet traveled smoothly across the floor. As they approached the illuminated room, she paused, reaching down to pull a pair of tri-stars from her boots. Her hand lingered on the doorknob for a fraction, enough time for him to consider forcibly removing her from the lead and taking over the mission to ensure no harm came to the petite woman.

But Bianca deserved her revenge.

The door flew open, revealing a hulking, foul-smelling man sitting at a desk surrounded by empty food containers and stale beer bottles. He instinctively stopped scenting the air, his nose overpowered by the stench of unwashed human and rotting meat. The man scrambled to his feet, grasping for a handgun lying carelessly atop the computer tower as Bianca adjusted her stance and sent the first star flying through the air.

****

Focus, bunny.

Bianca ignored the blood spilling from the wounds her tri-stars left in the wrist and chest of the howling man. Secure with the knowledge Jagger remained at her back, she walked toward Clayton Jorgensson, digging her heeled boot into his ribs to push his injured body back into his chair.

"Clayton," she said cheerfully, yanking out the tri-star embedded in his breastbone and waving it toward him. "It is a delight to finally meet you."

"Who the fuck are you?" he yelled, struggling to stand while he made a feeble attempt to staunch the flow of blood pooling beneath him.

"Oh, honey." She nicked the man's cheek with her star, noting Jagger's movement into her peripheral. She angled her face slightly so her companion could participate in the conversation. "Bianca Schumann. Though I believe you incorrectly identified me as Bianca Holst."

She turned to Jagg, putting more weight behind the foot lodged against Clayton's chest. "I just couldn't bring myself to take on his name," she explained casually. "Bianca Schumann rolls off the tongue so much nicer. Don't you think?"

He grinned, providing a rare glimpse of his fangs for the benefit of their target. "I rather enjoy the way Bianca Schumann rolls off my tongue."

She rolled her eyes at the innuendo.

"Fucking blood whore!" Clayton snarled, spitting his disgust onto her boot.

She rose a hand to Jagg, pleased when his launch at the man halted. "Bianca," she corrected, taking the opportunity to slice at Clayton Jorgensson's lower lip. "I believe you've recently been in my home. Yes?"

A feral smile crossed the man's face, causing the cut on his lip to bleed more profusely. His injured arm rose slowly, angling awkwardly in a feeble attempt to reach for his weapon once again. She sighed, lowered her foot from his chest, and stepped back. "I thought we agreed when I arrived you shouldn't do that," she chastised, sending her star into his bicep. Clayton lurched forward, gripping his new wound, and spitting profanities.

"You fucking cock-sucking whore of Satan," he snarled, blood and spittle dribbling down his chin.

A blade embedded into the man's calf. She looked over at Jagger with disapproval.

"Sorry," he said flippantly, his irises elongating. "Instinct."

She bent down to meet Clayton's eyes. "This will go fast, or it will go slow," she said, enunciating clearly so Jagger would see her warning. "I want you to turn around and show me the names of any other women your group intends to target."

As the man launched into another tirade of curses, she righted herself and waited.

"He'll bleed out within the next thirty minutes," Jagg mused as he sauntered over to the computer tower and collected the handgun. "Sooner if he continues to yank at the one in the wrist."

The man froze, releasing the weapon but refusing to turn toward the computer.

"Clayton, honey, you are looking rather pale," she cooed. "Let's just get this done, and I'll put you down quickly."

"You're a fucking traitor," the man gasped out, his strength depleting. "Every one of you dirty whores."

Clayton's front teeth flew across the room, and she crossed her arms in annoyance. "For the love of…would you stop it?"

Jagger lowered his bloodied fist to his side, his ice eyes almost unrecognizable as they remained trained on the dying human. She huffed, removing two more stars from her pockets as she stepped back to ensure a lethal hit and released. The stars hit their marks, and Clayton Jorgensson fell forward clutching his throat.

"Be a dear and collect the computer," she instructed Jagg, her gaze locked on the dying man at her feet. She forced her attention away, scanning the cluttered room. Anti-vampire propaganda signs littered the walls and table.

Photos of women, some of whom she recognized as Tenders, were scattered across the desk, names and locations scrawled across them. Stepping over the pools of blood, she systematically collected the pictures, carefully placing them in a neat pile for later assessment.

Jagger didn't move.

"The computer," she said again, a rising need boiling in her to vacate the premises. In frustration, she huffed and yanked the cables from the wall, wrapping them haphazardly around the tower and hoisting it onto her hip. Slipping a hand into her bra to locate a photo, she dropped it on top of the dying man. "Fine. Let's go."

Clayton had yet to take his final gurgling breath as she led Jagg out of the basement. They made their way to the car, Jagg making no move to assist her with the bulky computer tower when she deposited it gently into the back seat. As the vehicle tore out of the tight alley and onto the main road, she closed her eyes and leaned back.

The kill had not held the thrill she had hoped it would. The need for revenge pulsating at the back of her brain was temporarily appeased, but the release was slow, not the burst of adrenaline she had expected to experience. The photos of the women, herself among them, were tucked securely in her back pocket. Between those and the computer, she'd gained a wealth of information from her first human kill.

They pulled into the motel lot, aligning the car tightly to their room. The pair got out and entered the room silently, Jagger moving across the floor like a caged lion. Ignoring him, she placed the computer tower on her bedside table and tossed the photos onto the desk, stripping her hat and boots off as she made her way into the bathroom.

The steady thrum of the hot water on her back

soothed the tension knotting her shoulders and the tension in her muscles. Tinges of pink swirled at her feet, spatters of Clayton Jorgensson's blood rinsing from her hands and face. She scrubbed her hair and skin rigorously, earnestly washing away the stench lingering in her nose.

The fresh smell of her bodywash began to overtake the room, the steam wafting a floral scent to indicate she had succeeded in eliminating Clayton Jorgensson from her body. Turning the water off, she wrapped herself in a coarse towel and entered the now empty bedroom.

Chapter Thirteen

Audra paused outside the common room to take a deep, centering breath. Mickey's long arm wrapped around her waist, his nose buried in her hair.

"I would feel a lot better about this if you let me join you," he murmured, pulling her closer to him and scenting her neck.

She shook him off, stretching up to kiss his cheek in reassurance. "Just monitor him, and if, IF, you sense anything, then you can come in. It'll be fine," she stated, attempting to convince both herself and Mick. "You'll be close, right?"

Mickey nodded tersely, obviously unhappy with her decision. He gestured toward the hallway juncture leading to the com room. "Kaius and I will be right over there."

As he reluctantly released her, she straightened her spine and strode into the common room where Rhys was lounging on the sofa, his bare feet kicked up onto the coffee table. Her nose wrinkled out of habit.

"Where's Mick?" Rhys asked, glancing toward the large French doors separating them from the rest of the haunt. "Ah. He and Kai are probing with full force."

"You can sense that?" she asked, curious. Although she was well versed in Mick's empathy abilities, she had much to learn about the intricate interactions they had with the other hauntmates.

Rhys's brows rose slightly in surprise. "I can. A

small line opens, similar to the intravenous tubes we use in the bloodslave quarters. Right now there are two. You can stop scanning me over, sweetheart. They're internal."

She glanced away, debating whether she should sit to project an openness to conversation or stand to portray her readiness for attack.

"Just sit already." Rhys huffed, bringing his legs off the table, and resting his elbows on them. His tattoos were on full display, the elaborate lines interwoven to create asymmetrical masterpieces on his skin. She took her position on the large wing back chair, crossing her legs and forcing her body to relax into the cushions.

They eyed each other for a few minutes, neither speaking, neither moving.

"I won't apologize for my anger," he finally said, looking down at his hands. "And I won't apologize for the reservations I hold against your ideas." She remained quiet, giving him time to collect his thoughts. "But I will apologize for what I said to you. The fucking and killing part. Not for all the times I called you a bitch."

She bit back a smile at his addendum. Though there was little humor in the situation they found themselves in, she could appreciate his attempt to lighten the moment.

"You realize Mickey wants to us to move, right?" she asked, not ready to let him off the hook easily.

He frowned and tilted his head. "Where does he want us to go?"

"Not you," she said slowly. "Us. Mick and I. He's looking into haunts in Eastern Canada willing to put us up until we can establish a home of our own."

He sat back, running a hand through his black hair. "You're serious," he said, more to himself than to her. He looked toward the doors of the common room. "Mikhail would actually break up the haunt for you. Jagger and Dominic, sure. I get that. I mean, that's connection. But…"

The incredulous tone in his voice stung briefly until she began reading his body language. His face was perplexed, arms crossing in defense. He was confused, struggling to understand the strength of the tie an unconnected vampire could form with a human. "You changed his mind," he finally stated.

She shook her head. "I bought time. It's all I could do for the time being."

He nodded absently and went silent once again. She waited, watching his dark eyes change and flicker as he processed the information. When it seemed he was no longer willing to talk, she rose.

"Do you have any comprehension of why I do what I do?" he asked to her back, causing her to stop and turn.

"Reputation. Money. I get it," she said quietly. "I don't like it, but I understand it."

He laughed humorlessly and leaned back into the sofa. "What's the longest you've gone without a relationship?" he inquired, leveling her with a stare.

"Aside from the two years in the bloodslave quarters?" she snarked, pursing her lips as she heard the bitterness in her own voice.

"Yes, aside from that."

She thought back to her time living among humans, when dating, work, and studying consumed her time. "I guess eight months. Maybe nine. Why?"

He began to stand, pausing to resettle himself on the seat when she took an involuntary step back. "And you're, what, thirty-three?" When she confirmed with a nod, he fixed his eyes on the blank television. "Mick is pushing two fifty. Jagger is sitting at four hundred fifty, I'm over seven centuries, and Nichol is twice my age. Some of my clients are closing in on Kaius's age. Others, like Dominic, are in their first century.

"The one thing bringing them to me, pushing them to pay astronomical prices for an item with an average fifty-year shelf life, isn't the sex. Or the talents. It's the companionship." He looked over at her again, his dark eyes tired.

"Over the decades, some of us meet humans who pique our interest. Of those, the lucky ones meet humans to share their existence. Humans who won't stake them in their sleep or bring pitchfork mobs to their doors."

She returned to her seat, listening as he quietly explained an aspect of vampirism she had never considered.

"Some of us crave the warmth and vitality a human brings into the haunt. It keeps us from becoming despondent and isolated. Forces us to retain a link to our humanity. My Tenders are strong, capable, intelligent women. Most of them thrive in their positions in ways they were unable to do living among the judgments and temptations their own species wallows in."

She sensed a change in his demeanor, a shift from explanation to defense of the women under his care. She took in every word, applying it to what she had personally witnessed within the haunt she now called home.

"We're a minority," Rhys continued, his voice lowering. "A despised minority surrounded by centuries of folklore and fear. We don't have the luxury of approaching multiple humans in the hopes we may connect with one, either physiologically or mentally. Our survival is dependent on secrecy, living on the outskirts of a world hellbent on destroying us. It doesn't make for an easy dating scene. And seven hundred, eight hundred, a thousand years is a long time to go without a partner."

****

Mick's blue eyes flickered to Kaius again, searching for reassurance the echoes he was receiving from Rhys were consistent with Kai's probes. The old vampire nodded, his gaze locked on the double doors as he listened for signs of trouble.

"You have my permission to leave," Kaius said quietly as they stood guard.

He side-eyed his creator. "I never said I would."

"Not to me," Kai replied. "But should you feel you must, you may."

Audra and Rhys were holed up in the common room for over an hour, their hushed discussion too quiet for him to make out. Rhys's emotions had rolled and changed frequently, teetering between anger and frustration, with a tinge of remorse filtering through in waves.

It was the remorse staying his position, forcing him to stand at the hallway junction while his lover remained hidden behind the common room doors.

"Is she going to be safe here?" he inquired,

unwilling to look at Kai as he admitted to his fear, his weakness.

Kaius tilted his head slightly in contemplation. "I cannot guarantee that," he posited. "Will any of us cause her intentional harm? No, I don't believe so. But we have many unknowns in our future, and I cannot promise you Audra will survive it unscathed."

Swallowing the quick tightening of his throat, he returned his attention to monitoring Rhys. Wherever their conversation had led them, Rhys was finding amusement in Audra's responses, an emotion he hadn't transmitted in a week.

"He would never follow through with his threat," Kai offered in the quiet of the hall. "Rhys has many demons and many, many flaws. But it's against his core to bring intentional harm to his brethren. And damaging your female would harm you."

His brow rose beneath his shaggy hair. "Audra. Lord help you if you call her my female in her presence."

When Kai responded with a small smile, he felt himself relax slightly. The discord between Rhys and himself was wearing, having never been at odds with each other in the over two centuries they had existed together. Small skirmishes aside, he had placed Rhys on a pedestal, the reputation of the suave elder vampire creating a sense of awe in his younger brother.

To witness his idol fall to such depths was disconcerting.

The doors opened as a spike in Rhys's temper flared, and the sound of what he had come to recognize as Audra's "therapy voice" echoed down the hall.

"It doesn't have to be an essay," she said over her

shoulder as Rhys appeared behind her, his large form looming over her despite her high heels. "Point form would be sufficient."

He tensed as Rhys's fangs bared at her back before Rhys realized what he was doing and fought his lips closed as he spoke. "I don't have any unresolved issues."

Chapter Fourteen

The ticking clock on the wall loomed over Jagger's head, keeping his movements quick and meticulous. The black garbage bags were heavy with the towels, sheets, and clothing he'd scavenged from the upstairs rooms to use in the bloody-basement cleanup. He was in the final stretch as he carefully removed the soiled clothing from the body on the floor and placed them atop the last trash bag. Heading topside to scrub his hands of spatter, he collected a clean set of clothes from the master bedroom and ventured back into the basement to complete his work.

The stench of stale blood held his mind in check as he went about his duties, washing the body clean and redressing it for show. Standing back to assess his progress, he steeled himself to complete the last of his work. The room was cleaned of blood to the human eye, the few specks dotting the papers and furniture easily explained by what he was preparing to do. Forensics would be able to piece together a more complete picture of the night's events, but there was little he could do to avoid it in his limited time frame.

Leaning over Clayton Jorgensson, he sank his fangs deep into the man's throat, taking care to straddle the wound Bianca's stars had left. With a jerk, he tore his fangs into the initial laceration, making it appear as though his fangs were the sole cause of damage. He repeated the action on the man's wrist, chest, and bicep, each tear showing a distinctive puncture as its origin. Pocketing the stars, he left his blade embedded in Clayton's thigh, resigning himself to the loss of his weapon as fair trade for the opportunity to bring a moment of pain to the disgusting creature now dead on the cold floor.

One last look throughout the room, and he began the arduous task of removing the garbage bags from the home and piling them into the car. With sunrise less than twenty minutes away, his drive was focused and precise until he arrived back at the motel. Killing the engine, he wondered briefly if Bianca would grant him access to their room.

He checked his appearance in the rearview mirror, schooling his face to appear unaffected and calm, a far cry from the rage of bloodlust consuming his features hours earlier as Clayton Jorgensson ranted and spat at Bianca.

He barely remembered the drive to the motel after their mission. Barely remembered the fury engulfing him as he scanned the pile of photos Bee had tossed on the desk. Barely remembered walking out of the room and returning to the scene with the faint hope the man would still be gasping for his last breath.

The photo of Bianca was a stealth shot, one taken of her in the sunlight surrounded by the wisteria hanging gracefully in her backyard. The sanctity of her garden was soiled long before the destruction of her home. Judging from the placement of the gazebo and lack of snow, the photo was taken months earlier.

Clayton Jorgensson was watching Bee for a long time.

He glanced at the sky, the arrival of the sun

sending a tremor through his bones as he fired off a quick message to Bee to let him in, his knuckles rapping on the wood. The door opened to crossed arms and wary blue eyes. Pushing the door closed behind him, he wedged a towel against the bottom jamb and debated briefly what to tell her.

"Hungry?" she asked, offering her wrist as her gaze traveled over his form in concern.

He shook his head. "I'm good." He spun slowly to allow the woman to assess him completely. When she reached up to lower his hood, he stilled to permit her inspection of his eyes. "See? I just had to go for a run. Get rid of some of the bloodlust before I snapped and drained a kitten."

She hummed in disapproval, rightfully unsure about how truthful he was being. He took the opportunity to bolt to the shower and escape the watchful blue eyes amplifying the guilt he was already feeling.

Her kill was intended as a message, her response on behalf of the Tenders who were, and would be, targeted by the hate groups spreading across the country. A message of solidarity those who knew her stars would recognize. A response in the only language the violent understood.

He had taken it from her.

The warm water washed the remains of Clayton Jorgensson from his skin, a visual cleansing of his wrongdoing. It hadn't been his intention when he arrived at the home to scrub Bianca's presence from the scene. The thought had not fully formed until the blood was already staining the heavy towels and he was facing the reality of burying his fangs into the foul human.

Instinct.

The instinct to place a barrier between the kill and the blonde spitfire who maintained complete control when a vampire with over four centuries under his belt lost his cool.

The instinct to pull the backlash onto himself instead of allowing it to creep into her home under the veil of darkness and biblical salvation.

The instinct to send the message messing with the vampire Tenders was a huge fucking mistake.

He rinsed the soap from his hair and took the last damp towel from the rack. Between their bloodied clothes and wet towels, laundry was becoming a pressing issue. When he entered the bedroom, she was repacking her throwing stars, layering them neatly between silk kerchiefs. Slipping the tri-stars from his filthy clothes, he doubled back to the bathroom to wash away Clayton Jorgensson's remains and tucked them into the bottom of his own pack.

"Tomorrow night should be just as quick," Bianca stated calmly. "Perhaps quicker. I don't know how long it will take for someone to realize Clayton is out of commission. Once it happens, I'm afraid the others will be prepared for our arrival. I'll make sure to watch the news tomorrow evening before dusk." Her arms extended to him, indicating she wanted him to pass her his bloodied garments. "I'll also be dealing with this tomorrow. Perhaps you should take the far bed."

Back in Tender mode, she straightened the room and fussed over how she would slip from the room without burning him in his sleep.

"Just wake me," he finally suggested when her

stream of consciousness ceased. "I'll hit the floor until the door closes. Good?"

Her stomach rumbled in response.

"For fuck's... Bianca. You need to eat," he scolded as he made his way to her. He took a good look at the dark circles forming under her eyes. "Eat and rest. You call for delivery. I'll call around for a laundry service. You aren't spending all day washing my cargos."

****

"I wish you could taste this," Bianca moaned as she devoured another slice of bacon. Her stomach had increased in its insistence until the driver arrived at their door, piles of bacon, eggs, and hash browns heaped into Styrofoam containers. Jagg had emerged from the bathroom with a grin, an automatic response to her giddy dance of joy over the food's appearance. Sitting up from his reclined position on the bed, he scanned the numerous boxes with curiosity.

"Pick one and put it on my tongue," he instructed. "But not that one. That looks horrendous."

Avoiding the eggs Benedict, she scooped a small amount of bacon grease onto her finger and offered it to him. He regarded it a moment before opening his mouth. Taking care to avoid his fangs, she touched her finger to his tongue and pulled back with a look of excitement and expectation gracing her face.

He made a show of his sampling, scrunching his nose and pursing his lips. "There is no way something so slick is good for you," he finally responded, licking his lips slowly. "It's still...how long does it take for the taste to go away?"

She huffed and grabbed a fork. "You aren't allowed to comment," she stated haughtily. "Given your preferred meals, your opinion is invalid." She dug into the eggs Benedict, smirking as he recoiled slightly. "Surely you eat alongside the Tenders back at the haunt," she said as she swallowed something that looked suspicious. "Johan always joined me at mealtime."

He rolled his eyes. "I assure you, his mind was more on your enthusiasm for the food than the actual meals themselves."

****

"This?"

Jagger scented the paper-wrapped package and nodded. "That one has at least another three days before it turns. Add it to the rest, and we should head back. You are looking tired."

Seline hummed in agreement and handed her purchases to the clerk. As the man chatted aimlessly with her, she brushed Jagger's hand from her back. From her buttocks. From her thigh. The small smile on her face only encouraged his roving hands and increased his anxiousness to return to their home for a meal and a tumble.

Once she realized he was capable of identifying the shelf life of perishables, she had begun shopping for her food in the early evening after the sun set but before the markets closed. Every decision was passed under his discerning nose for evaluation and returned to the shelves when he scowled in offense.

The walk home was quick, Seline driven by her hunger and him driven by his. He watched as the stunning brunette sashayed around the kitchen, stirring pots, tasting spoons, and pausing to send a quick smile his way. Mealtimes were becoming his favorite time of the night, a time when she was alert and happy, relaxed in the confines of her small house. Two years into their union, and he responded to the sounds of pots and pans as he once did the exposed thighs of an eager virgin.

She held a spoon out to him, her hand cupped beneath it to capture any wayward drips. "Taste," she ordered, her chocolate eyes narrowing as the scant liquid dropped onto his tongue.

"Vile," he replied with a grin, flashing a little fang.

Licking the spoon clean first, she wielded the utensil as a weapon, swatting at him playfully. "You, sir, hold no right to an opinion. It's delicious."

The ritual of dishwashing soothed him as their night drew to a close, the pair using the time to discuss her day and his plans for the night. Once the kitchen was clean, they would retire to her bedroom until she fell into a deep sleep and he could slip from the room unnoticed to wander aimlessly through the outskirts of the town, keeping watch on the advancing lines of the Turks.

Domestic bliss.

Chapter Fifteen

"Divorced. No children."

Bianca nodded absently as Jagg read off Nichol's notes on their second victim. The cheap detergent used by the company he'd contracted for their laundry had filled the room with an artificial odor of lavender, and a headache was beginning to form at her temples. Placing pressure on her forehead, she took a moment to close her eyes and will the dull ache away.

"You're injured?" Jagg inquired immediately, rising from the bed to assess her up close. His ice-blue eyes zeroed in on her as he began lifting her hair in search of damage.

"Stop it," she snapped, swatting the offending hands away. "It's just a headache. It'll disappear once we get outside and away from this horrendous-smelling stuff."

Jagger lowered his head to the pile of folded laundry. "What the hell did they do to this?" he asked, poking at the clothing in disgust.

She placed her throwing stars along the holster strapped across her hips, ignoring his question in favor of preparing for the evening. Her stomach was hollow, her head aching, and her mind unfocused.

She was feeling...older.

Over six decades with Johan and his constant blood supply had kept her body young, barely aging past nineteen. But in the fourteen years since his passing, she was beginning to feel the impact of her ninety-six years. While she visually appeared to be in her early thirties, her body was aging far quicker than she had anticipated. Fatigue set in after long nights. Muscle aches lasted for days after a rigorous bout of garden weeding. Stress knots had formed in her shoulders.

The level of concern etched on Jagger's face was, however, unwarranted. "Come," she said, taking his hand. "Be a gentleman and escort me across the road for a meal before we head out."

The ease with which he fell into the traditional vampire-Tender relationship helped to ease her mood. All worry for her well-being disappeared from his features, all tactical discussion of their mission ended. As they waited for her food in the empty cafe, he entertained her with stories of his youngest hauntmate, Dominic, and his connected mate, Molly. Despite the undertone of danger she knew was present at the time of the connection formation, he maintained a light tone, finding humor in many of the events that had occurred.

"Whenever Louis is around Molly, Dominic growls incessantly until one of them becomes fed up and smacks him." He smirked. "Sometimes Nichol will hunt him down and beat on Dom himself."

"Connection is so intense," she mused aloud without thinking, offering him a taste of the ice cream she was eating. "I heard you were once connected."

All humor fell from his face, his expression locking into an unreadable neutrality. "Once," he replied tersely, effectively ending the conversation.

She looked away from him, guilt over her unintended offense tinging her thoughts as memories of her training with Rhys came flooding back.

"Number one rule for Nichol is no questions. If he wants to talk, he will. But don't count on it, sweet cheeks," Rhys instructed as he gently pulled a brush through her long hair.

"This applies to most vampires, and your head may depend on remembering this. I know Mikhail has been pretty chatty with you, but he's a rare beast." He examined his work, placing a stray strand behind her ear. *"I'm easing you into this as slowly as I can, angel. Mick, Kaius, and I were the introductory lessons. Nichol is the true test. He's a miserable bastard. Do not give him a reason to request punishment."*

She exhaled slowly, closing her eyes to allow Rhys to apply a black liner to her lids. *"Why would vampires take such offense to interest in their lives, their experiences?"*

"Lips," Rhys muttered as he reached for a gloss. *"We've seen and survived things that would give you night terrors for years. It's not a road they, nor you, need to travel. Speaking of roads to avoid, stay away from Boy. Tall, silent vamp. Kaius reported seeing you in the hallway leading to the bloodslave quarters a few nights ago. He lives and works in that wing of the haunt and is best left to his own devices."*

She shifted in her seat, unwilling to disclose her interactions with the mute vampire.

"Stand," Rhys said, holding a hand out to assist her. He motioned at her to spin and watched with an unsatisfied scowl as she twirled for his study. *"It's your height,"* he finally stated. *"Unless you grow another six or seven inches in the next ten minutes, we need to keep you in high heels. You look too disarmingly breakable."*

She grinned and accepted the offered shoes.

Despite her best efforts, all playful banter ceased for the remainder of the meal. Jagg went so far as to openly flirt with the waitress, turning his icy gaze and lazy smirk her way while ignoring the jealous glare of the line cook. He navigated his movements precisely, the hood of his sweater providing cover for his markings and a shadow for his irises.

The motions were practiced, honed from decades of existence in the fringes of human society. The angle of his shoulders as he lounged back in his seat, the sprawling of his legs under the table, the pursing of his lips. Though her pride was piqued by his actions, she fought the roll of her eyes as she witnessed yet another subtle dominance display by a Kaius vamp.

Boy was the only one in the haunt who didn't move in such a way, who fought to remain invisible in spite of his size and his ethereal beauty.

Boy was far too pretty for her.

Observing Jagger as he made small talk with the server, she listened while his voice morphed into a hypnotic timbre. His words were double-edged swords of innuendo and innocent commentary. His attention to her drew attention to his own, a subconscious refocusing for the woman who was currently wrapping a strand of chestnut hair around her finger. There was no script for her to follow, no rigid outline of expectations, yet Jagg responded as he had to Bianca when she shifted into Tender mode.

Unattached.

Unencumbered.

Unnecessary.

"We need to get going," she interrupted, her face stony and eyes narrowed on the offending vamp across from her.

Jagger lifted a brow under his hood in surprise at her sudden change in attitude and reached for his wallet. Tossing her own money on the table, she smiled tersely at the waitress and walked from the cafe. The stomp of his heavy boots were quick to align with her pace.

"I am to pay when we go out," he growled in her ear as he grasped her arm. She shook out of his grip, continuing toward the vehicle and her mission. He stayed at her side, his chastised hands shoved deep into the pocket of his sweatshirt. When the pair reached the vehicle, she attempted to open her door.

"Unlock it, please," she grit out, teeth clenched.

"Not until you tell me what the fuck your problem is," he snarled back, placing both hands on the roof of the vehicle and staring at her.

"My problem," she hissed, "is you were blatantly disrespectful to me back there. Was that your retribution for my faux pas? I am NOT some new trainee ignorant on protocols and requiring punishment."

"No," Jagg snarked back, his light blue eyes ovaling. "You're a Former Tender who has forgotten her place."

****

Two more kills, Jagger thought to himself as he pulled off the freeway and into the lighted suburb. Two more kills, and he could return to his weapons room, return to his bunk, and return to women who didn't bounce between trained submission and bewitching independence.

The script of seduction came easily to him as he

used his functioning senses to maneuver through the murky waters of feminine desires. The targeting of women was second nature, an instinctual response from centuries of necessity. Even times such as tonight, when his goal was little more than a distraction from the thoughts Bianca's question carried, he was a master at reading and responding to women.

He monitored the subtle shifts in weight, the slight turns of shoulders, the subconscious jutting of a hip. With each word he spoke, he studied the woman's irises, her brows, and her gaze. The pursing of lips, the tilt of the head, the scent of arousal. He used each cue and responded on demand. Pavlovian.

The script for Tenders was even simpler, with each side well versed in the expectations and outcomes. There was little surprise in the revolving door of Tender trainees gracing the halls of the Kaius haunt. Sure, the women varied greatly in personality, appearance, and talent, but the core behaviors Rhys ingrained in each woman passing through his capable hands remained rigid and predictable. Sometimes the hauntmates grew bored of the practiced perfection and looked street side for a warm meal and a hot bed, but the ease and availability of the Tenders always drew them back.

A security blanket.

When Bianca was adhering to the traditional Tender role, he found himself mindlessly responding in kind. It was a practiced interaction with mutual benefits. Bianca gained protection. He gained a safe meal. Bee received the benefits of the Kaius haunt's investigation work. He received the benefits of companionship and a day guard, tiny as she was.

The sex was an added treat.

It was when Bianca broke ranks, when she abandoned her training and spoke through wit instead of rote, that he became withdrawn. It was when she acted or reacted on impulse instead of calculated purpose that he became flustered.

When she disregarded his internal compass of chivalry, he became pissed.

And when he was pissed, he instinctively bit back.

A Former Tender who has forgotten her place.

He risked a glance at Bianca as he turned off the engine. Her plump lips were tight, eyes trained on the apartment complex across the road. Something had shifted in those bright blue eyes when he spat back his retort. A hardened resolve. He'd seen this look before, and something knotted in his gut at the recognition.

Chapter Sixteen

William Ambrose lived on the fifth floor of an apartment building without an elevator. By the fourth, Bianca was breathing far deeper than she liked. Jagger followed tight behind her, a silent shadow in the empty stairwell. As they reached the landing on the fifth level, she leaned against the wall to catch her breath and complete a final weapons check. With exaggerated movements, she patted her chest, waist, and thighs under the guise of counting her stars as she stretched out the cramps rippling through her torso.

"Let me go in first," Jagger said softly, the first thing spoken since the motel parking lot.

She shook her head and straightened, the sting of his earlier words still winding itself through her plans. She didn't trust her ability to speak yet, knowing both her breathlessness and her thoughts would reveal far more about her current state than she was prepared to showcase. Pulling her lock pick from her pocket, she led Jagger to suite 53, placed her ear to the door, and began manipulating the knob.

The apartment was sparsely furnished, lacking both a dining table and a sofa. One large brown armchair sat in front of an old tube television, close enough for the watcher to turn the channel by hand. She moved slowly across the floor toward the bedroom, conscious of Jagger's presence at her back. The bedroom door was slightly ajar, allowing her to peek inside for her target.

Empty.

She pushed the door open slowly, anticipating an ambush.

Completely deserted.

"Where is he?" Jagg muttered, doubling back to scan the barren apartment.

She rifled through the dilapidated dresser drawers and examined the closet before she joined Jagger in the living room. "It doesn't look like he bolted," she said quietly, flipping the lock on the exterior door. "He must be out."

Jagg sank onto the old chair. "Then we wait. Bars close within the hour, so we can expect William back soon. Be prepared."

She hoisted herself onto the kitchen counter, setting her tri-stars within reach. Jagg's eyes were trained on the door, his muscles tensed, and body positioned for a launch across the room. The minutes ticked by as strained anticipation clouded the small room.

"You'll be returning to the haunt with me, correct?" he finally said, interrupting his monotone hum. "The others have been asking."

She nodded, put off by the addendum to his question.

"For how long?" he pushed, sitting straighter in his seat.

She narrowed her eyes and crossed her arms defensively. "I suppose I'll be staying long enough to relearn my place, won't I?"

His eyes darkened as he grit his teeth. "It was a slip," he growled. "You're extremely well trained. Probably overtrained."

She hopped off the counter, forgetting her tri-stars as she stormed over to stand in front of him. "What exactly do you mean by 'overtrained'?" she bit out, matching his accusing tone.

He rose to his feet, the shadow of his hood making his stance more menacing in the dark room. "How many years have you been out of the Tender trade?" he asked, the vast difference in their heights amplified by his looming posture.

"Thirteen? Fourteen? Yet your home didn't hold a single scent of a human lover. No photos of friends. No indication a man had breached the sacred premises. You've remained completely immersed in vampire politics. Just when you begin to sound real, like you have an opinion and thoughts of your own, you slip right back into that perfect Tender mode without a blink. So yes, overtrained."

His voice rose with every word. She opened her mouth to argue back as his eyes flicked behind her and a burning pain radiated through her core.

****

William Ambrose fell backward into the hall, six of the nine inches of Jagger's blade embedded in his skull.

Another of Bianca's kills marred by his interference.

The scent of O positive overpowered the tiny apartment as Bee struggled to push her bloodied body from the floor. He lifted her into his arms, placing one finger on her wrist to monitor her weakening pulse as he bounded over Ambrose's body and began his sprint down the stairwell. He paused his escape for a moment and skidded back to the scene.

Reaching into Bianca's shirt, his fingers fumbled

for the photo tucked securely inside and dropped it onto Ambrose's body. Eyes scanned him through peepholes, memorizing his face and that of the blonde woman bleeding in his arms. He barreled down the stairs, jostling his panting cargo as he did.

"Just give me five minutes, Bee," he murmured as he fought to get his car keys in the lock. Faint red and blue lights crested down the street as he placed Bianca in the back seat and tore off down the road, keeping his speed on target to avoid detection as he passed several police cruisers ripping down the street. "I need you to hold on until I find a safe place to pull over and check you out," he muttered, watching his rearview mirror anxiously.

Slowing into an abandoned church parking lot, he circled around the building and pulled in snug to the exterior, out of sight from the road. He fired off a group text to his hauntmates, asking, begging, them to be on standby as he assessed Bianca's injury. Her blood was pooling under her, staining her blonde hair, and dripping down the leather seat. He crawled into the back, his eyes scanning for rips in her clothes as he did.

"I need to turn you over, honey," he warned as he slid his arms underneath her. When she clenched her teeth in response, he awkwardly lifted her slight form and placed her stomach down. His hands began searching for the entrance hole, ripping her clothes as he became more frantic. "Got it," he muttered, grazing a hole on Bianca's lower left hip. He snapped a picture on his phone and sent it off to the others.

Her body shook incessantly under his hands, an unnatural tremor as her systems sank into shock. He watched his phone nervously for advice, stroking her wet hair in reassurance. "Nichol and Mick are old hats at this," he conversed, forcing a calm tone despite his distress.

"Here's what we're going to do. I'm going to give you my wrist. I need to…fuck…okay. I need to get the bullet out, and we need a link for monitoring. Bite down as hard as you want. Bee? I need you to do this."

She opened her teary eyes, turning her head slightly toward him and nodding. Her mouth opened as he tore into his veins and pushed his arm against her. He adjusted his position, one arm fastened to Bianca's lips. Angling the other, he began hunting for the wayward bullet.

"This is going to hurt, hon. But if I don't get it out, you'll heal over it, and Nichol says that's definitely not anything we want." As his fingers began their search, she released his wrist and wailed. He shoved his bleeding wrist back into her mouth forcefully, burying his fangs into her neck to get just enough to begin the link. "Not a choice, Bianca," he growled, unhooking from her delicate throat. "Bite. Down."

Her teeth broke skin as he made contact with the slippery metal of the bullet. He grappled with the object, snarling in frustration as it escaped his grasp over and over. The burst of her pain through the blood link pounded at the back of his head, forcing him to ignore both his overwhelming tension and the agony she was experiencing at his inept handling.

His phone was alight with messages. Nichol and Mick continued to text instructions and warnings regarding the back-alley doctoring. Kaius sent encouragement. Rhys coached him on Bianca.

"You're doing great," he said softly as his fingers

found purchase on the bullet once again. "Rhys thinks I should be barking orders at you right now." He tugged the metal slightly, effectively dislodging it enough to begin extricating it from her body.

"He's blowing up my phone with helpful suggestions like knocking you out if you struggle and speaking with 'the tone of authority.' " She bit down harder as he gave a final yank and dropped the bullet onto the floor. "All done."

When Bianca didn't immediately release his wrist, he carefully pried her lips open. "Any more and Kai will flay me for creating a female vamp," he cautioned. Her pain was easing slower than he anticipated, the bursts of distress only slightly reduced. He sat up in the cramped back seat, photographing the wound and sending the picture to the others.

—*Jagg: Pain isn't ceasing. Advise.* —
—*Kai: Wait five.* —
—*Jagg: If not?* —
—*Kai: Hospital*—

He resumed stroking the red-tinged hair and alternated between staring at the injury and glancing at the clock. He had three hours until dawn. Not enough time to make the journey to the haunt. Bianca's breathing continued to labor, her body rising and falling in short, spastic movements. Reaching into the front seat, he pulled up the GPS system and began scanning for hospitals in his vicinity, finding one halfway between the church and the motel.

"Bee," he whispered, "I need to get you to a doctor."

She arched in response, attempting to shake her head.

"Not your decision right now, honey," he stated, unfolding his large form from the back of the car, and resettling in the driver's side. "I need you to hang on for a few more minutes. If you fight me on this, Rhys has recommended I tether you."

He moved swiftly through the empty streets of Lincoln, skillfully maneuvering through secondary roads and alleyways until he pulled up to the emergency doors of the hospital and hesitated. His fangs were on full display, irises ellipse.

Not even his blood-soaked hood could hide what he was under the glaring fluorescent lights. Rifling through the glove box, he found what he needed and scribbled a quick note before he exited the running vehicle and delicately lifted the dying woman into his arms.

"I'm going to need you to be compliant," he warned as they entered the automatic doors. "No arguing. Okay?"

Her head lay against his chest motionless, not a flicker of movement behind her lids. A nurse scurried to the pair, her eyes wide as she took in the bloodied garments and unconscious woman. He kept his head down, burrowing his head into Bee's hair for cover.

"Please," he murmured, to both the nurse and Bianca, "she's been shot. She needs help."

A flurry of activity erupted in his periphery. His hood left him blind to most of the movements surrounding him until an old hand appeared on Bianca's face. He looked up enough to see the lips of the man assessing Bianca's state.

"I'm going to need you to put her on the gurney," the man said, his attention entirely on Bee. "We'll get to work on her, and you can check in with triage."

He glanced at the rolling bed, at the two orderlies standing beside it ready to assist the doctor. With calculated slowness, he lowered her onto the gurney and backed away as swarms of white coats took control.

****

The sun was due to rise within the hour. Jagger took his time carefully folding Bianca's clothes and setting them neatly inside her suitcase, placing the most comfortable-looking items to the side. The passenger side of the vehicle was slowly becoming more orderly, a small victory after his rushed exit from the motel room he had shared with Bee.

The trip to Bianca's safe house in Omaha was uneventful, save for the continual buzzing of his phone as his hauntmates inundated him with texts. In the safety of the underground parking garage, it was easy to focus on the mind-numbing task of organizing the clothes, beauty products, and throwing stars he had tossed haphazardly into the hatch in an effort to remain out of the line of police scrutiny.

It was Nichol who had mentioned it, a scathing message to stay alert and protect his own worthless ass.

With a final check of the vehicle, he locked it up, loaded his arms, and ascended into Bianca and Johan's bolt-hole. The lock groaned under his hand, snapping off with little resistance.

He activated the shutters and stripped naked on the entrance tile, abandoning the soiled clothing in favor of a shower, a cleansing from the night. He shoved image after image of Bee's bloodied body from his mind, shook off the ghosts of her tremors rippling through his hands.

Pure floral scents filled the steamy shower as he scrubbed his skin with Bianca's soap and lathered his hair with her shampoo. Wrapping a plush white towel around his hips, he proceeded to wander the spacious condo for the washing machine.

—*Jagg: Put a Tender on* —

—*Rhys: WTF for* —

—*Jagg: Now, fuckwad* —

—*Rhys: Audra here. How are you holding up? Have you heard anything from the hospital?* —

He ran a hand through his hair and leaned against the large red machine.

—*Jagg: Fine. No. I need to do laundry.* —

—*Rhys: Good. That will occupy your mind.* —

His head lolling back in unnecessary annoyance, he gave in.

—*Jagg: How do I do laundry?* —

Audra's precise instructions made quick work of the job. When the first machine finished its cycle, it would be time to place the clothes and a scented paper into the dryer.

Amid his failures of the week, his success at his first load of laundry was mildly calming.

He meandered through the rooms, checking out artifacts older than himself and needlessly straightening paintings on the walls. Every item of the eclectic collection of artwork displayed throughout the home told a story. Held a memory.

And the only one who knew them was last seen turning gray on a rickety gurney.

The rumbling against the soles of his feet stopped, and he carefully moved each piece of wet clothing one by one to the dryer. He set the scented paper on top and turned the machine on.

Done.

The sun was an hour into its rise. He stood in the doorframe of Bianca's bedroom, staring absently at her vanity.

The faint smile of contentment once gracing Seline's features was no longer. He couldn't remember the last time he'd seen it, seen her gazing mindlessly into her mirror as she pulled a brush through her curls.

Her dark eyes now alternated between apprehension and resolve when she forgot he was observing her, forgot he was in the room. The excitement and joy once swirling in his mind through their blood link had become dulled and gray as excitement turned to longing and joy became jealousy.

"Jagg?" she called out over her shoulder. "Could you help me?"

He accepted the brush silently and began running it down the cascade of black hair falling to her waist. He scanned her hands, noting the burns were healing with ease. "You'll be careful today," he stated, his voice holding less authority and more concern.

She slipped from her chair and held her injured hand out for her brush. "I don't require coddling," she grumbled, avoiding his eyes as she slowly bandaged her palms. "I'll be home before sunset. Like always."

A burst of resentment accompanied her words as she gave him a perfunctory kiss on the cheek and strode out the door. A look to the sky told him there was an hour until sunrise, an hour in which he could accompany her, perhaps speak to the owner of the bakery regarding her workload until the oven burns healed completely. As though reading his thoughts, she turned her head back and glared.

Five years.

Her wedding ring was no longer a point of contention, the circular band laying in a small dish beside her bed and worn on a whim a few times a month. He closed the front door and retired to the small, dusty hole beneath the house, undressing and placing the worn clothes in a pile for Seline to attend to later in the week.

His core was restless, aching for the woman who had frozen him from her bed months earlier save for the odd frenzied romp before she was too tired, too busy, or too occupied to draw out their lovemaking.

The packages from Kaius continued to arrive periodically, the money sitting in a scattered heap in the corner of his lair. Seline's insistences he use it to "buy himself something" went unheeded. All he wanted was currently unlocking the door to a small bakery and entering a world of which he would never be a part.

He settled back to rest, closing his eyes, and ignoring the unhappiness radiating from the small tunnel linking Seline to him.

It was nearing sunset when he rose to a burst of excitement and desire.

He shook himself from his thoughts and crossed the room. Collecting an ornate brush and several containers of sweet-smelling lotions, he made his way back into the living area and began packing.

Chapter Seventeen

Rhys sat across the com room table from Audra, keeping his eyes locked on his phone. A bidding war had erupted for his two newest Tenders, the rare opportunity for a bulk deal causing a frenzy among vampires searching for the last of the Rhys-trained Tenders. It provided ample distraction from the assessing cat eyes monitoring his every move. Nichol sat to his left, hunched over his laptop and muttering curses as he scanned news articles.

"Have you given any more thought to my offer?" Audra finally asked, her hands clasped on the table in expectation.

Keeping his attention on his phone, he grunted. "What's keeping Mickey? You leave him tied to the bed posts?"

In the fringes of his sight, Audra pursed her lips and breathed out. "His bed doesn't have posts."

Louis wandered into the room, his eyes green and mischievous. "Gonna need your help with Dominic tonight," he called over to Nichol as a faint possessive rumble echoed down the hall. "I may or may not have complimented Molly's shirt on the way over."

Rhys grinned as Nichol slammed his hand on the table and glared at the red-haired vamp. "I am getting sick of fixing your shit," he snarled as he rose to his feet. "Dom!" he barked toward the door. "End it before I rip your goddamn throat out."

The growl ceased, punctuated with a snort from Molly as she entered the room. Dominic followed, his face sullen.

"Nice shirt," Rhys tossed out, winking at the raven-haired woman, and ducking quickly to avoid the swing of Nichol's arm. It was a nice shirt. Good grunge band from a couple decades back.

Molly rolled her eyes, her tongue sticking out at his obvious attempt to stir the pot. She and Dominic took up position on his right, giving wide berth to Louis who had turned his attention to a hushed conversation with Audra.

Mickey and Kaius finally arrived, Kai choosing to stand behind Nichol and follow the rapid scanning of the news as Mick pulled his chair tight up against Audra. His large hands covered hers as he listened in on her discussion with Louis and ignored Rhys's presence for the time being.

It was expected.

Kaius glanced over at his group, his unreadable face locked down. "Once Boy arrives, we will begin."

"Will the Tenders be joining us?" Molly inquired, her fingers aimlessly tangling through Dom's hair.

"Nope," Rhys replied, scanning his texts again. "Given their inevitable sales within the next few weeks, there's no point in arming them with sensitive intel."

Boy slipped into the room, taking position in the corner at Audra's back. Mickey angled his chair slightly, providing himself with a good view of the mute vamp and tossing a look of challenge his way.

One of these nights, he mused to himself. *One of these nights, Boy is going to snap and obliterate the entire haunt. And with how we've treated him, it'll be well-deserved.*

Kaius stood at the head of the table, the tension in his stance indicating this would be a tough, and likely long, meeting.

"We'll begin with the most pressing issues," he said quietly, meeting the eyes of each hauntmate. "Nichol has worked his way into the hospital files where the Former Tender Bianca Schumann is being treated. She's been placed in a medically induced coma and is currently stable in the hospital's intensive care ward.

"A second bullet was removed from her liver during the night. The police are involved and are in the process of linking her shooting to the man Jagger killed. Nichol has assured me when Bianca wakes, she will spin the events to her advantage."

"My hope is she implicates Jagger," Nichol interjected, receiving glares from the table. "Security footage has been released, and his image is on every online news site. Audra, your photo is back in play as well since the connection has been made between last night's events and you and Jagger's escape from the prison in Vansburg. Prepare to stay inside for a few years."

Audra crossed her arms and acknowledged the warning with a nod.

"With attention focused on Jagger," Kai continued, "it should skew the investigation long enough for Bianca to recover and make her way here. Our network, combined with her own, will provide adequate protection."

"And Jagg?" Rhys asked, leaning back in his chair and setting his booted feet on the table.

"Leaving Omaha tonight. The backroads will lead him up to Chadron, Nebraska and loop him back here," Nichol answered, angling his laptop toward him to show a map. "We expect him in two nights."

"Does he know this?" Mick inquired. "Because we're two hours past dusk and his mood and location are pretty static. Right, Kai?"

Kaius nodded. "He's aware. He's also wrapping up some loose ends. I'll update everyone through text message once he makes contact. Mick, your update."

Mickey pushed a paper toward Kai and sat back. "Two more missing people reported in Mississippi. Following the same path as those in Florida and Alabama. All women."

"Not our concern," Nichol grunted, snatching the note, and sliding it atop a pile of loose papers on his workstation.

Audra huffed out a breath and stared Nichol down. "Is there any reason to suspect this is not Dovidas? Or Chen?" she posited. "Their locations are unknown, the missing women have been taken from along a highway stemming from a major international port, and the movement is extending in this direction. At the very least, it bears monitoring and preparation. If Dovidas and Chen are working together to amass an army, we need to be on top of it."

Nichol's brows furrowed, his freckles rippling across his nose as he did so. "All women? It's a human man. Monitor the situation, and if we get a higher head count, we will revisit the issue."

"Is it really that far a stretch a woman would be inducted into the almighty testosterone vampire brethren?" Audra mumbled as she settled against

Mick's arm.

"Only if you believe in Armageddon," Rhys piped in, holding his hands up in a show of truce when a snarl tore out of Mick. "Calm the fuck down," he grumbled as he lounged back. "Female vampires are the most dangerous beings who ever existed. By the time they pass their first century, they're a hundred times more powerful than a male vamp, have twice the control, and quadruple the rage issues. It took a concerted effort on behalf of every haunt on Earth to find and destroy the few female vampires created over the centuries. Trust me, not even Dovidas or Chen is stupid enough to think they can control an army of female vampires."

Kaius leaned slightly across the table, placing his large body between him and Mick. "Dominic, Louis. What can you two tell us about the progress in the bloodslave quarters?"

"Physically, the humans are faring better under Audra's nutritional plan. It's made them stronger and surprisingly less feral," Louis began. "We had to eliminate Audra's presence from the quarters, though." He glanced from Boy to Mick. "There are several bloodslaves who recognized her when we attempted to select the first round for reintegration. Audra?"

Audra motioned for Louis to continue, placing a hand on Mickey's thigh. "She's being viewed as a traitor, to put it bluntly. Most of the attacks have been verbal, but there have been a few grabs for her. We've made the decision to relegate her role to advisor and reviewer."

Mickey's blue eyes were darkening quickly, their shape changing as Louis spoke. "When the fuck was I going to be told about this?" Mick snarled, his fangs bared at Louis.

"I guess that would be now," Audra stated, reaching up to Mickey's jaw and redirecting his attention. "No harm done. Nothing to tell. Louis and Dominic have been excellent escorts. As has Boy."

Rhys crossed his arms behind his head and waited patiently for the meeting to resume as Audra and Mick launched into one of their trademark arguments. Within minutes, the couple settled into a frosty silence, and Louis resumed his report.

"Molly has been invaluable," he praised, chuckling as Dom growled and Nichol reached over to punch the youngest hauntmate in the shoulder. "After Audra makes the selection based on Boy's recommendations, I collect the human and isolate it in the cement cell."

"Him, her, or they," Audra interjected. "Never 'it.'"

"Him, her, or they," Louis repeated. "Then Dominic does his funky pheromone relaxation thing, and Molly starts the interview. So far, four have shown positive signs. They seem to take to Molly, and she's been able to pull a lot of information regarding home states, skills, training, and family. Audra creates a profile for them based on Molly's notes. Then, Nichol? I assume you're the one putting together the identification and filling Audra's orders for clothes and bank cards?"

Nichol nodded. "I have a standard supply kit based on Audra's recommendations and have secured apartments in a few locations around the country."

Kai straightened and crossed his arms. "Impressive," he muttered. "Louis, you're certain your hypnosis will hold as we release the humans?"

"Positive," Louis said confidently. "When Dominic does his thing, the human minds are far more pliable than usual. Providing I'm not altering their core morals or base behaviors, human hypnosis is pretty straightforward."

Kai turned to Rhys, who glanced down at his phone again.

"The—what was Audra's term? Tramp Twins? I should have the sale of the Tramp Twins complete tonight. Good price. Capable master. Our delightful Frenchman. Delivery should be fairly quick. Simone is the final hurdle, and I can turn the Tender training rooms into a secondary sparring facility," he reported, his voice flatter than intended. "Once Simone's price is paid, I'm completely at your command."

****

Jagger fought the urge to double back toward Lincoln, to swing by the hospital and ensure the freight company delivered his packages as guaranteed. The bitter cold of winter filled the vehicle as it flew down the gravel road. The scent of Bianca's blood was muted by the open windows and frigid air, the overpowering odor no longer coating his nose and tongue.

Even as it aged, her blood called to his fangs.

Chadron remained hours away, and he knew his late start would make his arrival at the vampire stronghold uncomfortably close to a good frying. His phone continued to buzz incessantly, his hauntmates filling him in on the night's meeting and updating him on Bianca's hospital records.

A second bullet.

Had he stepped back and assessed Bianca's state from afar, the presence of a second bullet fit. The tremors, her small body fighting between the foreign object lodged inside it and the healing powers of his blood. Her lack of response after ingesting enough to risk an accidental Deviant.

The vision of Bee's head lolling to the side as he placed her on the gurney pounded at his psyche, a constant reminder of his failure to protect and shield the woman. It was the loss of his temper that had left them vulnerable, his attention wholly diverted to the unloading of his frustrations.

A second bullet.

Ambrose was a good shot, striking Bianca twice between the opening of his door and the knife becoming embedded in his skull. He had to wonder how many shots the man got off in total. How many had he not heard? He pulled his hood tighter to his ears and checked his phone. The Gagnon haunt was anticipating his arrival and preparing the home for a race from the sun's light.

In his current state, the threat of the beams didn't faze him as much as it should. He was entirely unharmed, not a single scratch marring his skin. With the exception of the mild weakness from feeding Bianca, he was entirely whole, primed for battle.

His health marked his failure more than any weapon could.

"Fuck it," he muttered, channeling Rhys's blasé attitude toward existence. Fuck worrying about the well-being of a fragile human. Fuck clinging to those brief interludes when the woman responded to him with fire and humor. Fuck whatever witchcraft had brought about his intense attraction to the petite blonde. Fuck the jealousy pinging every time he remembered the object of his desire had been intimate with most of his hauntmates. One of them recently.

The vehicle sped up down the gravel road, closing in on the fortified Gagnon compound. The males who inhabited the swath of land were much like the Kaius haunt, prominent and respected in vampire circles. The exception lay with their numbers.

The head of the haunt, Jean-Michel, was over a thousand and a prolific breeder. Each child followed in their creator's footsteps, siring several new vampires every century. Their expansive territory housed dozens of separate residences connected by underground tunnels, forming a ring around Jean-Michel's dwelling. One of the Kaius haunt's greatest consumers of both Tenders and blood services, he was unsure how welcomed he would be in the face of the changes occurring within his own haunt.

Fuck it.

The large, electrified fence came into view, its breadth expanding past the horizon and disappearing in the shadows of the treed property. He slowed his approach, firing off a text to let Jean-Michel know he had arrived. The gates opened, and he sped along the path toward the main house and away from the rising sun.

Chapter Eighteen

"The FBI has been actively searching for the suspect, led by their Vampire Intelligence division. The alleged perpetrator is believed to be the same vampire who escaped police custody last month in Vansburg, West Virginia, one Luciano Othario. He is described as being six foot one, two hundred and ten pounds, light blue eyes, dark hair, with a goatee.

"Government-instituted tattoos are visible on both the right and left temple. He was last seen wearing a black sweatshirt with a hood and black military-style cargo pants. The suspect is considered armed and dangerous. Police are asking the public to call 911 if they see Luciano Othario. Do not approach him."

Jean-Michel chuckled and turned off the television. "Closed-captioning is really a wonderful thing, isn't it, Jagger? Or do you prefer the pseudonym Mr. Othario?" He grinned. "I watch more TV when I don't have to listen to it."

Jagger picked up his glass of A negative. "You're certain you don't mind housing a fugitive for the day?" He smirked, grateful for the old vampire's hospitality. "The FBI could be planning their assault as we speak."

"Good. That gives me a month, maybe two, to plan my defense," Jean-Michel countered. "If it doesn't offend, may I take a better look at those tattoos?"

He bristled slightly at the request, conceding with the knowledge the ancient vampire was more curious than scathing. He lowered his hood and leaned forward.

"*Connard*," Jean-Michel growled, walking closer to Jagger to get a better look. "Curse. Unoriginal and incorrect. I would expect nothing less from our fine lawmakers. At least the marking was done by one with talent. The lines are not bleeding or asymmetrical."

Cocking a brow, he took a sip from his glass. "Asymmetrical. Heaven forbid I be stamped by a novice."

"Ah, come now." Jean-Michel resumed his place and splayed out across the sofa. "Were they for any other reason, I might be tempted to mimic them. It's rare to find a vampire who can stand the mercury injections long enough to complete such an intricate design. Outside of your bloodline, I suppose."

He brought his hood back up over his head. "Must be a genetic deficiency in the Kaius line," he agreed. Rhys's tattoos were legendary among their kind as the mercury used to create the intricate designs burned deep with unrivaled pain. He'd barely held it together during his own markings at the hands of the human law enforcement. How his brother tolerated it over and over was a mystery he didn't want to think about. "I understand you spoke with Rhys earlier. Two Tenders? I must say, you are braver than I."

Jean-Michel's booming laugh filled the room. "For my youngest," he explained with a fanged grin. "It's time for him to stop mooching off the goodwill of his brothers' females and start learning how to maneuver the delicate balance of his own."

Grunting in agreement, he downed the remaining blood from his glass. "Best of luck to him," he grumbled.

The old vampire eyed him a moment before he spoke. "I hear you have spent some time recently with Ms. Schumann," he said slowly, choosing his words carefully as Jagger felt his face harden. "She is an interesting creature, isn't she?"

He studied the Pissaro hanging behind Jean-Michel, his sudden interest in Impressionist art not going unnoticed.

"I attempted to court her several years back," Jean-Michel continued, unconcerned with the low rumbling of warning and dagger stare coming from him. "I was quite taken with her. Beauty notwithstanding, she has a *je ne sais quoi*, something I could never identify yet desired, nonetheless. It was during one of our territory disputes. A room full of hostile vamps, and this tiny blonde pixie holding us all at bay with a look and a tongue lashing. I wouldn't suppose you have been at the receiving end of her chastisements, mannered as you are."

He clenched his jaw. "Maybe once."

"Ah." The elder vampire chortled. "Then you understand the dueling urges to fill her mouth with either your tongue or your sock."

Caught off guard by the accuracy of Jean-Michel's description, he grinned and shook his head. "So that's what the sensation was."

"Yes," the ancient said wistfully. "I believe some refer to it as being enamored."

He scanned his host, caught between curiosity in the vampire's story and agitation over its subject. "You were unsuccessful in your pursuit."

"I was. She was courteous enough, smiling whenever I arrived at her door bearing flowers and truffles. I might dare to say she was mildly interested in this old vampire's tales, too." He laughed, shaking his head.

"I spent two years and a fool's fortune attempting to convince Ms. Schumann to join my haunt as my exclusive Tender. I had hoped to gain from Johan's misfortune, to attain what he left behind. But alas…" Jean-Michel paused dramatically, and Jagger cocked a brow. "I did not possess whatever it is Ms. Schumann is searching for. Perhaps it is my visage hindering my attempts."

Rumors in vampire society placed Jean-Michel as the subject of several Renaissance paintings. He fought the rolling of his eyes.

"I don't think Bee knows what she wants. Or who she is," he speculated quietly.

"Bee? Interesting." Jean-Michel's green eyes narrowed in contemplation. "The young Johan referred to her by Bee. I, unfortunately, was never granted the privilege."

He slouched back in his chair, crossing his arms. "Yeah, well, I guess you hit that level of intimacy when you almost get a woman killed."

****

Kaius had not rested in days. The quiet of the haunt when the sun was high in the sky did little to detract him from his continuous monitoring of Jagger's emotions and location. His presence lifted the burden from Mikhail, a cross he bore willingly as he maintained an open link to his middle child.

While Dominic was considered the most volatile of the brethren, it was Jagger who caused him the most tension when his moods fluctuated. A century of melancholia had broken three weeks earlier, the shift from the predictable hum of ennui to spikes of jealousy, desire, lust, and self-loathing. The intensity of the deviation was reminiscent of a much earlier time.

"Connection is not to be taken lightly," Kaius *stated to his angry child, halting the swing of his sword before he caused damage. "There truly was no choice between staying and leaving. Someday, you may understand the pull."*

Rhys launched into another calculated attack, his weapon making light contact with Kai's wrist. "We're brothers in blood," he snarled. "That disposable whore is worth less than the dirt on her knees."

He countered Rhys's movements with ease, allowing him to work his frustrations out in the safety of the underground sparring room. "That whore," he cautioned, "may one day join our haunt. I have extended the invitation to Jagger to bring his connected mate to Berlin. He's anxious about the rising tensions in the Ottoman Empire."

Rhys attacked on impulse, his faulty movements leaving him open. "I will respectfully move on should he bring that siren to our door," he seethed as Kai took advantage of his open form. "You drew blood, you old bastard."

He straightened, allowing Rhys a moment to gain his footing. "Had I not felt the connection from here, I would be inclined to agree," he replied calmly. "An unschooled woman amongst us opens us to uprising. However, to separate the two could be detrimental to Jagger, and I'm unwilling to take the risk at this point in time."

Rhys looked up at him through his black hair, eyes

venomous. "But the time may come."

The time had come. It had started as a whisper and grew to a deafening howl.

****

The need to place as much distance between himself and the brunette under his fangs won out despite the urgent hunger radiating through his body. Jagger dislodged himself from her neck and began extricating himself from her embrace. The woman held tight, her hips swaying against him in the hopes of eliciting a reaction.

"Jean-Michel said you had two hours before you needed to leave," the Tender purred, her hands trailing down his spine toward the band of his cargos. "I don't have to be back home until dawn…"

Her brazen assertiveness instantly marked the woman as a Tender trained outside the Kaius haunt, a woman brought in to sate physical needs before all else. By the slight acidic taste of her blood, she was also a seasoned drinker. He gripped her hands firmly, removing them from his ass as she continued to rub against him.

"I'm afraid there's been a change of plans," he lied smoothly, not wanting to offend a Tender in Jean-Michel's home. "I must thank my host and head out."

Pouting with a feigned disappointment, she crossed her arms expectantly as he moved to leave.

"Thank you," he said, bowing. "I'll make sure to sing your praises to Jean-Michel."

Content with his dismissal, the woman allowed him passage from the room and into the receiving area. His host stood against the wall, a fanged grin on his face.

"She wasn't up to your standards," he posited as Jagg hefted his bag onto his shoulder. "Nor mine. The lesser adept trainers have the tendency to create simpering harlots instead of valued companions. Rhys's skills will be sorely missed by those of us with discerning tastes."

With a noncommittal grunt, he glanced back at the room where he could still see the brunette as she adjusted her bra. "I sometimes forget he truly is the best in the business."

"Indeed," Jean-Michel agreed. "Though I sense even the most exquisitely trained would not catch your eye at the moment. Safe travels, Jagg. I look forward to your return."

He thanked his host, placing his bag in the hatch when Jean-Michel waved over to him.

"Former Tenders straddle a delicate line between the human and vampire worlds. Sometimes they must be pushed wholly into one before they can embrace the other. Luck be with you, Jagger Kaius.

****

"Nichol's going to be pissed. That thing is filthy," Dominic warned as Jagger pulled into the garage.

He tossed the vehicle's keys to Dom and collected his bags from the passenger seat. "How are my beloved children?" he asked as his brother ran a finger along the hardened dirt caked along the four-by-four's body.

"Probably hungry," Dominic admitted. "I haven't had much time in the weapons room since Molly began working on the BRP."

"BRP?"

"Bloodslave Release Program. Audra came up with it. Said something about abbreviations lending credibil…never mind. That's what the BRP is," Dom muttered.

He walked alongside his youngest brother, the temporary relief of being surrounded by familiarity breaching the incessant guilt echoing in his mind. Dominic rambled on, filling him in on the successes and failures they were experiencing in the first round of the BRP. They walked straight to the weapons room, Dom recognizing intuitively he required a few moments in his own space before he took on the rest of the hauntmates.

"Everything's how you left it," Dom stated, grinning. "Exactly, actually."

He glanced around the room. Scribbled notes. Rags hanging haphazardly across chairs. A pile of boxes piled precariously in the corner. Knives on full display atop black silk.

He reached for the few sets of throwing stars on display, flicking them into a drawer and shutting it tight. "I guess I should be grateful you didn't fuck anything up," he deadpanned.

Dominic flipped him off and walked out, leaving him alone in his sanctuary.

He took his time unpacking his bag, placing each used weapon on one table for cleaning and sharpening and placing the others back in their various boxes and drawers. He sat in his worn chair and grabbed a clean rag. The ritualistic movements of oiling the soiled blades calmed his head and refocused him solely onto his work.

It wasn't until Rhys appeared at his door, he realized dawn had come and gone without so much as a tremor in his limbs.

"Bianca knew the risks when she walked into that apartment."

He looked away from his older brother and began the arduous task of scrubbing the oil from his skin. Rhys's boot knocked at the side of Jagg's chair until he looked up again in anger.

"She knew," Rhys continued. "The guy is dead. Revenge is sweet. All that happy-hearted bullshit. Regardless, her condition isn't on your head."

He nodded, seeing the words on Rhys's lips but refusing them passage into his consciousness.

"Her condition has been updated to stable as of an hour ago."

Another nod. Another piece of information ignored.

"Kaius would like you to feed and rest," Rhys stated, picking up a freshly oiled blade and turning it over in his hands. "And if you're hungry, now's the time to fill up. We'll be down to one Tender within the week."

He dropped the hood from his head and leaned back. "Fine. Send me over whoever. No blondes."

Rhys's hardened eyes narrowed briefly before he nodded and stomped off. He followed suit, watching the halls for shadows in the hopes of avoiding the rest of his hauntmates until dusk. When he made it into his bunker without being accosted, he sank against the door and waited for the knock of his meal as he clung to the small flicker of life in his blood link to Bianca.

Chapter Nineteen

The brunette had yet to wake, her hair splayed across the pillow and clothes spread across the room. Jagger sat on the edge of the bed and stared aimlessly at the dark red bra wedged between the back of his sofa and the wall. His cargos were strewn over his bedside table. Only one sock was in his line of sight.

The place was a fucking mess.

The woman shifted her position as he stood, taking up as much of the large bed as she could. Moving silently through the room, he began picking up clothes, separating the dirty pieces, and folding the clean ones. Grabbing a blade from his coffee table, he headed into the shower to wash away the day's activities.

Jean-Michel was right. Rhys-trained Tenders were leaps above the rest. The woman who had kept him from lying restlessly in his bed until dusk had not pushed him into conversation. She had held his eyes, never straying her gaze to the tattoos marring his temples.

Her only advance on him was her submissive stance of availability and encouragement, hands clasped at her back and head tilted. She had responded eagerly without the overt dramatizations other Tenders felt were required.

She was perfectly, beautifully interchangeable.

As the water pelted his skin, his mind wandered to Bianca's time at the Kaius haunt. Had she arrived in the haunt compliant? Or had Rhys trained the compliance into her? Did her seamless adaptation to every vamp she encountered come naturally? Or had she learned to adjust her mannerisms to suit his vastly different hauntmates?

The shampoo ran down his chest in rivulets as he dropped his head forward.

He didn't know the brunette's name.

The realization Bianca had spent years as one of the interchangeable, nameless beauties in the haunt tore at his psyche. How many of his brothers watched her walk from the room with a fleeting thought they hadn't known her name? How many times had she entered one of their rooms, offering her veins to a hungry or injured vampire only to be weakened or injured herself?

A sharp vibration coming from outside the bathroom snapped him from his introspection. He stilled his feet and felt the movement of the Tender toward the bunker door. Turning off the water and wrapping a towel around his hips, he exited the shower and came face-to-face-with Kaius.

"You're expected in the com room," Kai said, his blue eyes perusing him.

"I'll be right over," he replied, pulling a clean singlet from his drawer.

"I'll escort you."

Kaius sat on the sofa, politely keeping his eyes averted as the naked Tender strode over to him and collected her neatly folded clothing. Jagg motioned to the privacy of the bathroom, mildly pleased when she shot him a smile and disappeared behind the door. He turned his back to Kai and pulled on a pair of cargos, slipping his blade into the thigh pocket.

"Anything I should know before I head in there?" he asked as he pulled a sweatshirt over his head.

"I would appreciate it if you sat between Mikhail and Rhys," Kai stated. "It's best if Audra is not directly across from Rhys for the time being. Or Boy. She's an interesting addition to our haunt."

Jagg chuckled and laced up his boots. "And I thought Molly would be the monkey wrench."

Kaius pulled out his phone, frowning. Jagger's brows rose.

"Did you just search up that term?" he asked the old vampire.

Kai placed his phone back in his pocket. "Louis suggested it would help when the females, and apparently my own bloodline, use colloquialisms I'm not familiar with. The vampire with the bright red hair believes my inquiring about certain inane phrases inhibits my role as a figurehead within the haunt."

Sarcasm.

The pair walked wordlessly to the communication room as he steeled himself for another update on Bianca's condition. Mickey and Louis were testing each other's reflexes across the table, flinging pens at each other's eyes. Audra stood at Mick's side, her arms crossed and a disapproving frown on her face.

Nichol sat hunched over his laptop, tapping the keys in rapid succession and muttering obscenities to himself. Molly sat on Dominic's lap, swatting his roving hands with a notebook as her voice grew louder. Unnoticed in the din, he took a seat beside Mick, hoping Rhys would take the hint and situate himself accordingly.

"Don't fucking bump me," Mick mumbled as he

caught another pen, firing it back with precision. "I'm not in the mood to be blinded by this waste of space."

"Waste of space." Louis huffed, the pen missing his retina by a fraction. "I'm not the pussy who had his pencils taken away."

"If one of you was to stake the other, my shoes would be destroyed," Audra snarked. "Jagg! Welcome home." She placed a hand on Mick's broad shoulder. "Mickey."

"Yeah. Good to have you back," Mick grumbled, swatting a projectile away and sitting back. "Game's over, man. I give."

Louis held his victory pen in the air and kissed it. "I'd like to thank Audra for pussy-whipping her man. Nichol, for providing quality pens for our use. And Jagger, for distracting Mickey before he took out my eye."

Nichol booted Louis's chair in response, effectively calling the meeting to order as Rhys and Boy slipped into the room. Rhys pulled his chair up at Jagg's back, yanking his hood down and dodging his arm as it flung back.

Nichol met everyone's eyes, a sneer on his face. "If we are ever overrun by Deviants or the FBI, I will be shoving each and every one of you to the floor, except Kai, and saving my own ass. Audra, I may drag you behind me if you can keep that mongrel of yours under control."

Audra curtsied in response.

"Jagg. Finish the Deepfryer assembly and begin assessing it for weakness. Senator Green is still pushing for legalization, and we need intel," Nichol instructed. "Dominic, you, Louis, and Molly need to get the first round of bloodslaves ready for integration immediately. Audra and I will prepare the locations and determine the least invasive, most effective transfer route. Rhys go do your thing. Kaius?"

Kai rose, positioning himself behind Mickey and placing a hand on his shoulder. "Mikhail and Boy, you will be coming with me to the sparring room."

Mick's shoulder muscles rippled under the pressure of Kaius's grip. The slight tensing of Kai's fingers were met with a wince as Mick stilled. "Got it."

Nichol and Kai exchanged a look. "Last thing," Nichol said, drawing the group's attention once again. "Bianca will be lifted from the coma in the morning, providing her vitals remain stable. Guards have been placed outside her room. The local news is reporting protesters outside the hospital, but the numbers are currently sitting under twenty. Any changes in status and I will alert you through text. Now get the fuck out of my workroom."

Dominic and Louis jostled for position out of the room first, Molly tearing after them. Kaius whispered into Mick's ear before leading him and Boy out and down the hall. Jagger rose slowly, cognizant of Nichol and Audra's eyes on him.

"Thanks for the update," he said quietly as he moved toward the door. "Is it possible to get any eyes on Bianca from our end?"

Nichol's brows furrowed. "I'll confer with Kaius. It might not be a bad idea to have someone monitoring her until she has recovered and is able to transition underground. Am I correct in assuming you don't wish to be considered for duty?"

He nodded. "I would recommend Boy."

****

The multitude of Deepfryer boxes provided the perfect distraction from the increasingly violent visuals passing through his head. Each opened package gave Jagger a small thrill, another piece of a project he was itching to finish for months. Screwdrivers of various sizes littered the weapons room floor, flattened boxes were propped against every upright surface, and tiny washers and screws rolled aimlessly across the cement. His sweatshirt was yanked off hours earlier and was now serving as a cushion for the most delicate of bulbs.

Completely engrossed in his task, the appearance of a large boot in his periphery almost knocked him off balance. He arched his head up to see Rhys leaning in the doorway, unable to maneuver through the chaos overtaking the room.

"Care to take a walk?" Rhys asked casually, arms crossed and eyes scanning the mess.

He rose slowly, allowing numerous bolts to fall from his lap. "Where to?"

Rhys motioned for him to follow, backing away from the door to allow him to complete a final leap over the last of the unintentional obstacle course. Leading him to the sparring room, Rhys held his ear to the door before reaching for the knob.

"They're either on a break or dead."

The scent of Mick's blood intermingled with Boy's and wafted through the open door. He and Rhys slunk in, staying tight to the wall as they took in the scene. Kai acknowledged their presence with a sharp glare before returning his attention to the bleeding vamps knelt before him.

Mick was the more injured of the two, blood

slicking his long blond hair back and dragging an unwanted memory into Jagg's mind. His naked back was a canvas of slashes and bruises already beginning to heal. Boy appeared to have fared better, his bare torso less marred but bearing more fang marks.

Mick was a biter.

"Tired yet?" Kaius inquired, his face immobile.

Boy remained still.

"Mickey wants more," Rhys mouthed to him.

The guys rose to their bare feet and took position on opposite sides of the sparring room. Kai stood in the center, laying out the fight's parameters. It was an effective training method, one he had adopted for the sessions he himself ran with the hauntmates.

Rhys tapped his arm, mouthing Kaius's instructions for him. "Fangs and holds only. Stay within the blood. Boy to stay within the strength level of four to five hundred."

He watched as Kaius delegated the sparring perimeter, puncturing his own wrist and slowly dropping the lines. Mick and Boy remained against their respective walls, their eyes memorizing their reduced fight space. As Kai backed away, he and Rhys followed suit and tightened their positions on the wall. The flick of Kaius's wrist and the blond males launched themselves into the ring.

Boy had the advantage of age, despite Kai's boundaries. He guarded his vampiric age rings carefully, keeping his ankles wrapped with bandages to avoid revealing the number of thin gray lines ringing his legs. No hauntmate knew the extent of the old vampire's strength or speed, his limited sparring alongside the others always constrained within limits.

But despite the age factor, Mick held his own, fueled by rage as Kai maintained a steady verbal tirade.

"Perhaps tomorrow evening I will bring the female down here so she can decide for herself which of you is more capable of protecting her should the need arise," Kai taunted calmly. "Maybe award her to the victor. Focus, Mikhail. You cannot afford to be distracted. Boy is older, stronger, and more skilled. Though I dare say equally invested in the outcome."

Jagger's eyes flickered to the skirmish in the middle of the room. Mick was on his back, fangs embedded in Boy's bicep as the older vamp held his arms to the floor. With the amount of Boy's blood Mickey was starting to ingest, the playing field began to level, the senior vampire's blood providing a boost in Mick's strength, speed, and healing.

He turned his attention back to Kai.

"…ossible she may decide neither is suitable. Her bond with Nichol could override both of your desires. Which would make this entire exercise moot. Keep your leg in the ring, Boy. Mikhail, rein in your core and respond with your brain. I have witnessed more control in a fledgling."

As Boy adjusted his legs to remain within the boundaries, Mickey took the opportunity to flip the elder vampire onto his back and dove for the jugular.

Kaius continued to observe, ending the match as Boy bucked Mick out of the ring, tearing open his own throat in the process.

"Kneel," Kai ordered, eyes assessing the gushing wound at Boy's neck. Mick and Boy dropped to their knees before the haunt leader, the fire of their battle no longer evident in their tense expressions. "Whatever hostility you hold for one another will be limited to this room, and under my supervision. There will be no more shows of aggression in the halls or meetings of my haunt.

"I will no longer be making decisions based on your FEELINGS. This has gone on too long and for no purpose. Boy, the decision of her mate resides with Audra. You will no longer disrespect her by ignoring her choice. Mikhail, you will no longer disrespect the honor of your mate with your subtlc implications her affections may be easily swayed. Jagger?"

He stepped forward, hands clasped behind his back in a rare show of acquiescence. "Hose them off."

Chapter Twenty

Bianca's second cognizant waking fared far better than the first. IVs stayed in place. The oxygen mask remained intact. No sedatives were administered by a physician while a surprisingly strong nurse restrained her.

It was pleasant.

She waited patiently on the uncomfortable bed, knowing the changes in her readings would bring a medical team to her side shortly. She flexed her fingers and stretched her toes, pleased with the sensations of tightness and discomfort she experienced in doing so. Her mind wandered, latching indiscriminately to random thoughts passing through her drugged mind.

She should use the credit card with the travel miles to pay for her stay.

There is nothing redeemable about the green of hospital walls.

It was a long time since she used her purple nail polish.

Her physician eventually appeared in the doorway, his movements rushed as he and the strong nurse assessed her vitals and asked her a litany of basic questions. Yes, she knew where she was. Yes, she knew what year it was. No, she did not require more sedative. Yes, she would be willing to talk to the FBI once the doctor deemed her fit.

As the drugs began to wane, her mind sharpened.

What remained of Jagger's blood continued to course in her veins, her bullet wounds healing quicker than was medically justifiable if she stayed under the scrutiny of professionals. Reaching back to feel under her bandages, she was quick to realize she would likely be unmarked by morning at the rate the older vampire's blood was working. She sat up, gripping the metal rail of her bed as she steeled herself.

Three.

Two.

One.

The hole to the left of her spine gave under the force of her fingers, reopening the wound and sending a surge of pain throughout her body. She grit her teeth and repositioned her hand at the second injury. It was far further in its recovery.

Try as she might, she couldn't breach the newly healed opening. She tried time and time again, resulting in little more than an uncomfortable pressure at the site. Looking around her bed, she caught sight of a wired call button strung loosely to the head of the bed. She tugged gently, bringing the button and cord neatly into her hands.

Pausing to listen for sounds of movement outside her room, she brought the metal plug of the cord up and under her bandage and positioned it, awkwardly wrapping her fist tight around the base, and flung her body back against the mattress.

The searing pain indicated her success.

The sensation of blood leaking from both wounds eased her mind for the moment, the slicing pain a focusing point for her brain as she used a flimsy tissue to clean what blood she could from the metal prong.

It would buy her a day. Maybe two if Jagg's blood became more sluggish and worn in her system.

Dusk slowly drew in, the room darkening incrementally until the only light source was the glaring fluorescent lights on the ceiling. Another assessment by the hurried doctor, and she was cleared to talk to the FBI come morning. Shifting in place, she called out to a passing nurse.

"May I shower?" she inquired, her eyes trailing the IV lines leading from her arms to a rolling metal stand.

The nurse checked her chart through, flipping pages and clucking her tongue in concentration. "Let me wrap those IV sites for you and change your bandages. Then you should be good," the woman replied, pulling a roll of white tape from a drawer.

She sat patiently, watching the nurse work. "Is there soap? Shampoo?" she prodded, desperate to rid her skin of the scent of drying blood but unsure as to the protocol of hospitals.

With a satisfied nod at her handiwork, the nurse opened the tiny closet at the foot of the bed, pulling out towels, a clean gown, and a bag she recognized instantly. "This was sent in a few nights ago," the nurse stated, carefully arranging the items at her feet. "The men outside went through it, but I believe whatever was packed in here was undisturbed."

She thanked the woman, keeping her curiosity in check until the door closed and she was alone in the room. Placing the bag on her lap, she emptied its contents one by one.

A change of clothes. Slippers. Bodywash and shampoo.

The brush from her vanity.

A scribbled note identifying the contents. *A fresh start.*

It took her three trips to the bathroom to prepare for her shower. The rolling IV stand slowed her progress, its wheels turning inconveniently and the base catching on doorframes and hooking on furniture. Once she was ready, she carefully undid the ties holding her bloodstained gown on her body, kicking it to the side and shimmying carefully out of her panties.

The water heated slowly, never reaching a fully welcoming temperature. The scent of her own beauty products soothed her as she took her time to wash, moving slowly to avoid tangling herself in the IV lines. Using four small towels to wrap her hair and body, she applied the floral-scented lotion Jagg had included in her bag.

Jagger.

He had obviously made it as far as her Omaha condo. Shaking her memories of her last moments spent with him, she began the task of returning her things to her bag.

****

The tall figure at the window ran his fingers along the track permitting the glass to open marginally to the open air. He bent, studying the construction intently despite the darkness of the room. Bianca lay still, watching his movements and inching her fingers toward her reattached call button. The figure straightened to an impressive height, turning slowly to reveal a familiar pretty face, and squinting eyes.

"Boy," she whispered, sitting up. "What are you doing here?"

He moved closer to her, the light from the hall

providing an eerie illumination as he blinked his eyes repeatedly, a slight flinch every time he did so. She reached toward his jaw.

"You poor thing," she muttered. "Brown does not do your eyes justice." She prodded lightly at his lips, sighing when she saw blunted teeth in place of the silvered fangs she knew. His eyes continued to twitch, fighting against the intrusive contact lenses.

He moved in closer, assessing her IV sites and running his fingers up the lines to the stoppage points. With a flick, he turned off the machines before he crimped the lines and rifled through a drawer for tape, pulling two pieces off and holding them out for her to latch on to. With capable fingers, he dislodged the needles and taped the sites off skillfully before he turned her wrists over, tapping various places before motioning his desire to check her back.

The wounds no longer bled, a slight pressure the only sensation as he examined the twin holes. Content with her condition, he returned to the windows, gripped a pane, and worked it gently from its track.

She moved swiftly, pulling off her hospital gown and slipping into the first comfortable clothing she had in a week. Packing her bag, she stood to the side as he eased the removed glass under her bed. She looked out the open window, a tight fit for someone Boy's size.

"We're five stories up," she hissed, stepping back from the opening.

He took her hand, gesturing to a ledge three feet below the window and pointing toward the lower roof of another wing of the hospital.

"No."

Taking her bag and tossing it with ease to the roof

below, he knelt on one knee and waited.

"How did you get in? Let's go that way."

He remained still.

She gave in, acknowledging the old vampire was likely taking the path of least resistance. She wrapped her arms around his neck tightly, flexing a little in protest as he rose and attempted to back out of the window.

"We won't both fit," she whispered. "You first."

He paused, assessing her, and blinking unevenly. Ducking his head, he allowed her to climb off him awkwardly before he dropped to the small ledge. She took a breath and climbed through the window, breathing out only when she felt large hands guiding her descent. He led the shuffle, his strong arm held out to provide a balance for her.

He dropped to the rooftop first, arms open to catch her as she followed suit. Throwing her pack across his back, he fell to a crawl as he began his trek. The closer they moved to the edge, the louder a chant below grew.

"Blood whore will be no more."

She stopped, sitting back on her heels. "That's for me," she stated. He glanced back at her and nodded, jaw set. Undeterred, they made it to a three-story drop at the back of the hospital. He leapt off the edge, landing hard on the cement below. She backed away for a moment, settling her nerves before she worked up her courage and aimed for the vampire below.

He caught her midair, with not even a grunt of exertion, and placed her on her feet. The noise of the crowd grew louder, chants and shouts intermingling into a din of hate. Her breathing labored as they ran across the lot, his pace significantly slowed by her human speed. He knelt again, hefting her up high on his waist and continuing into the treed park at the back of the parking garage.

Her mute companion maintained his steady pace, cutting across paths and dodging trees until he arrived at a familiar vehicle. Setting her down, he pulled out his phone, fired off a text, and folded his large form into the driver's seat.

****

"Rhys. Phone."

Jagger sat back from his project and waited for Rhys to accept Nichol's cell. They were working on the final wiring on the Deepfryer, and any interruption to his concentration would add another hour or two to the process.

"Yeah?" Rhys answered, his phone manners as lacking as Nic's. The older vamp stilled, then glanced up at him. "I'm going to take this in my room," he muttered, leaving him alone to complete the intricate task.

He pushed his hood from his head and cursed, reaching for one of his newer blades, a retractable switch, spinning it absentmindedly as he awaited his brother's return. Counting down from five, he gave himself permission to reach toward the tunnel where Bianca currently resided.

Five.

Locating her was simple, her life force pulsing stronger since her reported waking three days prior. No longer a faint pulse in the recesses of his mind, it now took concentration to ignore the throbbing reminder of her existence.

Four.

Determination lined the tunnel, directing all other emotions as they meandered into his consciousness.

Three.

Relief. He glanced at the clock on his phone. Boy should have arrived on site hours ago, extracting Bianca from both the growing mob and the probing detectives standing guard outside her room.

Two.

Wherever she was, she felt safe. He clenched and released his jaw, knowing wherever she was, she was safe with Boy. An older, more powerful, more adept protector. A familiar vampire she trusted, had known for decades.

One.

He broke from the small link, retreating from the unsettling thoughts stirring in his head until a movement in the doorway caught his attention.

"Might want to come up to the com room with me," Nichol said. "Call it a night down here."

He stood reluctantly, turning off the lights and following Nichol up through the halls of the haunt. Kai joined them at his side, walking a fraction too close for his liking. The communication room was already full, the hauntmates crowded around the table as they awaited the arrival of the last three stragglers.

Rhys tossed Nichol's phone at him. "I've just gotten off the phone with Bianca," he began, avoiding all eye contact with him. "She and Boy made it out and are en route to Broken Bow. The Gagnon haunt is expecting them tomorrow night. From there, the decision will be made to bring Bianca here or cross into Canada and hide her up there until things settle in the region."

"She'll come here," Mick tossed in, Audra nodding at his side. "We have the room."

Rhys sat back and crossed his long arms. "This isn't our choice. It's Bee's. And if I had to wager on it, I believe she will choose Canada and try a vampire-free existence. I can get her established, place her on the local haunt observation list. The usual."

Nichol frowned. "A Tender doesn't get a choice."

"Former Tender," Jagg corrected quietly. "Therefore, the decision is out of our hands."

"This is Bianca's final shot at a white picket fence, a potbellied husband, and two kids. It can be a big draw for the Formers, Nic," Rhys added. "It's time she picks a side."

Chapter Twenty-one

The ceiling of the cave began to collapse, shards of stone and dust falling to the ground only to be kicked up again by the raging vampire. Walls cut smooth by water over millennia now bore fissures and jagged pockets from the assault of bloodied fists and boots. Howls reverberated in the enclosed space, bouncing around until one was indistinguishable from the next.

Jagger's swath of destruction was contained to the cavern as the sun rose higher in the sky, his rampage slowly easing as blood loss rose and blood lust waned.

Her smell had changed subtly over the past three months, the faint, almost undetectable intermingling of two separate yet complimentary scents within a single body. He had dismissed the shift, believing it to be little more than the result of residual odors from those Seline interacted with in her day. The slight bulge of her belly, the sudden fullness of her breasts, all clues as to her condition.

A child.

He sank against the cave wall, drained and emotionless. His connected mate was ripe with another man's seed, her womb nurturing another man's baby. He lay his head against the stone, closing his eyes.

Seline's restlessness had increased month after month, her moments of joy all but gone as she moved by rote through their lives. Her mealtimes, once filled with lively gossip and hushed speculations, became wistful laments about the new mothers arriving at the bakery with their babes in arms. He had sought to distract her, to entice the despondent woman with promises of travel and luxuries, far from the routines and reminders of the human society in which she existed.

Her hand had rested protectively on her stomach as she told him, pleading for him to understand why she'd gone to another's bed. A fulfillment, one he could never provide.

It would be theirs, she whispered. Theirs to raise. Theirs to love. A semblance of a normal life.

He had escaped the tiny home, bags in hand, before he succumbed to the torment and rage radiating from his core and encompassing his mind. The remnants of her scent on his clothes, once a calming reassurance, tore at his sanity as image after image flashed through his head.

The man. The child. Seline. Visions of her traitorous act pounded into his skull, warring with the immense guilt he had carried for months over his inability to provide her the life she so desperately craved. With each image, he grew emptier until numbness settled over him, engulfing his mind and body.

He'd been a fool to believe he could sentence her to a life of darkness.

As dusk settled on the land, he began his trek to Berlin.

He adjusted his stance and released the blade, cursing softly as it curved slightly to the left, missing its mark. He stalked forward, retrieving the dagger from the wood target, and examined the trueness of the curve, keeping his eyes averted from the hauntmate at his door. With a gentle bend to the blade's arc, he backed up and aimed once again.

A strong hand grasped his arm as he threw the knife, sending its course reeling off point.

"Not the time," he muttered, attempting to shake off Rhys's hold. He struggled a moment before relenting, ice eyes scowling at his older and closest brother.

"Want me to give it a few months?" Rhys inquired, his dig scratching the surface of Jagger's control. "Eight? Nine? State your preference."

A low growl formed in his throat, a warning to Rhys to back off.

"Yeah, yeah." Rhys huffed dismissively. "Been there, done that. Here." Rhys released him, stretching over to grab a pen and paper. He scribbled frantically for a few minutes, stopping every so often to assess his work before resuming. When he was satisfied, he turned back to him and held the paper up. "This is you. See? Hood, creepy eyes, and those little triangles are your pathetic excuses for fangs. That's me. You can tell because the fangs and bulge are bigger."

His scowl set on his face.

"This is us ripping each other's throats out. Then this is us not talking for a few years. As you can see, I'm occupying myself with Tits McGee, and you're sitting by yourself in the corner. See? There you are, miserable as shit and digging your goddamn heels into a pile of manure."

Rhys turned the paper over, tapping his artwork. "Now here you are lying in a coffin. I'm piling dirt on your pathetic ass because you're as good as dead for the next few decades. In case you forgot, I'm the one with the big dick and the shovel."

With an irritated snarl, he snatched the paper away from Rhys, gesturing to an unidentifiable drawing at the bottom. "What the fuck is this?"

"You're such a fucking moron," Rhys barked. "That's Bianca burning in a Deepfryer along with some century-old weakling because she didn't know you were a fucking option, and when she realized she wasn't cut out for the fence and the kids and the dog, she turned to the wrong fucking haunt for protection."

Rhys slammed the paper onto the workbench, rearing up inches from his face. "Like I said, we've been there, done that. This time around, you know the outcome. I'll leave some of my stash in your bunk for when the shit hits the fan."

Rhys balled the paper, tossed it at the Deepfryer, and stormed from the room, his shoulders rolling out the tension. Deliberately ignoring the crumpled note on the floor, Jagg retrieved his blade and sat down to hammer out the curve.

****

"It's fine," Bianca murmured, kneading the small pile of hay into something resembling a pillow. Boy looked away, returning his attention to running his fingers along the seams of the plank walls as she eased herself down on her makeshift bed, her freshly opened bullet wounds no longer healing at the accelerated rate she had cursed only a day earlier.

The FBI interrogators were relentless in their questioning, finally backing down when the doctor arrived and put an end to the charade. The men had entered her room prepared, security footage images set on eight-by-ten glossy photo paper and a personal file on her twenty pages thick. Their disdain for vampires dripped from their voices as they questioned her on her associations with the suspect, setting photos of Jagger on her lap to examine.

And examine she did.

Every photo was pulled from the hospital security cameras, her lifeless form draped over the secure arms of a hooded vamp. He was diligent in hiding both her face and his, the only facially recognizable photo placed before her a blurred profile of him, his eyes obscured by shadows. She hid a smile at the ingrained defensive movements amid the flurry and strain of the night.

It had taken her a few moments into the questioning to remember the details of her file, the carefully assembled background Nichol had created years earlier to cover her years of absence among human society.

She had forgotten she had a degree in political science.

The less forthcoming she was with her answers, the more agitated the interrogators became until their voices rose enough to summon the physician, and she was temporarily freed from the onslaught.

She adjusted her position, hips growing sore on the cold wood of the barn. Boy stood in the far corner, his eyes flickering from board to board as the sun began to rise. He moved rhythmically through the barn as thin rays punctured the darkness.

"This area is secure," she called out quietly, motioning Boy toward her. "There are no breaches. Come. Rest."

Boy walked over to her, stepping over her reclined

form and wedging himself into the dark corner. The brown of his contact lenses was barely visible as he monitored her movements, her shifts and stretches. Lowering himself to the floor, he gently pulled her onto his lap and locked his gaze on the barn doors.

****

"*Mon ange!*" Jean-Michel called out, arms outstretched as he descended the staircase. "You look like Godiva in the flesh. And you smell like her horse."

Bianca stepped into the familiar embrace, a slight satisfaction in knowing the vampire's horrendous blue overcoat would be tainted by the barn odor and would likely meet its fate in the fireplace by morning. Boy stood at her back, his lean-muscled body primed for attack. "I would sell my soul for a shower," she stated, using her pleading eyes to encourage Jean-Michel to waste no time in releasing her.

He stepped back, bowing, and motioning down the hall. "Down the stairs and to the right is your quarters. I trust your beast of a guard will be accompanying you?"

She swatted Jean-Michel, a scolding look on her face. "My companion will be accompanying me, yes. Behave yourself, Monsieur Gagnon."

Bowing with a glimmer of mischief in his eye, Jean-Michel stepped aside and allowed them passage. The pair moved swiftly into the basement quarters, taking no time to admire the opulent decor before Boy began his sweep of the quarters and she entered the bathroom to start the shower.

Scrubbing her hair, she kept up a steady stream of chatter at Boy. "You aren't bound to me on the grounds. The compound is quite secure and offers much to keep you entertained should you find the monotony of flirtation and small talk uninteresting. Both bedrooms are quite nice if memory serves. One, however, has a significantly larger bed. Make sure you move your things in there. I think you are at least an inch or two taller than I."

The bathroom door cracked open slightly, bringing in a cool waft of air. She peeked around the curtain and smiled at the sullen vampire. "Fine. You are at least three inches taller."

Apparently satisfied with her amendment, he closed the door, and she finished rinsing the scent of hay and animal from her hair. The shadow of his feet remained outside the bathroom as she took her time brushing her hair and wrapping herself in a large white robe. She gestured for him to take her place as she exited, crossing her arms, and cocking a brow when he remained in place.

"I'm not going anywhere," she argued. "Get in there. You smell horrific."

Leveling her with a glare of warning, Boy closed the door, and the water began running. She held position until she heard him step under the spray, then padded upstairs to visit with her host.

Jean-Michel was waiting for her in the large sitting room, the fireplace blazing and not a single blue overcoat in sight. She smirked at the handsome vamp and hoisted herself into the oversized armchair to his left.

Ignoring her obvious pleasure in adjusting his wardrobe to her liking, Jean-Michel stood, bringing a plate of fruits and cheeses to her. "If memory serves, this will be an opening course to the multiple others I have being prepared in the kitchen as I speak."

She swallowed her first bite of strawberry and leaned back contently. "This is why I love you. You know that, right?"

The duo had a long history, one of tumultuous politics and failed romance. But she counted Jean-Michel among her top-trusted vampires after the Kaius haunt. The Frenchman was fair in his dealings, chivalrous to a fault, and spoke his truths with conviction.

"The ancient is a Kaius male, is he not?" Jean-Michel inquired. "Rhys informed me you would be accompanied by one of his haunt, but his scent…"

"A hauntmate not of the bloodline, yes," she replied, recognizing the vampire's concern for security, both hers and his. "One I have known far longer than I have you, kind sir."

Content with her assurances, Jean-Michel relaxed in his seat and turned the conversation toward the stagnant vampire political arena in the face of the anti-vampire uprisings. Despite his seclusion from human society, he was well aware of the unstable social and political climate North American vampires were facing. He paused his musings as Boy entered the room, hair damp and a hint of anger in his empty blue eyes.

"I was hungry," she interjected into the silent stare-off, bringing her host's attention back to her and temporarily appeasing the ire of her bodyguard. "Sit, sweetie. Monsieur Gagnon, may I trouble your staff for an AB positive?"

With a flourish, Jean-Michel sent off a text to his staff, a warmed carafe of AB positive appearing within minutes. "I'm sure you will find it to your liking," he said to Boy. "It is, after all, Kaius haunt stock."

Boy nodded as he accepted the meal but made no move to drink it. Instead, he retreated to the far corner of the room and stood motionless, observing Bianca's surroundings with the attention of a predator on foreign soil.

"Not much of a conversationalist, is he?" Jean-Michel mused. "The males of the Kaius haunt are a different breed entirely."

She smiled. "That they are. Have you much contact with them?"

"Rhys and I maintain an open line. He will be delivering two of his lovely creations next week. He's informed me, however, both the Tender sales and blood sales will be eliminated within the year. Pity. Quality in both is severely lacking elsewhere."

He paused as an overly made-up woman entered the room, exchanging Bianca's empty plate with a steaming bowl of soup, a tinge of jealousy on her face. He waited until the woman was out of earshot before huffing. "That is what passes for quality outside of Rhys's scrupulous eye. It's the class, the mannerisms of his Tenders setting them apart. *C'est la vie*. Let's move on to a more pleasant topic. What will it take for an old vamp like myself to be placed back in the running for your affections?"

Chapter Twenty-two

Kaius released the wrist of the Tender standing at his side, murmuring his gratitude by rote as his mind continued to compose, assess, and eliminate game plans. Though they were moving in the right direction, the haunt was dangerously unprepared for the months and years ahead. Despite his best efforts, he knew his inability to balance his dual responsibilities were the cause, his lack of foresight into the bigger picture a decade ago the source of their precarious position.

The colorful curls of the Tender bounced from the common room, her duty complete. With a quick check on Mikhail's state, he slowly shut down the links to his kin. He needed to focus, to eliminate the emotions of the others to determine the most advantageous course of action. He couldn't afford to be influenced in his decisions.

He reclined on the sofa, stretching his legs, and closing his eyes as he began envisioning the first crucial steps to make his hauntmates self-sufficient amid the pressures bearing down on them.

Unity.

Throughout the centuries, the intense solidarity of the hauntmates was a key factor in their survival. Unlike most haunts, the Kaius vamps didn't move on as they grew stronger, establishing their own bunkers and filling them with their bloodline. Instead, they remained a cohesive unit, their strengths adding to the overall power of their line instead of dissipating it throughout the continents. They worked as a finely-tuned machine, each component an integral part of the whole. Short separations through distance over the span of over a millennium had placed little strain on the cohesion, as each member's individual pursuits consistently aligned with the growing influence of the Kaius name.

But now, when facing insurmountable odds, fissures were appearing in the once impenetrable fortress of the haunt.

Mikhail and Rhys.

Mikhail and Boy.

Rhys and Jagger.

Dominic.

Nichol.

The disputes were manifesting themselves as anger, the posturing and physical aggression nothing more than a symptom of the underlying malignant crux. The violence cloaked what lay at the center of the dissensions, masking it thoroughly from even the hauntmates themselves.

Doubt.

Throughout centuries of intermittent bloodshed, forced confinements, and movements across thousands of miles of hostile territories, the Kaius vamps had maintained an unwavering belief in their strengths, their endurance, and their survival. Their bloodline was powerful, a combination of both the sire and the vampires themselves.

Unlike many of his contemporaries, he had purposely chosen to create a lineage with enough strength, skill, and intelligence to someday overtake him, a line powerful enough in their own right to no longer require him.

The allure of mere companionship or the desire to spawn an army of mindless subservients had little appeal to him. He wanted, needed, a haunt of prime specimens from across the centuries, a small and cohesive unit of virtual perfection capable of bringing down whatever crossed their path.

The uncertainty creeping among the brethren was debilitating to their survival.

Mikhail had little confidence in his ability to keep his mate safe within the confines of his own haunt, let alone the forces building around them.

Rhys held no faith in his future, seeing the bleakness of another cell in his imminent path.

He held no faith Rhys would survive again.

Jagger believed himself expendable.

Dominic felt his connected woman was settling.

Nichol refused to see himself as the true leader of the haunt.

They could run. Take shelter to the north for a few decades until the undercurrent of vampire hate swelled and abated. Plot and prepare as Dovidas revealed his intentions and his connections. Amass an army of faithful, training in the harsh terrain of the Canadian north.

"Kaius?"

He lifted his arm from his eyes and focused on Mikhail's female. Audra.

She walked over to him, crouching at his side in an impressive balance on her uncomfortably high heels. "I would like to propose something to you."

Sitting up, he gestured for the cat-eyed woman to join him as he listened for his hauntmates. "I'm intrigued. You don't often seek me out. Never, in fact."

She extended a paper toward him, her impeccable handwriting covering the page. "I've discussed this with Molly, and she's on board. We would like to be trained to fight alongside you. I've made a list of the pros and cons, as well as required equipment and weapons needing to be ordered."

He looked over the notes, feigning interest long enough to mimic contemplation. "I assume you've come to me first, knowing Mikhail, Dominic, and Nichol would not agree."

Her lips pursed as her brown eyes narrowed. "You're the haunt leader. The decision is yours, not theirs."

With a chuckle, he handed the paper back. "The repercussions would be mine as well, then." He sat back and observed the woman for a moment. "You understand if I agree, training would be defensive, not offensive." Another twitch of her lips.

"You would train under Jagger in blades, firearms, and hand-to-hand combat. He runs an intensive program, one even Mikhail struggles to uphold. You would be prepared for this?"

She leaned forward and took a deep breath. "You push it past Mickey and Dominic, ensure Nichol doesn't interfere, and Molly and I will do whatever is required to defend ourselves and our home."

Home.

He had yet to adapt to the concept of these women calling his haunt "home."

****

Jagg began pulling open drawers, rifling through his vast collection until his eyes fell on his target. "We could start them on something small and lightweight," he stated, gently placing the blades on his workbench. "Something allowing them to get a good understanding of the balance and movement without shanking themselves or each other."

Kaius lifted the hilt of one knife. "You are willing."

Looking back over the list, he paused. "Very willing. The Deepfryer is wired and functional, but I can only do so much with it until Nichol gets a shipment of dead pigs in. And even then, I probably shouldn't spend too much time standing beside a cooker." He tugged a rag off his wall and began working on the first blade. "The more Audra and Molly know, the less we have to worry about them when things heat up."

Kai wandered over to the Deepfryer, touching the glass panels hesitantly before turning back to face him. "It would be helpful if you could create a general training outline. Tonight. Something I can use to present to Mikhail and Domi…"

He grinned. "Audra came to you, didn't she?" he asked, shaking his head. "She made noise about it a few days ago, and Nichol shut her down pretty damn fast. I'll have something drawn up within the hour, and I'll back you up when you approach the beasts."

Grunting his thanks, Kai left, leaving him to work out a regimen for the women. Human women. His dark brow furrowed, and he began typing into his phone. The Internet had thousands of routines to select from.

As he perused the web pages, he began to compile a list of appropriate training activities to blend into his own routines for the rest of the hauntmates. Wrapped up in his work, the time passed quicker than it had in weeks, and soon he found himself striding into the com room, papers in hand.

Kai sat at the head of the table, the slight hunch in his back indicating he was prepared for an argument. Possibly a fight. Kaius extended his hand to him, taking a moment to read over the regimen and nodding tersely as the others trickled in slowly. Dom and Molly arrived first, jostling through the door in a flurry of activity and playful competition.

He watched the pair as they pushed and pulled each other to gain their preferred seat until Nichol interfered with a sharp word. Louis sauntered in, nodding toward Kai, and taking his place on the outer edge of the room. While fully immersed in the haunt's activities, Louis appeared to prefer observing during the meetings, his eyes often glinting with amusement when things became heated.

Rhys rounded the corner, purposely looking past him to Kai and taking up a position across the table, angling his chair to avoid directly facing him.

Mick and Audra were last to appear, Audra's skewed ponytail and Mickey's pleased smirk belying their pre-meeting activities. He turned his paperwork over, hiding the contents as he peered at the pair from under his hood. The transformation Mick had undergone in recent months was fascinating to watch, his former restlessness replaced with an overall contentment despite the continued emotional fluctuations bombarding his mind from his volatile hauntmates.

He suspected Mick had yet to link to Audra.

Catching the flick of Kaius's wrist in the corner of

his sight, he turned his attention to the haunt leader as the meeting was called to order.

"There is not much on the docket tonight," Kai began, shifting in his seat and leaning forward. "I would like a summary from each division before I address my pressing concern. Louis?"

"Molly, Audra, and I will have the first three humans ready for reintegration on schedule. They've taken well to my suggestions, though I'll have to wait until they are off site before I try to eliminate the quarters from their memories," Louis stated, glancing at his cohorts for confirmation.

Audra flicked her hand quickly. "The arrival of their clothing has had a huge impact on the mental states of the candidates. I would like to request a bulk order of track suits for the remaining bloodslaves, Nichol," Audra said, turning her attention to her vampire counterpart. "I can provide a list of common sizes, and we can sit down later to select a brand."

As Nichol nodded and made a quick note on his laptop, he caught Rhys's movement in the corner of his eye.

"…no different than those eggs you put hats on," Rhys muttered, stretching back in his chair.

Jagg looked to Audra, smirking as her cat eyes narrowed. "You did not just liken humans to hard-boiled eggs, did you?" she asked.

"It's an apt comparison," Rhys replied, smugness forming on his face. "One of my trainees a while back became ill eating uncooked cookie dough, and I had the revelation. When properly prepared, eggs are a source of nutrition for you, correct? However, they can also be a threat to your well-being when processed incorrectly.

Same with humans. If we don't prepare them right, they're a threat to our health. Therefore, humans are like eggs, and now you want to put hats on them."

Being unable to track the entire argument irked him as Rhys and Audra launched into a fast verbal sparring across the table. He turned his focus onto Mick, who had relaxed into his seat as his mate went head-to-head against Rhys until Kaius rose.

"Rhys, you're goading for reaction," Kai chastised. "Audra, you're feeding it. You and Nichol can figure out the details later, but this report is over." Audra's lips pursed, and she angled her body away from Rhys. "Now," Kai said, redirecting the attention of the hauntmates, "Mikhail, an update."

Mickey ran his hand along Audra's back absently as he spoke. "The trail of missing women I've been tracking has halted in Oklahoma. No new reports for two weeks. I'll keep watch, but it may be a dead end in our hunt for Dovidas."

With a nod, Kaius motioned to him, and he adjusted his hood. "Still waiting on pig corpses to begin testing the Deepfryer and assess the incremental damage levels. The glass is bullet resistant, heavily wired, and held fast in its frame once assembled. I need to build an enclosure around it, allowing me access to the control panel during testing but keeping those rays off me.

"The one test I did for residual UV through the glass proved we cannot be in the vicinity of one of these bad boys when it's activated. My secondhand burns were quick to develop and healed at the same rate as full sun exposure burns would."

Nichol stretched his arms back over his head. "The

pigs will be here next week. Molly, you will need to bring Audra on your mail run when they arrive. They'll be heavy. We'll store them in the bloodslave freezers until Jagg needs them. Boy should be back by then and will clear out two of the top access freezers."

Kai made a quick note and looked across the table. "Rhys?"

Rhys hefted his booted feet onto the table and lounged back. "I'm bringing the retrainees to the Gagnon haunt in two days. I announced a time-sensitive bidding on Simone and have received a large number of offers, which will empty out the Tender training area completely. However, we have a small issue with Lis."

The guys around the table sat up a little straighter, their allegiance to the Tender Lis comparable to what they felt for Bianca. He caught Audra's side-eyed glance to Mickey before her head shook slightly and her expression turned to concern.

"Her current master is exercising his right to maintain her position in his haunt. However, Lis has messaged me, reporting his unfulfilled connection to a local woman has drastically altered his personality and temperament. It's a situation I'm monitoring, but should she require a safe house, I would like to have a room available for her."

While everyone nodded their agreement, Molly spoke up. "If he's a danger to her, why are you not pulling her out now? It's not right to leave her there."

He noted Dominic pulling himself closer to his connected mate.

"As of yet, Lis is in no reported danger," Rhys reported. "There's been no mention of abuse, and Lis continues to have contact with me through text and email. Her master maintained a continuous link to her, so we currently have no grounds to extricate her from the situation without repercussion."

Molly and Audra's arms crossed simultaneously.

Kaius's wrist flicked quickly. "I have one final issue to address. I have discussed this with the parties directly involved, and we all feel it is in our best interests as a haunt to move forward. Jagger has prepared a training schedule for the fem—" Kai paused. "For Audra and Molly. It's imperative they become educated in both weapons and hand-to-hand combat."

"No," Nichol stated as he began closing his laptop, indicating the meeting was adjourned.

Mickey and Dominic pushed their chairs back slightly.

"If we don't," Jagger interjected, ignoring Nichol's display, "we leave the women exposed with nothing standing between them and whatever human, Deviant, or vampire they meet." He met Mickey's eyes, staring him down. "I understand neither of you want to accept you might not be around to fight for them, but it's an antiquated ideal we cannot afford right now."

Pushing his notes across the table, he gave Mick and Dom a moment to look them over. "I've prepared a variety of methods increasing incrementally as the women strengthen. I'll be focusing on firearms first, as it has the lowest strength or endurance requirement, moving on to blades and hand-to-hand. And frankly, whether or not you agree is moot, as Audra and Molly already have. They start tomorrow. This is merely a formality."

As Dominic's mouth opened in protest, Kaius leaned forward. "Should either of you, or you, Nichol, be anything other than supportive of the women's decision, I will chain you in the sparring room for a week to provide them with a live target."

Chapter Twenty-three

Bianca leaned against the door of the room Boy inhabited in the Gagnon haunt, her arms crossed and brows raised. The object of her ire sat rigidly on the bed, his normally empty blue eyes flashing with anger. The standoff was into its third hour, neither participant wavering, and only one vocalizing throughout the battle of wills. The sun had risen two hours earlier, its arrival noticeable only in the small shiver passing through Boy as the sun crested.

She dropped her arms to her side, deciding to approach the one-sided argument from a less combative stance. "Honey," she began, holding her place but purposely softening her tone. "I'm just worried if you don't feed, you won't be at full strength. It's been a week, and despite my affable relationship with Jean-Michel, we are residing in unknown territory. I know little about his children and even less about the humans on the grounds. I need you."

Boy's expression changed for the worse. His brows furrowed beneath his long blond shag, and his lips drew tighter, the outline of his fangs more prominent.

She had come to Boy's room as dawn neared, having noticed his refusal once again to drink the warmed blood supplied by Jean-Michel. The sullen vamp had yet to feed since he had pulled her from the hospital, and it pricked at her Tender side fiercely. She had entered his room quietly, locking the door behind her and wrapping her arms around his waist as he stood against the wall texting his hauntmates.

His muscles had stiffened at her touch as they always did at first, his stance adjusting slightly to one of attack before schooling itself into a less hostile pose. As he relaxed fractionally into her hold, she had nuzzled his broad back and lifted her wrist in submission.

While often recalcitrant to her offerings, Boy had periodically relented and allowed her to fulfill her duties to his kind, to ease her mind of the misplaced guilt she felt whenever she looked at the neglected Kaius hauntmate. Tonight had started no differently, his refusal to feed displayed through little more than a stoic denial of her presence.

As she remained pressed against his cool body, she had trailed her hands along his arms, running her fingers along the sensitive skin of his triceps. He continued to ignore her, and she became more insistent, skimming the band of his cargos and inching her hand up his black shirt. When he finally relented and set his phone on the bedside table, he gently lifted her hands from his torso.

And placed them on her own hips.

The blatant shutdown of her sexual advances hadn't stung, but the refusal to take her blood had invoked her indignation. She had glared at him as he maneuvered around the bed and leaned against the wall, arms crossed and staring blankly at the ceiling.

Determined to ensure the stubborn vampire in her care was fed, she strode to him, tightening the belt of her robe as she muttered her frustration with him. Reaching up to his mouth, she had forced the issue by slipping her pinkie under his lips and slicing it along his fang. Holding the bleeding digit in his line of sight, she waited for Boy to concede.

He had turned away, setting off two hours of irritated arguments from her and two hours of hostile silence from him.

With a sigh, she crossed the room and crouched in front of him, brushing the stray hair from his face and ignoring his slight flinch from her touch. "I know you're refusing me out of some misplaced loyalty to Audra, but she is not, nor has she ever been, yours," she whispered.

His crystal blue eyes lowered to hers, his head shaking his hair back into his eyes. "No? This isn't about Audra?" His head shook again, jerking back when she reached up to his jaw. "Is it me?" she inquired, her anger slowly being replaced by concern.

When he nodded slowly, she sat back on her haunches. Vampires had refused her numerous times over the decades for a variety of reasons, none of which stemmed from her. Mick had sent her away during a particularly low mood swing. Nichol had turned his back to her wrist while engrossed in a radio broadcast during the lead up to the second World War.

Numerous cordial offers to vampire guests were politely declined, the respect they held for Johan outweighing their desire to sample her. Even Johan himself had turned her away periodically during times he felt his control was too precarious to risk injuring her.

But never had she herself been named as the reason for refusal.

A twinge in her knees from her position pulled her

from her reflections. She adjusted her hips slightly to alleviate the discomfort. "Is it my age?" she asked quietly, well versed in the vampiric preference for youth and vitality in both blood and body. He shook his head quickly. Scooting back against the wall and ensuring her robe covered her completely, she arched her neck and stared at the ceiling. "My blood? Does it smell different?"

Another adamant refusal.

She smiled wistfully for a moment. "So it's me, but not me?"

She looked to Boy. His brows knotted, and he leaned forward to grab his phone. His thumbs flew across the screen, pausing periodically before resuming at the lightning speed. When he was content with his work, he handed the phone to her, his note application open.

—You are no longer a Tender. Or a Former Tender. The burden of our care is no longer yours to bear. Rhys, with approval of the Kaius haunt, has released you from your duties. A notification of your new status has been issued across the continents, bearing Kaius's signature. My assignment now is to ensure you are safely integrated into a human community, alert the resident haunt of your location to secure protection, and to leave you to live out the remainder of your life as you see fit. —

She reread the message over and over.

A full release.

A pardon.

"Jean-Michel is aware," she said, no question in her voice.

Boy nodded, taking his phone from her, and typing

a reply.

—Jean-Michel has been tasked with securing transportation into Canada and has identified a small community where you can establish residence in a home owned by the local haunt. Transfer of ownership is being made into your name. Your only tie to vampires will be the unseen providing your security. Nichol is preparing your new identification and transferring your bank accounts into an alias. Mikhail is familiar with the area haunt and has facilitated the communication between them and Jean-Michel. Rhys has approved the accommodations and will be arriving tomorrow night to oversee the details of your disguise, your updated papers, and to review safety measures you will be required to take. —

Rhys. Kaius. Mick. Boy. Nichol.

A single question pushed through her suspended thoughts.

"Will Jagger know where I am?"

****

"No."

Jagger looked back to his trainees, ignoring his best friend standing in the doorway. Audra's face was flushed with exertion, her normally impeccable makeup smeared as she wiped the sweat from her brow. Molly was in similar shape, her smart mouth silenced by deep breathing and intermittent gasps for air. Two hours into their second session, and all the effort the women had put into jovial complaints over sore muscles from the previous evening was now channeled into tackling tonight's agenda.

Rhys stepped back into his line of sight, calling to the women over his shoulder. "Take five for a water break," he growled. "You're no use to us if you drop dead from dehydration."

Making a quick note on his training regimen to allow for more frequent hydration breaks, he continued to pointedly ignore his brother.

Until Rhys's fist connected with his jaw.

He spat the blood filling his mouth onto Rhys's boot, pushing his hood off, and baring his fangs.

"Oh good," Rhys snarled. "You aren't fucking dead yet. I leave for the Gagnon haunt in twenty minutes. So do you."

Shoving Rhys aside, he stormed away to adjust the height of the punching bag dangling from the concrete ceiling. As he extended his reach to the links, Rhys's body pummeled into his, throwing him into the metal-covered cement wall. Debris from the ceiling rained down on the duo, scattering in a flurry when he swung back at the older vamp, his fist connecting with Rhys's cheekbone.

They grappled on the floor, neither holding back as they beat their frustrations out on each other. Rhys's strength of age was countered by his speed, and the upper hand was gained and lost amid the blows and blood.

Kaius's appearance in the sparring room went unnoticed until he was wedged between them, his long arms holding the brothers apart as he spoke. "Thank you for notifying me, ladies," Kai called out, his gaze fixed on Jagger. "I believe you may take the rest of the evening off."

Kaius's grip on his neck had stilled him immediately, recognizing he would be wise to calm down in the presence of his creator. Rhys, however, continued to buck and swing, his movements halting only when Kai released Jagg and focused all his strength on restraining the snarling hauntmate. Bringing Rhys to the floor, Kai sat on him calmly until Rhys finally relaxed under his weight.

"Am I correct in my interpretation of your surprise earlier Rhys hit first?" Kai inquired casually, raising himself off Rhys and offering him a hand.

He nodded, refusing to acknowledge his closest brother as he popped his left thumb back into its socket.

Stepping alongside Kaius, Rhys crossed his tattooed arms. "First and second hit," he bit out, running a tongue along his fangs to ensure they remained in place. "Most of the ones in the middle. Though I think Jagger got the last one in."

Kaius pointed to the door. "Go get cleaned up," he said quietly to Rhys. "The Tenders are ready to go, and it would be rude to keep them waiting much longer."

Rhys hesitated, his dark eyes flashing to Jagger before he turned and stormed from the room. He held his position, awaiting his own instructions. Kai remained still, his head cocked as he listened for Rhys's departure.

"He is concerned for you," Kai finally spoke.

He lifted his hand, silencing the haunt leader. "Not his business," he grunted. "Nor is it anyone else's."

Kaius nodded thoughtfully. "I will respect your privacy. For now. However, I retain the right to intervene should I feel the need to."

He began to walk toward his weapons room. "Your interference turned out great last time," he grumbled. "I'll hose this place down before dawn.

****

Rhys perused the grounds slowly as he approached the door, scanning the vast fields and scenting the air for unrecognized bloodlines. His Tenders walked alongside him, flanking his entrance as the head of the Gagnon haunt opened the door without a word.

The formality of the Tender trade had begun to wear on him over the years, the posturing and the exaggerated inspection of the goods being sold. The younger buyers were by far the most irritating, asking ridiculous questions and probing for discounts. Ancients like Jean-Michel tended to hasten the process slightly, their expectations and knowledge firmly in place prior to his arrival.

The Gagnon home was opulent, almost garish in its decor. He motioned for the women to walk ahead and took a moment to scan the room for signs of Bianca and Boy. Finding none, he followed Jean-Michel into the receiving room and flopped gracelessly onto the red velvet sofa.

"As discussed, these lovely specimens are a resale," he began, gesturing for the women to turn for inspection. "Slightly rough around the edges, a little on the simpering side, but skilled and knowledgeable. Your kin should find them to his liking."

Jean-Michel remained on his feet, his eyes narrowing as he watched the women walk the Persian rug and return to stand before him. The minutes ticked by as he scanned them for obvious defects before he chuckled and sat. "They're fine," he stated. "Roland will be pleased, which pleases me, which fills your bank account. I will transfer the remaining sum at dawn." He pulled out his phone and sent off a text.

Rhys hummed his agreement as a Tender he didn't

recognize entered the room, her mascara caked on her lashes and lipstick two shades too dark for her complexion. With the flick of his wrist, he dismissed the Tramp Twins for the final time. "Who did you purchase her from?" he muttered, watching the woman's hips swing a little too much.

Jean-Michel's composure dissipated slightly, his hands gripping his knees. "A trainer out east," he growled. "A gift from my youngest. I'm hoping your products, rough as they may be, will encourage better taste in his future purchases."

They chatted as the imperfect Tender arrived with warmed carafes of AB positive. He accepted it with a fangy smile, not hiding his amusement when she blatantly assessed him. Jean-Michel rolled his eyes as the woman retreated with a final look over her shoulder. "You are free to have her during your stay," the ancient offered, lifting his glass. "Perhaps you would rethink your retirement from the training path if you experienced what others are attempting to peddle."

Sipping at the cooling blood, he shook his head. "Should I ever decide to return to the business, the subpar trainers will only boost my sales and my prices. A few decades of their wares should pave the way for a Rhys-trained resurgence." He set his glass down and glanced into the hall. "Speaking of trainees, where is my pride and joy?"

Jean-Michel sighed, a very human reaction momentarily throwing him. "She and her male companion have been holed up in their wing all evening. My human staff overheard Ms. Schumann yelling shortly after dawn but reported the disagreement as ending shortly after. I have selected not to step into their business this evening."

He laughed. "Selected not to? This is Bianca Schumann. The choice was never yours. She's been made aware of the plans to relocate her and is adapting to the idea. According to her companion."

"Strange fellow," Jean-Michel mused. "Everything is prepared to go in three nights' time. She will be escorted across an underground border port and transported by my allies into the Canadian prairies to a home on the outskirts of the city of Regina. Chogun is expecting her in five nights and has assured me she will be observed without interference."

He stood slowly. "Then I believe it is time for me to make my way into the den of the beast," he announced. "Care to join me?"

"I'm a fool for that woman," Jean-Michel stated. "But I am not stupid. I will pray for your safe return."

Snarling for emphasis, he followed the hall into the descending stairwell. Bianca's voice drifted up the steps, her one-sided conversation light and pleasant.

"Honey, I'm home," Rhys called in warning, knowing Boy would already be alerted to his arrival.

A door opened, and Bee launched herself at him, wrapping her arms tight around his neck and burying her head into his shoulder. "I'll beat on you later," she said, her voice muffled in his shirt. "It's just so nice to see you again."

Boy emerged from the room, standing in the doorway, watching Bianca cling to him before he slipped past them and went topside. "Where's he going?" she mumbled into his shirt.

"I'd bet on a quick perusal of the grounds," he replied, attempting to extricate himself from the tiny woman's grip and finally conceding defeat when her arms tightened. "The next two weeks will be long, sweetheart. Are you up for it?"

The blonde head nodded against him, her small hands tightening around his waist. "I should let Jean-Michel know his post office box will be full tomorrow. I did a little online preparation today."

She finally released him, pulling him into her room and bringing up a few images on the desktop computer. "I'm willing to have any of these colors and styles replicated. No black. No red. No purple undertones. They're horrendous with my skin tone."

He looked over the cuts and colors on the screen. "Pity to cover that crown of yours," he stated, his fingers flying over the keys. "This one."

She would be stunning in that color, he thought to himself. A rich coffee hue interwoven thickly through her honey blonde would be enough change without completely eliminating her unique shade.

Gently nudging her aside, he pulled up another image, an actress with a layered cut skimming her shoulders. Bee's fingers grazed her long locks thoughtfully.

"I've never gone so short," she murmured. "Who will do it?"

"I brought two Tenders who are good. Not as skilled as some, but competent. You can summon them in the morning to collect the supplies, as well as some contouring makeup. We need something fairly drastic. Thin your lips, lower your cheekbones, pull emphasis off your eyes. Nichol sent me with a few choices of colored contacts, so once your hair is done, we can match up a suitable hue. Perhaps a dark brown."

She was relatively silent, nodding absently as he reviewed the changes to her appearance required before they could create new photo identification and courier it from the Kaius haunt.

"Bee?" he probed quietly. "I need to hear you want this," he said softly, turning her to look at him. "I want to hear you say it. I can put a stop to this tonight, but after tomorrow, it will be significantly more difficult. Databases will be altered, your alias will appear on government sites, and Johan's assets will be transferred through a series of untraceable accounts until they settle in your new name.

"Your Schumann accounts will remain open, untouched to avoid suspicion. Your location will be known by only myself, Jean-Michel, Mikhail, Boy, and the local haunt leader, Chogun. Protection decrees have been made in your birth name, ready for invocation if needed."

She continued to stare at the brunette on the computer screen.

"You have three, maybe four fertile years left. It's now or never, and I need a definitive yes or a no, angel."

Chapter Twenty-four

Mickey adjusted his position, filling the doorway completely to block Rhys's view.

"You're a selfish bastard," Rhys grumbled behind him, giving a swift kick to the back of his leg before resigning himself to standing against the wall. He chuckled, his eyes locked on the view before him.

Two months into training, and the nightly sparring sessions between Audra and Molly had become a sport unto itself. Both women had proven themselves competent with firearms, their aim faltering only when given weapons too heavy for their frames.

Molly had become particularly adept with a gun, her ability to cock, aim, and shoot coming as a surprise to herself and her trainer. Bets had begun circulating on how accurate she could be against moving targets, and Nichol was currently in the process of rigging a contraption emulating the unpredictable movements of an attacker.

Despite his own initial reservations, observing Audra's skill in hand-to-hand combat had provided an unexpected mixture of reassurance and lewd thoughts.

Lewder thoughts.

More frequent lewder thoughts.

Tonight found Audra's hair slicked back, her shirt damp with sweat and clinging to her curves as she brought Molly to her knees. Dominic sat cross-legged in the opposite corner of the room, grinning as Molly released a string of curses and fruitlessly attempted to extricate herself from Audra's hold. Jagger finally sauntered over, signaling to Audra to release her opponent, and the women retreated quickly to their water bottles.

"Ask Jagg when we can start rotating into the ring," Rhys called over to him. "I want a go at Molly for making us watch that movie last week."

"No way am I interrupting training," he replied, keeping his voice low. "Nichol has another three days of banishment until he can observe again."

By the fifth week, Nichol had become obsessed with the training regimen Jagger had instituted. He had begun measuring knee angles when the women jumped, carrying tiny flashlights for continual concussion checks, and printing off articles on freak training accidents for the women to read prior to each sessions.

Jagger placed a four-week suspension on Nichol.

Kaius concurred.

He returned his attention to Audra, grinning when she pulled a mirror from her bag and checked her smudged makeup. Her arm reached back, flipping him off while she put the mirror away and joined Molly in the sparring ring to listen to Jagger's notes on the match.

Jagg had thrown himself fully into equipping Molly and Audra with the skills necessary to hold, maybe even gain, a fighting chance against both human and vampire attackers. Never one to use guns in the past, Jagger learned alongside the women and had become proficient and knowledgeable about every weapon he brought into the room or toted into the forest for target practice. He had even begun incorporating the women's firearms training into the vamp sessions, barking insults and instructions as he stood behind them in the woods, critiquing their stances.

Louis, as it turned out, was the only capable shot amongst the vampires. Bets were being laid as to whether Molly or Louis was better. Mick had placed his money on Molly.

Jagger dismissed the women, motioning for the guys to enter and begin their own nightly training. He kissed Audra's sweaty forehead as she passed him, ignoring her grumbles about how gross she felt and how desperately she needed to shower. Jagg strode past his pupils, his eyes focused on the door to his weapons room. Kaius and Boy entered the room, Louis and Nichol hot on their heels.

"Tonight's training is going to be a little different," Jagger announced, reentering the room with Rhys at his side. Rhys's expression was locked down, his formerly relaxed expression taut and a cooler tucked under his arm. "Shirts off. Pair up."

Nichol squared up against Dom and Rhys as he and Louis lined up alongside them. Kaius and Boy took their places, all eyes on Jagger.

"Nichol, Louis, Kaius, you three will be armed first. Hand-to-hand, fangs are fair game, only rule is no outside weapons," Jagger began instructing. "The purpose of tonight's training is to maintain focus in the face of pain and to use that focus to disarm your opponent. Bagged blood from the stocks is in the corner of the room for use as you require."

Thy exchanged looks. While surface injuries were common in practice, those severe enough to require a feeding were a rarity.

Jagger reached into a bag and pulled out three flashlights, and a quick shiver ran through his body. Jagg aimed one light at the door, passing his hand across the beam and allowing his hauntmates to recognize the effects.

"UV flashlights are becoming a known weapon against us," he said calmly. "Detective Whitman has been touting these on every news site interviewing him since my time in the Vansburg jail. He claims they're the 'common man's defense' against vampires and is recommending every household contain one per member. Tonight, your job is to disarm, neutralize, and subdue your attacker."

Jagger continued to move his hand through the light, pausing to hold the beam steady on his smoking palm with every pass. "If humans are using these against us, it's in the realm of possibility vampires will utilize them as well. The goal is to gain control of the light and turn it on your opponent. Questions?"

Rhys scoffed, refusing to look toward Jagger. The rest remained silent, turning their gazes downward in mental preparation.

Jagg passed the first three attackers their lights. "On," he barked. The lights flickered on, beams held to the ground. "Go."

The slash of pain across his chest froze Mickey's response momentarily, halting his normally intuitive responses. His skin began to heal, tingling uncomfortably as it did so. A second slash along his thighs. Another over his jaw.

The intensity of the pain mingled with the recurrent healing of the burns as the UV light passed over both unmarred and burnt flesh. Despite his attempts to focus on Louis's movements, the unpredictable streaks of light were continually punctuated by stray beams from his other hauntmates. Even as he positioned himself atop his partner, the rays of the rocking flashlight out of his reach burned him in a painfully predictable motion.

"Stand down," Jagger called into the fray, picking up Louis's flashlight and turning it off.

He rose up, offering his friend a hand and noting the bands of burnt skin peppering Louis's lithe frame. Glancing around, he noticed each hauntmate, Jagger included, was covered in red and black wounds crisscrossing their bodies.

Passing the cooler of blood to his hauntmates, Jagger took a seat on the floor and watched wordlessly as they regained their equilibrium. Nichol spoke quietly with Dominic and Rhys, explaining the holes in their attacks and suggesting alternate methods. Boy and Kaius sat side by side in silence, eyes staring blankly at the far wall.

Louis's gaze was affixed on Jagger, his attention wholly focused on Jagg's ice eyes.

"That would have been helpful eight minutes ago," Jagg stated, the strength in his voice drawing attention as his ice-blue eyes turned to Louis. "Prior to Mikhail gaining traction, your hypnosis may have bought you enough time to flatten your opponent and ensure the light remained under your control. Now, it's merely an annoying pulse at the back of my head."

Louis smirked, took a sip of cold blood, and turned his ire toward the bland meal.

Jagger rose, motioning for the others to stay seated. "Kaius. Boy. You both adapted your attacks to the weapon at hand and remained cognizant of your surroundings. Moving your sparring location in response to the others' beams limited the injuries inflicted by them and allowed for increased attention to your opponent." Kai nodded his acceptance of the appraisal.

"Dominic, you froze in Nichol's ray. Rhys's interference in the beam is the only reason you don't have a hole burnt straight through your torso. Next time, use your sedation pheromone right from the start and reduce your attacker's ferocity." Dom glanced down at the charred circle on his chest, flinching as he poked at it.

"Nichol," Jagger continued, the red slashes across his face lightening as he drank. "You focused on the weakest link before disabling the strongest. Had you affixed the beam on Rhys, you would have depleted the stronger opponent and taken both down with less injury to yourself. Mick, you had the chance to drain Louis of his aggression and didn't. Why?"

He leaned back on his arms. "I was too focused on avoiding the light."

Squatting, Jagg pulled his hood a little lower over his brow. "None of you used your strengths to disarm the others. Or your skills. Not a single one thought to disarm the weakest opponents or join forces against the attackers. The only rule I provided was no outside weapons. I said nothing about uniting against a common enemy.

"Every one of you approached this with a singular mindset, and you have the injuries to prove it. Tonight your assignment is to reflect on your greatest weakness, a shortcoming each member of this haunt has in droves." Jagger rose to his feet and began placing the flashlights back into the duffle bag.

The hauntmates rose, their gazes averted from each other as they collectively pulled their shirts back over their heads.

"Do tell, oh Learned One," Rhys's voice broke the silence with a harsh staccato. "What exactly is this weakness?"

"Avoidance. It was the instinctive reaction for every one of you."

"Ah," Rhys sneered as he moved toward the door, his face angled toward Jagger. "From the lips of the king."

****

"You could come along," Audra offered, her fingers caressing the barrel of the semiautomatic pistol hanging on his bulletin board. "Maybe take a break. Get some fresh air. Change of scenery. New Mexico is really beautiful during the summer."

Jagger chuckled and finished securing the clasp of the small knife pouch for Audra. "The convoy is already fully stocked, and I'm not exactly on anyone's buddy list after last night," he grimaced.

She accepted the pouch, slipping it into her back pocket. "Then thank you, and I'll see you when we return."

He waited a few moments until Audra's shadow was no longer visible in the hall before he slumped into his chair. For precisely ten seconds, he indulged in the security of Bianca's life force buzzing quietly in his body, its strength no longer waxing and waning since the distance between them had increased. Sealing her back in her place, he resumed leafing through firearm magazines as he awaited the others.

Dominic finally appeared in the doorway, his hands shoved deep into his pockets.

"Got your stash here," he muttered, reaching back to collect the knives and ammunition the group would require on their mission.

Dominic shifted his weight, his lips taut and brows furrowed.

"Problem?" he inquired, stacking the shell boxes on his desk.

When Dom remained quiet, he fixed his glare on his youngest brother.

"You know," Dominic finally said, the tightness in his face making his mouth hard to read, "I really can't stand the smell of honeysuckle. Too sweet. It's never subtle, either. It just kind of bowls you over and makes you notice it."

He leaned back in his chair, cocking a brow. "I'm not sure I could identify the scent myself," he said slowly, uncertain what Dom was meandering toward.

Crouching onto his haunches, Dominic relaxed a fraction. "I'm pretty familiar with it. My mom used to grow it along the back of her garden. On a trellis. Anyways, it can be really intense. But that's not always a bad thing."

He crossed his arms. "Okay."

"See, the thing is, Molly smells like that to me. Like honeysuckle. Maybe she doesn't to anyone else, but everything she touches has that scent. And even though I don't particularly like it, I crave it. Need it. Does that make sense?"

Lowering his hood, he hunched over his knees. "Not at all. What do you want?"

Dominic's turquoise eyes blinked a few times, a

stark reminder of his youth. "I was talking to Mickey last night about Audra, and it kind of came to me. I have no choice in this connection with Molly. None. But she does. So does Audra. So we can't keep behaving like Neanderthals. I mean, Molly and Audra aren't Tenders."

"Obviously," he interjected, amused by Dom's ramblings.

"This applies to you, too," Dominic continued. "We're all pretty used to women just doing what we want, agreeing with us, letting us take the lead. And we've always been able to get rid of any of the women who didn't follow it. Kind of like walking away but making them do the walking. Make sense?"

"No."

Dom pursed his lips. "Fine. You've been an absolute prick since you left Bianca in Lincoln. If you've fallen for her, which everyone thinks you have, you need to stop moping around here and let her know. Whatever martyr shit you think you have going on isn't working. It didn't work last time, and it sure as hell isn't working this time. Rhys says…"

Jagger's fingers had tightened around Dom's throat before his head caught up with his actions. "Rhys," he hissed, "has no say in anything I choose to do or not do. Take your supplies and walk out that door before I get angry. Safe travels."

As his hand released Dominic's throat, the younger vampire steadied his footing, collecting the boxes into his arms and shooting glares toward him. He stormed toward the door, hesitated, booted it closed, and turned back.

"What the fuck is your problem?" Dominic

snarled, holding his ground when Jagger stalked to him. "I'm maneuvering through this connection shit blind. It would be a whole lot easier if I had one of you old fuckers to ask, but no. No one's allowed to breathe a fucking word of it around you. And whenever one of us screws up and does, you lose your shit or go all sullen and moody like some punk ass little bitch."

Ignoring the growled warning coming from him, Dominic stepped into his space, finger pressed to his chest. "Know who I have to ask? Louis. The bastard has never been connected, but he's the only one around here who doesn't get all weird whenever the word is mentioned. Did you know linking with Molly would intensify everything? I figured it out the hard way.

"What about the constant urge to kill every one of you jackasses in her vicinity? How long is that going to last? And did you know it fucking hurts, like, physical pain when I get further than downtown Denver? That separation is fucking painful? Because I thought I was dying the first time. This is all shit you should have been telling me. Instead, I'm tiptoeing around your moody ass and pretending everything is fucking fine when a little advice would be abso-fucking-lutely appreciated."

Dom turned, steadying his packages as he opened the door and strode through the doorway.

"Three years," he said quietly. "By the end of third year, the rabid desire to kill stabilizes. The separation pain…if you can push past it and make it about a thousand miles away, it becomes little more than a throbbing ache in your rib cage."

Dominic refused to face him again, holding his position and keeping his shoulders tensed in anger. He sat back in his chair, rocking it slowly from side to side. "I'm no help with the linking. We had a weak one, but…we never solidified it. Seline was…it was a long time ago." He huffed, stretching his arms behind his head.

"She knew what I was. Obviously. But she merely dealt with it. Molly is different. She understands what you are, who you are, and she embraces it. The same thing goes for Audra. She and Mick may not be connected, but there's an accceptance there most of us pre-outing didn't have. It's a different time, now."

He waited for his neglected younger brother to respond. Dominic had a right to be furious, he realized. As the only hauntmate with experience in connection, he had provided little guidance outside of clinical advice. Dom finally relented, turning to speak.

"Different time. Same result?" Dominic asked, his bangs obscuring his eyes.

Chapter Twenty-five

Jagger remained in the shadows of the darkened hallway, silently observing the interactions between his hauntmate and the haunt's final Tender. Her fingers flitted over the piano keys, jaw set in concentration as her blue eyes traveled along the sheet music. Rhys prowled around the woman, adjusting her posture while murmuring unreadable commentary. He suddenly dropped to one knee, carefully tilting Simone's knees together and grinning up at her when she became distracted.

She stood, allowing Rhys to sit in her place and demonstrate her positioning and proximity to the keys, flopping his knees open and gesturing toward his crotch as Simone laughed and nodded. She resumed her place, restarting the piece with her knees tilted together while Rhys stood behind her, a look of satisfaction on his face.

For over an hour, he had watched from the corner undetected. The emptiness of the haunt was acutely noticed upon rising, the absence of the growing Bloodslave Release Program contingent leaving a large vacancy in the life of the hallways. With Kaius and Nichol grumbling in the communications room and Boy in the bloodslave quarters, he sought out his closest hauntmate.

And proceeded to lurk like a creep.

Rhys leaned over Simone, his tattooed arm

reaching for the sheet music and hesitating until she gave a quick nod, curls bouncing. He turned the page, the steady vibration traveling through the floor indicating Simone didn't miss a beat in her performance. Straightening up, Rhys extended one hand in Jagger's concealed direction.

And flipped him off.

Cover blown, he emerged from the hall and moved silently to the large sofa. Neither Rhys nor Simone acknowledged his presence again until the woman lifted her hands from the keys and placed them in her lap. With a quick tousle of her hair, Rhys dismissed Simone and took his place on the high-backed leather chair facing Jagg.

"Does she play well?" he asked softly. "Her tempo is very steady."

Rhys nodded thoughtfully. "Classical and Baroque, yes. Anything Romantic gives her some trouble. As does jazz. The swing beat trips her up every time."

He pulled his hood down off his head. "I missed the entire Romantic Era," he mused. "But I can remember what I heard prior. Baroque was always too rigid for my liking."

Rhys sat back in his chair, crossing his arms. "You would have enjoyed swing music in the thirties." He grinned. "Shorter skirts than the twenties. Lots of thigh flashing. It was a good decade. Scandalous without the trashiness." When he grunted in response, Rhys's face locked down. "Too bad you weren't around. Why are you here?"

Running a hand through his hair, he sat up and faced his older brother. "Tell me how she is."

"No."

He felt his brows raise slightly in surprise before he schooled his expression. "I know she's alive. I just need to know she's in a good place."

Rhys's jaw tensed. "You want to know, ask her."

"I don't have her info."

"Good luck getting it," Rhys stated tersely.

"You're such a dick," he growled, standing up. "Yes or no. Is Bianca happy?"

"Why would you even ask?" Rhys snarked, no longer meeting his eyes. "If I say yes, you'll hide out with your knives and guns in the weapons room, torturing yourself with images of who or what has made her happy. For at least two decades.

"If I say no, you'll piss around here, debating and ignoring your options for a few years until you finally make the decision to seek her out, only to discover she's evolved so far past you, you'll never catch up. You want to know, you find her, and you ask her. Her file is sealed and frankly, brother, you are not on the Need-To-Know list."

****

Rhys joined Kaius at the edge of their grounds, watching the barren road.

"Tonight?"

Kai nodded, his eyes fixated on the moonless sky.

"How is Mick holding up with the proximity?" he probed, attempting to subtly search for clues as to the state of his prodigal brother.

"I've tightened my link to Jagger since the discomfort began. It has eased significantly these past weeks," Kai replied distractedly.

He scanned the dark horizon. "What can we expect when he returns?"

His question was greeted with silence from the haunt leader, a clear message Kai would neither answer, nor speculate.

It was deep into the night when a figure appeared on the deserted road. His feet moved forward instinctively, carrying him toward the hulking, hunched vampire trudging across the muddied ground. Kai remained stoic at the gates, his hands pushed deep into his coat pockets. As he drew nearer, Jagger's head lifted, the hood keeping his eyes obscured in the darkness.

"Rhys," he greeted in acknowledgment, passing his threadbare satchel to his hauntmate's extended hand.

Rhys threw the sack over his shoulder, slowing his pace to remain alongside his brother. They approached Kaius, stopping at the gate for the eldest vampire's perusal of his wayward child.

"Your room is waiting," Kai said quietly, stepping aside to allow Jagger passage through the grounds. Kaius paused Rhys's advance, shaking his head, and motioning for him to hold back as Jagg walked slowly up the veranda steps.

"Rhys?" Jagger called out, shoulders slumped. "You were right. You were right and I..." His head dropped momentarily, and he disappeared into the house.

Rhys remained on the leather chair long after Jagger departed the training rooms, alternating between rereading Bianca's unanswered text messages and playing solitaire. Bee had settled easily into her new home, her vampire security obeying the strict orders to remain on the fringes of her life. She often reached out to him, her long texts detailing the mundane events of her new human existence. Her gardens were coming along nicely. Mail delivery was sporadic. She despised her new name, as it didn't "roll off the tongue."

She had inquired after Jagger frequently during her first month, peppering the question in among a litany of lighthearted commentary. But after weeks of receiving no response from Rhys, the phone had gone silent.

It was better this way. For everyone.

It had to be.

And he had to keep reminding himself of that.

He lolled his head back, closed his eyes, and rubbed circles on one of his most recent tattoos. Years later, the burning sensation was becoming stronger, a long-lasting discomfort in the sites where new mercury intersected with old. "He isn't ready to pursue another relationship," he said quietly to his approaching creator.

Kai crossed the room and sat on the sofa. "The decision is not yours to make," he replied.

"Bianca has earned a vampire-free life," he grumbled back. "One where she is kept awake at night by squalling infants and an amorous husband, not by posturing vamps and vengeful mobs."

Kaius's chuckle echoed in the lifeless haunt. "My personal preference is the latter, but I understand your point. Is she still reaching out to you?"

Shaking his head, he waved his phone in Kai's direction. "Radio silence on my end. Nichol continues to receive weekly updates from Chogun. The gag order on all involved in Bee's placement should keep her out of everyone's sights. Including Jagger's."

Kai hummed in acknowledgment. "Perhaps it's best for all involved."

He opened one eye and caught sight of the piano. "Sometimes, I think it is. Other times, I'm not so sure."

Chapter Twenty-six

Nichol's nimble fingers danced across the back of the computer tower, expertly removing the wires from his personal unit and attaching them to the dusty one sitting askance on his desk. Jagger waited patiently, smirking as Nichol muttered profanities and disbelief at the unkempt state of the computer. A small rag was produced alongside a spray, and the auburn-haired vampire gave in to his compulsion to wash the specks of dried blood from the unit.

"The power button sticks," Nic mumbled, lowering himself to the floor to get a better view. "Green means it's functioning. Orange is not good. Neither is no light. Watch the monitor and let me know when the log-in page opens."

He adjusted his angle to face the screen, noting the time lag between this unit and Nichol's personal computer. "Is that it?" he asked, looking back at his eldest brother.

Nichol stood, leaning over him, and tapping the keys rapidly. The computer whirred to life, the first screen replaced by a second. "We're going in the back way," Nichol explained. "No risk of a dead man noticing, so the new password is 'iamnicholsbitch.' All lowercase. No apostrophe." A few moments later, the monitor filled with a mess of folders and icons.

"I need to feed," Nichol stated before lifting a small duffle bag onto the com room conference table. In it, he placed two burner phones, a wad of cash, and a set of keys. "Monitor the station until I return at dawn. I'll inform Kaius you're working on a project for me and are not to be disturbed."

He nodded and watched his brother stroll from the room, leaving him to his own devices.

His devices, and those of Clayton Jorgensson.

After a few minutes of fumbling, he located the file he was most interested in and, after another few moments of confusion, successfully printed the information. He tucked the papers into Nichol's bag, lifting his own sack from behind the door and tossing the bags onto his shoulder.

Dropping his phone onto the table, he moved silently through the halls to the topside garage and climbed into a four-by-four. Keeping his emotions muted to avoid detection by Kaius, he carefully detached the vehicle's GPS system wires and tucked them snugly into the glove box. Then, timing the start of the engine with the rise of the garage door, he pulled out onto the highway and began a winding trek to Lincoln.

****

Nichol's arms remained crossed, his fangs digging deep into his lower lip as he waited out Rhys's rant. Jagger's absence had gone unnoticed until dawn broke, providing him enough of a head start to avoid interference from both his creator and his hauntmate.

"Just pull up the fucking tracker and show me where the fuck he is," Rhys snarled, his hand moving the computer mouse across the desk. "This isn't even your fucking computer, is it?"

He maintained his silence as Rhys began

haphazardly removing cables from Clayton Jorgensson's filthy tower and attaching them to Nichol's pristine unit.

"Nichol," Kai said, warning in his voice.

Refusing to look Kai's way, he continued his mute observations of Rhys as the raging vamp snapped the delicate plastic Ethernet cable, rendering it useless. "Fuck." Rhys turned to Kai, his eyes narrowed. "I'd place my bets on a northern road. I'll call Jean-Michel and ask him to keep an eye out. Notify Chogun, as well. Jagg'll turn up in Bianca's territory. He knows she's in Canada."

"He doesn't know her precise whereabouts," he finally stated as Rhys pulled out his phone. "Canada is a large country, and the Tender pardon continues to be in full effect. As does the gag order."

"Then where the fuck is he heading?" Rhys barked.

Silence.

Tossing the broken cable to the floor, Rhys stormed from the com room, scratching at his arm.

Kaius sat back in Nichol's preferred chair. "He's worried for Jagger's safety," he stated. "Rhys carries much guilt over the events in Berlin."

Taking a seat across from the haunt leader, he leaned forward and clasped his hands. "As do the rest of us," he replied. "We were all culpable in molding his decisions regarding his connected female."

"Yet you are interfering once again."

He sat back, stretching his arms behind his head. "I was merely beginning to gather intelligence from the computer Jagger brought back from his time in Lincoln. Any information he gained without my permission during his unaccompanied time in this room lies outside my control."

Kaius cocked a brow. "A few nights ago, I overheard Audra provide Mikhail with a warning of his behavior I believe is suitable now. You are treading on thin ice, mister." He rose and strode from the room, leaving Nichol alone.

Taking the vacated seat, he leaned back and closed his eyes. Jagger would gain a substantial lead come dusk, his movements untraceable. He pulled his phone out, rereading Chogun's message from the previous evening.

—*Woman is AWOL. Examination of house indicates premeditation. Advise.* —

He had kept the intel to himself, alerting neither Jagger nor Rhys. After all, he was complicit in her disappearance.

The calls had begun sporadically, his phone buzzing to life in the early morning hours as he settled into his bunker to rest. Initially, Bianca had maintained a formal distance, her conversation limited to updates regarding her home, the shopping selection in the nearby city, and her forays into human interaction.

She had participated in something she called "paint nights."

She had spent many hours drinking burnt coffee with neighborhood women at a local cafe.

She had met a "nice young man" and had spent several evenings with him.

He had responded to her contact accordingly, grunting in acknowledgment at her narratives and huffing at her frustrations. The calls became more frequent as the weeks passed, her voice becoming tinged with ennui as she rambled on about the repetitiveness of her new lifestyle. Blaming Audra for his slight softening toward the Former Tender, he answered his phone every morning and sat in relative silence while Bianca nattered on until she was appeased.

The tone of the calls had changed the previous week.

Two mornings of silence had come and gone. As dawn broke on the third day, he stared at his phone, debating whether he should reach out to Chogun for an early report on Bianca's whereabouts or wait out the week. During their last conversation, she had mentioned her plans to spend another evening with the human man who was sniffing around her home.

Nichol, knowing nothing about the guy, felt Bianca was above him.

His phone finally came to life, the screen lighting up and buzzing in his hand. "What."

He could hear Bee breathing on the other end, hear the shuffling of her blanket as she settled herself into her bed.

"Bianca. Speak."

A mirthless chuckle rang through the phone. "Ah, Nichol. My charming, genteel Kaius vampire." She sighed. "How are you, honey?"

Ignoring the jab at his phone manners, he sat back. "You altered your contact regime," he stated, annoyed.

"Awwwww," Bianca crooned, "you were worried about me, weren't you? Such a doll. No need to fear, Nicky. I was in the very mundane hands of my suitor."

He frowned. "The human male."

"Of course, the human male," Bee snapped back. "Aside from you, every vampire I know has refused

contact. Jean-Michel. William Conall. Even Rhys. I am, after all, dismissed from service."

"You're displeased."

"I'm bored, Nichol. Bored, eating myself into a coma, and jittery from excessive caffeine."

The anger in her voice was new, a bitter irritation he had not yet heard from Bianca. *"Perhaps you need to expand your experiences."*

His suggestion was met with a long pause. *"This is harder than I thought it would be,"* she finally replied. *"I'm lonely."*

"You've maintained an active schedule," he pointed out. *"Every time we've spoken, you've mentioned repeated interactions with your community."* He winced slightly at the realization he was sounding frighteningly like Audra.

"I have nothing in common with these people," Bianca said softly. *"I have almost a century of memories and experiences, and I can't share any of them. When they talk about their time in university, I'm thinking of my training years. When they discuss their mothers, I'm reminded mine passed away thirty years ago. They gossip about their friends, and my mind travels to you brutish beasts and Jean-Michel."*

"You could spend more time with your male companion," he suggested, the realization of Bianca's unique situation slowly unfolding before him.

She laughed humorlessly. *"How, precisely, do I address over six decades of pledging with a man who brags about a two-year commitment to an old girlfriend?"* She sighed, blankets rustling against the phone. *"Let's discuss something less upsetting. How is everyone?"*

"Fine."

Bianca huffed into the phone. "How is Boy?"

He hesitated at the query. Aside from Audra, no one considered Boy. "I believe he's fine."

"And Rhys?"

"Fine."

A pause. "Jagger?"

Taking a moment to formulate his thoughts, he shifted in his bed. "He is keeping himself heavily distracted with his Deepfryer and training regimens."

Bianca hummed in reply. "So he's fine."

"I did not say that."

The phone calls resumed like clockwork afterward, Bianca returning to her lighthearted banter and Nichol doing little more than listening as her tone drew more assured. Thinking back, there was no defining statement, no moment of clarity when he realized she would run. It came in hints. A wistful memory of her time with Johan. A playful mocking of his "phone voice." A pensive sigh when all the Kaius hauntmates were "fine," but Jagger was "busy." When he last spoke to her two mornings earlier, the sounds of an engine hummed in the background, her voice made tinny by the vehicle's Bluetooth technology.

"Where are you," he demanded, no question in his voice.

She laughed, her voice lighter than he had heard it in weeks. "I have a few errands to wrap up, and time's wasting."

Chapter Twenty-seven

Jagger sat on the bottom stair of the tornado shelter, watching the last of the sun's rays disappear through the cracked boards of the hatch. With summer's decreased moonlight hours, he was under a tight timeline to get to Lincoln before dawn broke.

And he needed gas.

As the final beam disappeared into the horizon, he bolted into the car and tore onto the interstate. Falling into a comfortable gap in the heavy traffic, he set the cruise control on and began preparing for his fueling, reaching into his backpack and pulling out the small lens case, making use of the rearview mirror to place the contacts in his eyes. He blinked repeatedly, the roundness of the lenses at odds with the slightly oblong shape of his cornea. Grabbing the metal snips, he angled the mirror toward his mouth and squared his fangs.

Unevenly.

He spit the removed enamel onto the floor and leaned into the mirror to assess his asymmetrical fangs. His tongue ran across the jagged edges. It would have to do. Attempting to even out the damage would only make things worse. Experience had taught him that lesson repeatedly.

The detour through Cheyenne was a pathetic attempt to throw off his brethren should they decide to pursue him, but he didn't have time to waste. He needed to be in Lincoln yesterday, and the vehicle was traveling at a mediocre 80 mph.

By the time he made it to an open gas station, his fuel light was on long enough to whiten his knuckles on the steering wheel. He pulled up alongside a pump, checked his reflection, and headed inside the busy store to lay out a wad of cash for gas. He tightened his hood over his brow as he entered the store, a reflexive reaction to close proximity to humans. Largely ignored by the patrons, he muttered his pump number to the clerk and tossed a handful of bills onto the counter.

The gas tank filled slowly, the pumps overloaded by the constant stream of vehicles pulling in for fuel. He kept his back to the vehicle, carefully scanning his surroundings and noting potential hazards.

The children emerging from a blue sedan were short enough to see up into his loose hood.

A truckload of young men was pulling up to the adjacent pump, bass thumping.

The woman in the ill-fitting bra was eying his car and sizing him up.

The woman's companion was noticing.

Bingo.

He adjusted his hood, pulling it tighter around his incriminating tattoos. Keeping his head down, he felt for the change in the fuel pump's pressure as a pair of unlaced work boots appeared in his peripheral, dirt encrusted into the seams. He released the handle, replacing the nozzle carefully and ignoring his unwanted visitor until a hand flicked across his bicep. Turning away, keys in hand as he opened the door, he allowed his body to mimic human stumbling when the hand pushed against his back.

Experience had taught him fighting back in these situations usually escalated the event to bloodier proportions than rolling with it would.

Rhys had never learned that lesson.

"I said, eyes off my fucking girlfriend," the man snarled, spittle building in the corners of his mouth. The stench of stale beer wafted from his breath.

He righted himself slowly, the commotion drawing the attention of the guys in the pickup. "Sorry, man," he muttered, anxious to end the issue and get back on the road. "I'm just leaving."

The boyfriend held his position, blocking him from entering the vehicle. "Better fucking be, bloodsucker," he hissed.

Bloodsucker.

The name drew the attention of the other men at the pumps, some of them advancing on him while others merely watched. He blinked his eyes a few times, cursing himself for not noticing his contacts had shifted and revealed his irises. Cover blown, he stood to his full height and lifted his head to ensure he eliminated as many blind spots as he could. "Move back," he growled at the man. "Back up, and I'm out of here."

Foul-smelling spit hit his boot, but the boyfriend stepped back. "Fucking animal," the man spat. "Can't wait until you all fry."

He climbed into the car and started the engine, refusing to lock the doors in defense. As he pulled away from the staring masses, the boyfriend booted the side of the vehicle in a final posturing act.

Life was easier before humans were introduced to the reality of vampires. Living in the shadows had its drawbacks, but becoming a recognized and despised minority was infinitely more troublesome. He longed for the time when human minds categorized his eyes as a defect of birth and not an indication of species. Moving among humans was less difficult when they were ignorant to the obvious physical traits inherent in every vampire. When they believed the myth vampires bore no reflection in mirrors. That crosses and garlic were effective repellent.

Now, vampires were simply the new target of the revolving hatred ingrained in human society.

Shaking off the incident, he continued the trek toward Lincoln.

****

Bianca eyed the broken lock of her apartment for a moment before she retrieved a chair from the kitchen and scooted it under the knob. After two long days of driving gravel roads, sleeping in her car, and eating gas station food, she was less interested in aesthetics and more focused on getting in a shower and ordering quality take out.

Leaving her hastily packed bags and laptop at the entrance, she turned the shower on to full heat and reveled in the rising steam. She stepped under the water and closed her eyes.

Freedom.

True freedom.

It was not the Kaius haunt's official announcement of her release from her Former Tender status, nor her subsequent reintroduction to human society granting her true freedom. It was not the forced separation from the vampire political arena. Or the opportunity to date or not date whatever attractive, albeit uninteresting, man she wanted.

It was a seemingly inconsequential comment from Nichol.

Four mornings earlier, as she was bemoaning her flippant agreement to embark on an afternoon shopping session with her neighbor, Nichol had replied in his blunt way.

"Fuck their plans. It's your life."

The pair had conversed for another hour, sticking to the safe topics of legislation, the spike in fanatical religious uprisings, and superior phone brands. After she hung up, her mind refused to let go of the words circling in her head.

Fuck their plans. It's your life.

She had then spent the entire day at home, cleaning and reading as the idea cemented itself.

Fuck their plans.

She had wandered around the beautiful home Rhys had deemed worthy of her. Looked out the window for signs of the security Mikhail had facilitated for her. Practiced the name Nichol had chosen for her.

She was not naive to the amount of work her relocation had required on behalf of Jean-Michel and the Kaius haunt. She knew favors would have been called in for her benefit. Hours upon hours were spent on the logistics of her reassignment.

But that's what it had been.

A plan for reassignment provided by vampires and adhered to without question.

Fuck their plans.

Her assignment for a vampire-free existence was her final task from a vampire. In releasing her from the realm of the vampire hierarchy, Rhys had inadvertently released her from obeying.

She grinned as the shampoo ran down her back.

Rhys would likely be pissed by his oversight.

And it was no longer her job to care. She did, but she did not HAVE to.

Wrapping herself in a towel, she noted its improper hanging before removing it from the towel bar. She padded around her apartment, loading her clothes into the washing machine, and frowning at the discovery her formerly full container of detergent now contained less than half a cup's worth.

A few hours of digging into Lincoln's increasingly vocal anti-vampire movement online, she fell asleep on the sofa still retaining the slight hint of Jagger's scent.

Chapter Twenty-eight

Falling asleep in a grungy motel bathtub had its drawbacks, but the incremental time save was enough of a benefit to keep Jagger from complaining. He stripped quickly, the cold water beating down on him before his shirt hit the floor. The rally had started an hour before sunset, and he was anxious to miss as little of the march as possible. His hoodie stuck to his damp skin as he tossed his bags over his shoulder and vacated the room.

He was grateful he was given a different room from the one he and Bianca had occupied months earlier. It would have been distracting, and distraction was unwelcome.

Following the notes he had printed from Clayton Jorgensson's computer, he exited the freeway and pulled into a cement parking garage. From the roof, he would have an unencumbered view of the rally and the first three blocks of the planned march. Patting blades and tucking his newly acquired firearms into his belt, he got out of the car and scanned the area for the optimal view of the Species Purification assembly. Selecting his position, he crouched down and carefully laid the bulkiest of his weapons at his side.

Although the cement construction impeded vibrations, he maintained one hand on the floor as his impeccable eyesight scoured the growing crowd for familiar faces. Four years earlier, the meetings drew fewer than fifty of the most ardent supporters. Now, close to five hundred people populated the grass. Bright red Species Purifier ball caps obscured many faces in the poorly lit park, misspelled placards doubling as stakes blocking others. A makeshift stage rose a select few above the others, the leaders donning megaphones and anti-vampire shirts proudly.

A light rumbling reverberated through his fingers, alerting him to a potential encroacher. He maintained his position, his free hand slowly gripping the shank of a stiletto blade. When the vibrations grew more intense, he spun in place and launched himself at the intruder.

The tiny intruder with brown contacts and a black beret.

The tiny intruder looking up at him from his iron hold, unimpressed brow lifting.

The tiny intruder with a large, strangely warm backpack slung over her shoulder.

"What the hell is in there?" he demanded, releasing Bianca and relieving her of the heavy bag. His muscles remained tight, slow to recognize the lack of physical threat the glaring woman presented.

"No hello?" Bee inquired, unzipping the bag to reveal an impressive collection of food containers. "I'm hungry."

He stepped back, her unexpected appearance throwing him off his concentration. His body thrummed at her proximity, distracting him from his night's mission.

"What are you doing here?" he growled as Bee began laying out her feast alongside his weapons.

"That," she retorted, turning toward him, "is what I was going to ask you. After I ate. I'm starving."

Pacing at her back, his mind whirled as it recalculated his goals to account for the added complication of an unexpected Former Tender. A Former Tender who was supposed to be hidden safely in another country, searching for a mate, and raising a passel of children. His eyes flicked to his vehicle.

He could leave.

Hole up in the motel for another night or two and reconfigure his plans.

"If you decide to run," Bianca said, arching her head back to look up at him, "I can't promise your targets will still be alive by morning."

"I'm not running," he snarled, pride piqued. He nudged a large box of spiced meat from his spot and resumed his place along the cement wall. The duo sat in silence, Bianca watching the increasing crowd and Jagger watching her fork in his periphery as it made its repetitive journey to her lips. After a few minutes, the fork detoured and found itself in front of his own mouth. He begrudgingly tasted the offering.

"Everything in that is artificially created," he grumbled as he debated using his hoodie to remove the taste from his tongue.

"Artificially created by angels," she replied, shoving the unnaturally pink concoction into her mouth. "It's a cake roll. The strawberry ones are extremely rare." She swallowed hard and narrowed her eyes. "They're preparing to march out," she said, setting her cake rolls aside and rising to her feet.

"Sit," he ordered. "There are too many innocent targets at this point. I suspect a large number of the mothers and children will vacate the area long before the march concludes. Right now, the goal is to identify the remaining ringleaders and prepare for their return."

If Bianca's displeasure at his instructions wasn't evident enough in the crossing of her arms, it was blatantly obvious in her pursed lips and set jaw. "You have no business here."

"Nor do you. Yet here we are."

He ignored her as she angrily collapsed the pile of empty food containers and shoved them into her bag. He kept his eyes trained on the mob as it made its way onto the streets, the leaders marching ahead, their megaphones held to their mouths.

He had their faces memorized before they turned the corner.

As the last of the protestors disappeared from view, he leaned back on his hands, legs dangling over the edge of the wall. "I expect the projected loop should take two hours at their current pace." He turned to Bianca, looking solely at her lips and ignoring the gentle curve of her throat. "This is just getting bigger, isn't it?" he mused. "The momentum isn't waning at all. Bigger. Louder. More organized. That group down there was one-third the size of the entire population of North American vampires."

She nodded. "Pariahs in our own world," she agreed. "The lofty ideals of coexistence are diminishing with every passing day."

The pair sat in silence for a few minutes, eyes scanning the roads for movement. He pulled down his hood and ran a hand through his hair. "What were they chanting down there?"

Bianca angled her position. "Fight the bite. Abomination cremation. Call outs to hunt the blood whores and brides of Satan. Nothing new." Her eyes moved to his tattoos, then across to his ears. "Were you born deaf?"

"No," Jagg replied, bringing his hood back up in defense.

"Then how did it happen?"

He glared at her. "Rhys trained you better," he growled.

"Funny thing about that," she responded casually. "Rhys no longer has any say in my behavior. And neither do you. How did it happen?"

****

Bianca kept her eyes locked on Jagger as he scowled toward the barren streets. His ice eyes refused to look into hers, choosing to fixate on a stray dog scrounging for food along the darkened sidewalks.

"Your connection played a role, didn't it?" she pressed as she leaned into Jagg's sight line, emboldened by his lack of violent reaction. "Did she do it?"

The nearly imperceptible shake of his head was as momentous a victory in Kaius male disclosure as she had ever experienced. She studied her companion brazenly, noting the flexing of his jaw as he tensed, the outline of his fangs when his lips grew tight, the twitch of his shoulders as he fought to ignore her perusal.

When she had arrived at the parking garage hours earlier, she had taken up position a level lower, hiding in the shadows as she observed the increasing mob. The arrival of Jagger's vehicle had sent her into a mild panic, her first thoughts flying to Rhys and his impending reaction to her conduct. She had traipsed up the ramp to the top level slowly, a secure hold on her meal and stars in the event Rhys attempted to forcibly remove her.

The sight of Jagger's hoodie spread tight across his broad back was met with relief and irritation. The lulling lilt of his hum had calmed her instantly.

"I know you can see me." She huffed, becoming incrementally more annoyed with every passing minute Jagger stared at the mutt on the road.

"I can see you," Jagger muttered. "I'm choosing to ignore you. The silent treatment." He frowned a moment. "Starting now."

She laughed, covering her mouth quickly when the loudness of her voice echoed in the night. She moved a fraction closer to the sullen vampire and waited.

"I left my connected mate in Turkey," Jagger finally said, his voice graveled with tension. "She knew what I was. And we were…good. But eventually she wanted a life I couldn't give her. So she took matters into her own hands and found a man who could. Her belly was swelling when I left," he mumbled, no longer tracking the dog. "I don't know much about pregnancy."

"Neither do I," she interjected.

He smiled tightly. "I am well aware. Anyways, I traveled back to our haunt in Berlin. It took three months on foot. Mikhail was still pretty young at the time." A quick smiled flashed across his face. "Nichol was still trying to convince Kai to put Mickey down. Insisted Mick was a scourge on the sanctity and prestige of vampirism."

Covering her heart in feigned shock, she bit back a grin. It was an easy image to conjure up. "Did you ever see her again?" she prodded, morbid curiosity piqued. She was unable to comprehend the heartbreak he would have experienced, seeing his connected mate pregnant with another man's child.

A lesser vampire would have walked into the sun.

"I did," he replied, his hands gripping the cement wall. "My hauntmates fought my decision to return to her. Kaius kept me busy preparing for our move to the Americas. Nichol and Mickey took me hunting in the more affluent brothels inside the city. Rhys went as far as to remove my fangs during the daylight hours prior to my departure." When her eyes narrowed, Jagg shrugged. "An act of desperation, I guess."

"Rhys has had many of those, from my understanding," she replied tersely. Fang removal was considered a final option in only the direst of circumstance among vampires. It was one step above staking.

Jagger's shoulders tensed again. "His intentions were good," he argued. "His execution was sloppy. And ineffective. I managed to attach myself to a caravan outside of Budapest and made it back to Turgutlu in under two months." He paused, eyes glazing over. "Maybe if I'd walked the whole way..." Shaking the thoughts from his head, Jagg looked over at her. "What do you hear?"

She sighed and listened to the night. The faint chants were growing louder again, the mob making their way back to their final destination. "This conversation isn't over," she warned, swinging her legs back to the ground and collecting her throwing stars.

"Fuck," Jagger breathed.

Chapter Twenty-nine

"Ladies choice," Jagger stated after providing a rundown on the four targets.

"Mr. Willis is mine," Bianca gritted, rotating her wrists and shoulders. "Red cap, red shirt, beard, and glasses. Yes?"

He nodded and returned his attention to the approaching crowd. "With him taken out, you'll have successfully removed the three instigators of the Lincoln branch," he said. "I'll aim for the two men with the megaphones. First to eliminate their game gets Money Man."

He was grateful for the distraction of the hunt. The shift into predator was smooth and familiar. From his earlier position, he was able to mentally match photos from Clayton's files to the rising leaders on the stage. Jeremy Willis was a bonus, his involvement in the desecration of Bianca's home having gone unanswered until tonight.

Money Man was the only man in a suit and tie, his profile an exact match to the financial backer of Jorgensson's local Species Purifier movement. He stood on the outskirts of the protest, eyes scanning the crowd and motioning periodically as local news crews marched alongside.

He passed his keys to Bianca. "Go start the car," he instructed. "Everything but our weapons goes in. Is there anything in your vehicle we need to grab on the way out?"

"Yes," she snapped. "My car."

The swarm of humans drew closer. "Getting two cars out of the mayhem about to ensue is foolish. We'll leave yours as a dummy. It will throw the cops long enough to get us out of the state."

When her hands flew to her hips, he turned away from her and feigned distraction.

The slight tremble of the cement through his boots told him she had followed through. The piercing glare she gave him as she took up her position at his side told him she was not pleased about it.

"Got your man in sight?" he asked.

"Got him."

"Now."

Jagger's bullets embedded themselves in his first target's thigh milliseconds before Bianca's stars sliced the tendons of Jeremy Willis. By the time the initial onlookers figured out two of their leaders were hit, he had taken down his second target.

"Money Man is mine," Bee said, batting his gun to the side to throw his concentration. He took a step back and watched Bianca take aim. The fluidity and confidence of her shot was beautiful, the two tri-stars cutting through the air and lodging themselves cleanly in Money Man's spine.

"No kills. Strong message," he announced as the man's legs collapsed under him. He cocked his gun. "Shall I?"

"Leave him," Bianca instructed as she motioned toward the car.

He took one glance at the pandemonium below and crawled into the driver's seat. "Is there anything traceable in your car?" he asked as the vehicle moved slowly down the first ramp.

"There may be a few food wrappers, but everything else is back in Omaha," Bianca replied, straining her neck to see the protestors as the ramp curved. "No one is moving this way," she reported. "Head out the back and get on the freeway. We can hook up to the interstate from there."

"Yes, ma'am."

"Don't be patronizing."

****

"Just. Fucking. Leave it," Rhys snarled as he paced the floor of the common room, his eyes locked on the news report while Nichol continued to adjust the balance of the speakers.

"I can't concentrate with a disproportional bass," Nichol snarked back as he continued to hunch over the sound system.

His ears pulsed from the constant imbalance echoing in the room. "I'm going to fucking stake you."

"We won't miss anything," Nichol groused. "This exact footage will be replayed on a loop for the next four days while talking heads regurgitate the narrative over and over until I turn Jagger in myself for subjecting me to this shit."

Kaius sat stoically on the sofa, scanning the video footage for signs of his hauntmate. "This constant flashing of angles is extremely distracting. There is no way humans are able to fully take in the visual information being presented when it's displayed this way."

"They aren't meant to," Nichol muttered as he cautiously backed away from the amplifier. "The more chaotic the event appears, the more frantic viewers become, the more likely they will continue to watch the channel for updates. There. Sounds good, doesn't it?"

Rhys stilled his pacing and joined the others in a silent viewing of the broadcast.

"An active manhunt is underway for suspects of the vampire species," a pretty blonde newscaster reported solemnly. "Weaponry found on scene indicate multiple attackers were responsible for the assault on marching members of the Species Purifier movement. Preliminary reports link one of the weapons to an assault three months ago that left one man dead and a woman in hospital.

"The injured woman disappeared shortly after and is presumed to be currently held against her will. Anyone with information on tonight's attack is asked to call their local police department. Suspects are considered armed and dangerous and are not to be approached."

The picture flashed away, the speaker of the nation appearing on the screen. "The attack in Lincoln was an organized, unprovoked attack on American citizens, led by and supported by the vampire community. Our administration will be addressing the threat in the upcoming weeks. This attack will not go unanswered."

Flopping onto the sofa beside Kai, he ran a hand through his hair. "Nichol," he growled quietly. "If you have any knowledge of how to get in touch with Jagg, now would be the time to share it."

Nichol cocked his head, his ears listening for any disturbance in the balance of his speakers. "Kai," he called, ignoring Rhys entirely, "should I send out a warning through the network to avoid traveling in noticeable groups for the foreseeable future?"

Kaius nodded. "Touch base with Mickey and the others as well. Hospitable territory or not, there will be hunters in New Mexico looking to capitalize on this event." He paused. "There is no evidence this attack was led or supported by us."

"Facts don't win votes. Altered truths do," Nichol stated grimly as he exited the room.

He resumed pacing, scratching his arm. "Bianca's with him," he stated with finality. "I fucking know she is. She has to be. Chogun isn't answering my texts. Neither is Bee."

"If they are working together," Kai began slowly, "we can assume she participated in tonight's ambush. A human woman traveling with a vampire will not garner the same attention as a lone male would."

He nodded, his rising temper waning slightly as resignation set in. "You realize this is the night the species war begins, right? This is already being spun by both the media and the government. They will answer, and it'll be war."

Kai smiled humorlessly. "The war began the night we were outed. This is merely the first time the Kaius haunt has fired back."

Kaius left the common room, phone in hand and a frown on his face. Rhys flipped absently through the news networks, flashing through the same video footage of the carnage in Lincoln.

Once uncovered, their haunt's responsibility in the attack would signal to others the time to retaliate had begun, that North American vampires were no longer going to remain complacent in the movements mobilizing against them. No longer going to jump through hoops for acceptance in a society deeming them lower than animals. No longer going to wait for the voices of reason to prevail over the simpleminded rhetoric of the bigoted.

He fired off a text to Simone, too comfortable to get up and search for her himself. As the final Tender in the haunt, Simone was his final tie to the very comfortable, relatively secure decades he had spent in America. When her sale went through, it would signal the true return to battle for him.

The golden-brown curls bounced through the door, their rainbow-hued highlights dancing as she walked. She approached him quickly, stopping at his side and assuming her perfected Tender pose as she awaited instruction.

"Sit," he muttered, flicking through the movie channels for a decent production.

Simone bowed slightly and joined him on the sofa. He selected a film, stretching out and kicking off his boots as he settled. Motioning for her to move in closer, he watched as her face slowly settled into an unguarded expression.

The slight smirk disappeared, a hardened line replacing the mischievous smile. The confident arch of her spine grew straighter. The sparkle of her scathing blue eyes was gone, a reptilian stare settling in place as she focused her attention on the screen and ignored the assessing vampire at her side.

Simone would fetch a high price. Her future master would pay heftily for her up front, and probably with his life later.

Chapter Thirty

"If we drop down through Topeka, we can spend the night on the way to Salina. There's an abandoned haunt there we can hole up in for a night or two, depending on the reach of the feds," Bianca muttered as she hunched over her laptop in the sanctity of her Omaha bolt house. "I can't see them spreading wider than Nebraska.

Jagger glanced at her phone as it vibrated again. "The feds will stay within a hundred miles for a few days before expanding further. If we stick to the back roads and avoid cameras, we should be fine. You going to answer that?"

She scoffed. "It's Nichol. Or Rhys. You can message them if you want. I don't have to." She picked up the phone and extended it toward him.

He grabbed it, turning it to glance at the messages piling onto the screen, and looked toward her again, hesitant to read through her personal messages. "Anything on here you don't want me to see?"

Deep in thought, she shook her head and resumed her search of the Lincoln Slaughter.

He flicked through the messages absently. Nichol was short and succinct, his messages an array of clipped chastisements in her assumed involvement in the attack peppered with suggestions of safe houses in the region.

Rhys was a verbal bombing of rambling lectures and capitalized demands.

"Rhys is a real ass sometimes," he grumbled, closing the offending texts and scanning Bianca's other messages in curiosity. "Some woman named Mackenzie is wondering if you'll be joining her for coffee tomorrow afternoon."

She grinned, her eyes continuing to skim across her computer screen. "I'm busy. Tell her I have a dreadful cold and will have to skip out."

He responded as instructed, adding a smiley face at the end of the text. "Lisa wants to know if you want to paint the daisies or the irises Sunday. Irises?"

"Irises, yes. I'll cancel tomorrow after Mackenzie has had time to complain about my missing our coffee date," she stated as she looked up at him. "I need to spread out the ire I receive, or my temper flares at inopportune times."

Replying with another smiley, he began reading through the litany of older messages on Bianca's phone. "These women text more in a week than I say in a year," he announced. "And in full sentences. With proper punctuation." Intrigued with the human life Bianca had obviously forged with gusto, he opened message after message until one caught his eye. "Who the fuck is Jamie?"

"Human paramour," she muttered, engrossed in an article.

His eyes narrowed as he read through the messages. "Yeah, well, your PARAMOUR wants a repeat of last weekend and is looking forward to tonight."

"Of course he is," she replied distractedly. "Tell him I've become ill and will have to reschedule."

"No fucking way," he groused, reading through the

previous texts with a combination of jealousy and morbid curiosity. Jamie was apparently as avid a messenger as the rest of her social group. And he fancied himself quite the photographer. "This guy looks like an ad for a wilderness camp," he snarked, noting the slightly unkempt beard and pristine red plaid. "No way a guy with hands that unmarked is a lumberjack. He shouldn't dress like one."

She stopped her perusal of the Internet and cocked a brow at him. "He's a nice boy," she stated flatly, obviously unimpressed with his assessment. "It's the standard fashion trend for men right now."

Glancing down at his black cargos and the mildly worn hem of his hoodie, he snorted and passed Bee her phone. "I'm not responding for you."

She snatched the phone, typed a quick response, and set it face down on the table.

He glared at her for a moment before settling back onto the sofa and throwing his arm over his eyes to drown out any communication. And to avoid the urge to read Jamie's reply.

Her arrival on the roof of the parking garage had thrown him. Although he had planned to hunt her down after he dealt with the loose ends in Lincoln, he wasn't prepared to see her and even less prepared to talk to her. Every word out of his mouth since her arrival was a cover for the three words he knew were lurking in his head.

I want you.

Her leg brushed his elbow as she stood and passed him. The vibrations of her movements around the apartment were quick, her tiny feet flitting from room to room as she prepared her bags to vacate the apartment at dusk. He tracked her location, subtly dropping one hand to the floor to gain a better sense of her presence. After thirty minutes, the vibrations became stronger until he could feel her proximity at his side. He lifted his arm from his eyes.

"I'm going to bed. When you finish your tantrum, you may join me. This sofa is excruciatingly uncomfortable and far too short for you." She turned on her heel and marched away. He sat up, his eyes locked on the tiny woman as she stopped at her bedroom door. "You may join me. You may not touch me. I've placed a divider on the bed, and it will not be breached."

****

He looked positively ridiculous, long legs sprawled over the arm of her Queen Anne and broad shoulders extending past the edge of the cushion. Bianca took pity on the obstinate vampire, preparing her large bed with a wall of pillows to remind him her invitation was limited to the length of a mattress and not the warmth of her skin.

A reminder for herself as well.

When he skulked into her bedroom, Jagger eyed the barrier with a mixture of curiosity, amusement, and disappointment. Snugly tucked under her luxurious comforter, she crossed her arms, daring him to attempt to defy her.

He moved silently to his side of the barrier and lifted the blanket.

"If women in the eighteenth century were this creative with their linens, those pesky chastity belts would have been less popular," he mused, pulling his hoodie over his head and searching the room for a suitable place to toss it. She looked down at her nails, feigning interest in her cuticles as she stealthily watched him drop his cargos to the floor, revealing those delightfully strong thighs. "What's the purpose of so many pillows, anyways?" he inquired as he dropped heavily onto the bed, bouncing her in her place.

"Aesthetics," she replied, raising her head so he could see her over the wall. "Aside from this purpose, of course."

He hummed in acknowledgment. "Not that I have any intention of breaching your fortress," he said, humor in his voice, "but this isn't the first room, or bed, we've shared."

"It's the first one we've shared under my ex-Tender designation."

"You've been a Former Tender for well over a decade," he countered.

"And now I'm an ex-Tender. I've extricated myself from all expectations and responsibilities stemming from vampire society. I am completely free to do as I please, with whom I please."

He reclined into his pillows and covered his eyes with his forearm. "I am well aware."

She narrowed her eyes at his reply. When he showed no signs of lifting his arm to look at her, she rose onto her knees, reached over the cushioned barrier, and poked him in the chest. Hard.

"Yes?" he said as his arm rose, his expression less than enthused.

"What precisely do you mean by that?" she demanded.

"By what?"

Huffing and adjusting her stance, she poked the vampire again. "You are well aware. What precisely are you well aware of?"

He sat up on his elbows. "Your increasingly confusing and contradictory statements and actions," he said flatly. "You harbor resentment for the position you held for decades among vampires, yet when provided the opportunity to relieve yourself of those duties, you continue to immerse yourself. Orders were given and favors were called in to ensure you could live out the remainder of your existence in relative obscurity, yet here we are in bed until we begin our trck back to my haunt.

"You've obviously begun forming attachments and relationships in human society, yet you took the first opportunity you had to fulfill the vengeance of your former life in Lincoln. You've also made it clear your past attentions to me were based solely on the expectations of your role, so yes, I am well aware I am no longer your obligation."

His arm returned to his eyes, effectively ending communication.

She returned to her side of the bed, stunned and chastened by his appraisal of her actions over recent months. The litany of mixed messages she had sent him had seemed appropriate when individually examining each interaction they'd had, but once she assessed them as a whole, she began to see how unintentionally confusing she had been.

The tentative flexing of her independence during their first nights spent hunting the local Species Purifier leaders were balanced by years of training and decades of immersion into vampire protocols. She hadn't considered the effects her hot and cold behavior would have on the vampire who was on the receiving end.

She had ignored the flickers of wariness in his eyes as she slithered close to him, offering her body and blood in perfected Tender fashion. Had ignored the flashes of interest when she argued politics and vehemently explained why one dessert was superior to another. Had ignored the sparks of jealousy when she flippantly discussed other men in his presence.

Even if he did ask.

She sat up slowly and smoothly, limiting the movements in the mattress the vampire would surely feel. She sat back on her haunches, watching him as he lay in perfect stillness.

This was her sounding board.

With Jagg, she felt safe enough to flip through her roles, experimenting with her own personality as she separated what was her and what was molded into her. Without the pressures of Johan's position or Rhys's expectations, she was freer to stretch her independence while retaining the security of the formalities she'd known for decades. Perhaps it was his absence during her years training at the Kaius haunt, but he had never approached her as a Tender.

Unless she forced the issue.

She ran a hand down her face and shook her head slightly. The Kaius vamps were clueless enough when their women had designated roles within the haunt. Her emotional and behavioral waffling had probably burned stress holes in the vampire's brain.

"It's unnerving to be stared at for so long," he grumbled in the dark bedroom, lifting his arm. "Are you determining the best position for a stake?"

"I've known the best entry angle for sixty years," she retorted, carefully removing the pillow barrier and setting them on the far side of the bed. She noted the guarded look passing over his face as he observed her. With the final cushion neatly piled, she lay back down and snuggled under the covers.

He adjusted his position slightly, moving fractionally away from her before he settled again.

Chapter Thirty-one

The focused intensity of her blue eyes was fascinating for Jagger to watch as Bianca poured over a plethora of delivery fliers from local eateries. Her pen was poised in her fingers, periodically marking the items she found most intriguing. When her agonizing decisions were complete, she picked up her phone and began placing her orders.

Waking alongside her was awkward, her tiny body pressed tight to his and freezing his arms above his head in fear of offending her with an incidental touching. He had awakened long before her, immobile and alert. Despite the slight guilt echoing in his head, he allowed himself to sink into the floral scent of her hair and the softness of her hands on his stomach. When his body began reacting to his indulgence, he had carefully slipped from the bed and went into the living room to occupy his head with regurgitated news reports.

The vampire suspects were still at large, and police were recommending citizens remain indoors between dusk and dawn until the perpetrators were apprehended.

He had wandered the small apartment aimlessly, restless with anticipation of what the night would bring. Bianca's mercurial reactions to him the evening before were expected, but perplexing, nonetheless. She continued to appear torn between autonomy and affection, opposite ends of her internal spectrum. Until she reconciled both could exist simultaneously, he surmised he would be best served by biting his tongue and waiting it out.

Even if she drove him mad in the meantime.

Becoming involved with a woman who was unsure of her desires and her goals was something he was anxious to avoid, even at the expense of his own cravings. A woman dancing between human men and vampire society was a dangerous creature, lethal for any vamp who became too attached and too involved.

He wasn't involved.

He was merely passing through.

Her flicking wrist caught his eyes, pulling him from his musings. She motioned to the door, smiling as he ducked out of sight. The scent of food filled the apartment quickly, minutes ticking by as each delivery was brought to the door, the smells intermingling and overpowering. When the last of her orders arrived, she sought him out, finding him halfheartedly poking through her closet.

"Johan's clothes would be too small for you," she commented, grabbing his hand and dragging him into the living room. Steaming boxes and containers covered the coffee table. "I'm famished."

Taking a seat on the sofa, he didn't attempt to hide his interest in her singular attention to her meal. Once the feast was laid open, she lifted her fork and hesitated over her choices.

"Start with that one," he suggested, pointing to a meat drenched in a red sauce. "I like the smell of the spices."

She dove into the dish eagerly, offering a taste of the sauce to him and resuming her meal without attention to his reaction. The red sauce was interesting, the slight burning on his tongue a unique sensation. She gorged herself, her small form hunched over the table as she ate. Every so often, a fork would find its way to his lips, and he would either sample the offering or turn his head, emitting a grunt of disapproval as he did so. When she was finally sated, she climbed onto the sofa, reclined back, and set her legs across his lap.

"We can leave soon," she moaned, rubbing her stomach. "I just need a minute."

"That was quite a workout," he said drily, grinning when a hand lazily swiped toward him. As she recovered from her gorging, he relaxed back, his hand absently stroking the calves draped over his knees.

****

The slight tensing of his jaw caused Bee's smile to grow, her hand outstretched impatiently. "Come on," she goaded. "Hand 'em over."

The keys to the vehicle were deposited hesitantly into her waiting palm, jingling as she dove into the driver's seat before Jagger could change his mind. She started the engine as he climbed into the passenger seat, his long legs bent awkwardly until he located the button to move his seat back.

"You look ridiculous," he grumbled, shifting in place.

She fumbled to adjust her own seat until her feet finally reached the pedals. "Is this better, oh Emasculated One?" She grinned, throwing the vehicle into gear and pulling out of the underground parking garage.

"This isn't emasculating," Jagger argued as he toyed with the GPS system. "It's dangerous. You have inferior human reflexes, and your brain isn't wired to multifunction with the precision mine reaches. Therefore, this is an exercise in unnecessary risk." He sat back with a smug lift of a brow.

"Channeling Nichol are we?" she said pointedly as she pulled onto the highway. "Besides, we aren't going far."

It didn't take long for Jagg to realize she had abandoned the GPS path and was leading them in the opposite direction. "Bee." The warning in his voice held no amusement.

She smiled sweetly at him and sped up slightly. "We deserve a fun night," she rationalized. "Tomorrow, we can begin our trek to the haunt and prepare ourselves for the backlash of our actions. But tonight, we're going out."

He pulled the GPS into his lap, frowning. "Out where? I…this is why you're dressed like that, isn't it?"

She glanced down with satisfaction at the stunning wine-colored bell-sleeved mini dress she had selected. The silver platform heels added a good six inches to her height, a benefit in their crowded destination. "I look incredible," she replied. "And you damn well know it."

"Your appearance isn't in question," he muttered. "Now where the hell are you taking me?"

"Underground pub outside Sioux City. Now hush."

The pair arrived at the rural auto body shop serving as a front for the exclusive bar buried underneath. She had spent countless nights at the location over the years, using it as a base for informal meetings among negotiating vampires. The owner, a rare male Former Tender from the southwest, was meticulous in his screenings of both human and vampire patrons and was backed by the reputation of his long-deceased ancient master.

She pulled into the rows of vehicles behind the shop, handing Jagger the keys as she loosened the ties at her bust and touched up her lipstick. "Behave yourself," she warned. "We are going to dance, drink, and be merry. Got it?"

Jagger exited the vehicle wordlessly, his shoulders tense and jaw set as he scented the air and scanned the darkness. She waited patiently for him to complete his initial assessment, acknowledging his unease with the unknown location. When he was content with the security of the exterior, he extended his arm for her. "I don't like this," he muttered. "And you're showing far too much cleavage."

"Hush," she replied, looking up at him with a smile and shimmying her shoulders, allowing the lace ties across her breasts to loosen a fraction more.

The shop doors were unlocked, the reception room dark to avoid unwelcome interest from any passerby. Steering him toward the heavy metal door to the basement, she allowed him to take the lead, his forearm muscles rippling under her hand. She squeezed him briefly, a silent reassurance of their safety. A red light lit the stairwell, providing an eerie aura for the unshaven man at the bottom of the steps.

"Anton," she called, releasing Jagger and hugging the burly beast. "You promised me you'd shave that animal from your handsome face."

"I did." The man grinned. "A year ago. Where have you been, sweet Bee?"

"Nowhere and everywhere." She laughed, releasing the man and attaching herself to Jagger's arm again. "Anton, Jagger Kaius. Jagg, Anton."

Jagg remained still at her side, nodding briefly at the introduction. She didn't miss the slight frown gracing his face when she moved in to hug her furry friend.

Anton's brows rose. "A Kaius? It's an honor. Bianca, you bring me the best clientele. I'll let the DJ know to keep the music pre-1987. Drinks are on me tonight."

Bowing graciously at her host, she walked alongside Jagger through the door and paused at his side as he assessed the room. The layout of the bar was intentionally stark and open, leaving the patrons with a clear view of everyone's position in the area. The dance floor lay in the center of the room, small tables and chairs peppering the exterior walls. The single bar counter sat on stacks of glass blocks, the wall behind it a colorful array of alcohol bottles for the humans and vintage refrigerators containing a variety of blood blends for the vampires.

She tapped Jagger's arm to get his attention, waiting until his eyes fell on her lips. *Well?* she mouthed, conscious of the numerous pairs of functioning ears in their vicinity that would easily pick up a spoken conversation.

He leaned down, his lips brushing her ear. "I'm not dancing," he breathed before straightening and leading her to the bar. Every vampire in the room monitored their movement across the room, the humans joining suit when they noticed where the vamp attentions were focused. Jagger ignored the scrutiny, sauntering slowly around the dance floor and steering her through the crowd with ease. The bartender appeared before the pair instantly, his gaze traveling down her body.

"Sight for sore eyes, Ms. Schumann," he purred, ignoring Jagg's presence and the low growl emanating from him. "That dress is sinfully delicious."

She rolled her eyes, accepting a pad of paper and pen from the man. She quickly scrawled the dress designer's name and handed it back. "Stop acting like a lech," she chastised, turning to Jagger. "He prefers you over me. Matthew, be good."

The wiry man chuckled and winked at Jagg. "Daiquiri for the lady, correct?" She nodded as Matthew turned to Jagger. "Name your poison."

"O pos," Jagger answered, the quiet growl lessening.

Drinks in hand, Jagg escorted her to a table along the side of the bar, close enough to the exit to flee, far enough to assess the incoming patrons without notice. Women strode past them frequently, hips swinging in an effort to gain the attention of the handsome guy at her side. The vampires in the room continued to monitor their presence, whispering among themselves and subtly pointing Jagger out to their human companions.

"What's it like to be a rock star?" She giggled, elbowing Jagger in the ribs. "What are they saying?"

Stretching his arm across the back of her chair, Jagg leaned in, his lips grazing her lobe. "Lots of speculation about the attack in Lincoln. Our appearance together here has validated a lot of rumors." He flashed his fangs at her. "The vampires are jealous of the stunning specimen on my arm, and the women are voicing remarkably impure thoughts about the guy on yours."

She sipped her drink, scanning the crowd of eyes

surreptitiously watching them. Jagger's trademark hood remained in place, his tattoos hidden from the curious gazes of the onlookers. The tension he had rippled with upon their arrival was dissipating as the crowd's mood remained one of intrigue and awe at the couple's presence. "I intend to dance tonight," she warned. "With or without you."

"And I intend to enjoy the visual," Jagger replied smoothly.

****

It was intentional. Pure, evil intention of epic proportions.

Following through with her threat, Bee danced, and danced often. Brushing off the rare admirer who dared approach her in his presence. She held position on the dance floor directly in front of him, ensuring his attention was focused entirely on the sway of her hips, the curve of her back, and the precariously held position of her plunging neckline as it fluttered enticingly at her breasts.

Maintaining an aloof, disinterested facade against such a vision was proving impossible for him. And for the other vamps who had placed themselves in his periphery to shrewdly witness the show. While he continued to monitor the room, he was decidedly distracted with keeping his mouth closed and fangs under wraps as the tiny pixie shimmied and spun before him.

The rhythmic base ceased, signaling the end of a song she "just had to dance to," and she hopped happily back to their table, a faint sheen of sweat on her skin. She sipped her daiquiri greedily, frowning when the straw stopped sating her thirst. "Another round?" she asked, her chest heaving with the exertion of her dancing.

He stood, offering his arm to escort her across the room. The bar was admittedly well planned and carefully staffed. There were no waitresses maneuvering through the crowds, the bartenders being the sole providers of alcohol and blood. The openness allowed him to relax at his table, his view of the entire room unobstructed. Pretenses aside, the barkeep, Matthew, openly flirted with him now, playfully ribbing Bianca about stealing her date.

Neither he nor Bianca corrected the man.

Providing he didn't think too deeply about their situation, he was able to immerse himself in the carefree happiness she exuded within the walls of the bar. She chatted with every vampire she came across, introducing him to the numerous young vamps she knew from her days as an esteemed mediator. The elder ones used their casual acquaintance with Bianca to present themselves to the elusive member of the Kaius haunt, lifting their pant legs to reveal their ages as they offered support for the revolt.

The revolt.

Upon their arrival back at his haunt, he would need to warn Nichol and Kaius vampires were already coining the Lincoln attack as a revolt, a term floating on the lips of every vamp in the barroom. Murmurings would not stay as such for long.

Clutching two brightly colored drinks in her hands, Bianca skipped at his side. "How many is that now?" he inquired casually, unsure of her tolerance for alcohol.

"Eight? No. Nine." She grinned cheerily. "Only the first one had rum. It's my standard rule here, and

Matthew is well aware of my preferences." She paused to sip each drink. "A drunk mediator is a sloppy mediator. And a dead one—ohmygosh this song was written for me!"

The drinks rocked as they were deposited hastily onto the table, and he sprawled in his seat, his attention wholly focused on her as she joined a group of women on the dance floor in the center of the room who had drawn the attention of the males, their eyes locked on the undulating hips and tossed hair. When one woman positioned herself behind Bee and began grinding her hips against her, he leaned forward intently in preparation to extricate Bianca.

Or to get a better view.

He wasn't sure which impulse was in the forefront.

The beat ended, pulling him out of his haze as she hugged her dance partner and returned to his side. Pulling a tube of lipstick from her purse and touching up her lips, she sighed and flopped gracelessly forward onto the table. "I'm exhausted!" she exclaimed, her blue eyes bright. "And hungry. I'll be right back."

He frowned as she hopped up and made her way through the crowds, her small stature disappearing through the throngs of humans and vampires. Keeping his face schooled into indifference, he scanned the room for her, relaxing once he spotted the red dress peeking through the throng. She approached him, a smirk on her face as she extended her hand, the rhythmic pound of the music replaced by a slower tempo.

"You can't refuse," Bianca mouthed, grinning. "Every vampire in here will see, and one of them will happily take your place."

Cornered, he rose, placing her hand on his arm. "You're a sly negotiator, honey." He chuckled. "Lucky for you, I said I won't dance, not that I can't."

The pair joined the other couples peppering the dance floor, assuming a more formal stance than their counterparts. Her hand disappeared in his, her small fingers covered entirely. Resisting the urge to pull her obscenely closer, he locked his elbow in place as he rested his other hand on her hip.

"I dare say you rival Rhys." Bianca laughed as he smoothly dipped her. "Where on earth did you learn to do this?"

"Rhys," he replied, flashing his fangs. "He called it an essential hunting skill. You're slightly easier to dip than he is."

Relishing the feeling of her laughter as it echoed through her body, he momentarily wished he could hear the happiness he had drawn from her. The reverberation of the beat adjusted slightly, a new song bringing Bianca's head to his chest as her hand slipped under his hood and rested on his skin. He tightened his grip on her waist, drawing her dangerously closer until the music ended.

Keeping his hand locked around hers, he led her off the dance floor and toward the door. The sentry, Anton, stepped into their path as they exited.

"Jagger Kaius," he opened solemnly as he held out a folded paper. "My patrons requested I present you with this. Ms. Schumann"—he turned toward Bee, his face hard—"we are all aware of your new official status outside the vampire realm, as ordered by Rhys Kaius. But as your friend, Bianca, I hope you understand the status you have been handed tonight through your association with the face of the revolt."

Chapter Thirty-two

Bianca was silent for the first half of the drive back to Omaha, her face turned toward the window as Jagg drove down the dark highway. Anton's note lay unread on the dashboard, tangible proof of the sudden shift in mood his solemn proclamation had caused. His hand still felt the loss of warmth from her sudden pull from his grasp as Anton crowned her with her new unwanted status.

Her silence now spoke volumes.

"Perhaps you should return to the north," he suggested quietly. "It isn't too late."

She shifted slightly, angling her face toward him. "I don't want to discuss this."

She turned away.

He grit his teeth and ran a hand through his hair, pushing his hood off. "Fine," he snarled as he pulled the car off the road. "Then I will."

Her arms crossed, her eyes refusing to look his way.

Snatching the keys from the ignition, he jumped out and stormed around the vehicle, tearing the passenger door open. "Out."

Her hands flew to her seat, gripping the sides. "What the hell are you doing?" she yelled. "We have two hours until dawn. Get in here, and let's just deal with this tomorrow!"

"Get. Out." He knew his eyes were changing as he

reached across her and unclipped her seat belt. "If we continue this shit your way, nothing will ever get dealt with. Get the fuck out of the car."

He stepped back, looking away from the angry blue eyes boring into him. She slowly exited the vehicle, inching herself along the side until she was a safe distance from him. He extended his hand toward her, keys dangling from his finger. When the tiny woman flinched quickly, a hollowness filled his gut.

"Take them," he said, forcing his temper down and keeping his voice quiet. "And whenever you decide to leave, go. But this time, know there's no return. This time, I will have Rhys denounce you. Contact with you will be considered treason to the species, punishable by death."

Her hand reached toward his tentatively, her gaze locked on the keys. Clutching them in her fist, she drew her arms around herself and stared at the ground.

"Bianca," he started, hesitating as he siphoned the multitude of thoughts swirling in his head. He leaned into the open car door, picked up Anton's note, and scanned the contents. Looking to the sky for guidance, he found nothing but clouds, stars, and a few mosquitos.

"It's not avoidance if you never return. If you make the decision to walk away for good. If you stare down both paths and choose the one you can live with. Avoidance is this," he said as he gestured between them. "Straddling both paths in the hopes one takes the lead, takes the decision from you."

He carefully folded the note, placing it in his back pocket. "I avoided dealing with my connected mate. Ran away. Took the coward's way out. Choose your semantics." He crossed his arms and locked his gaze on the woman before him. "I returned to Turgutlu in early September of 1922, approaching from the northern roads on foot. The Greco-Turkish War was waging for two years before I left the region but had remained a distance away from the town Seline and I inhabited. Had I read the turn of the war correctly—"

He pursed his lips. "The town was razed when I arrived, most of it burnt to the ground. The stench in the air has clung to my memory for decades. The streets were deserted of life, littered with bodies and rubble. I recognized many of the humans from my nights in the market months earlier. Good people."

Bianca's eyes flicked to his momentarily, then returned to their intent study of the weeds at her feet.

"There were cries," he continued. "Men, women, infants. Cries and screams. Some clear in the night air, most muffled by debris. I sought out our—Seline's— home. What was left. It was little more than a pile of charred wood and shattered glass. I was digging through the mess, searching for any sign of my connected mate when I heard her scream."

He took a moment to properly describe the sound reverberating in his ears. "No. 'Scream' doesn't portray the sound Seline made. It was the wail of agony. Loss. Hatred. I dug through the rubble until I reached the hatch to the underground room where I could locate her heartbeat. It was strong. But it was the only one in the chamber."

Bianca's shoulders lifted a fraction, her arms tightening around herself.

"She came at me blindly when I descended into the room," he muttered softly as he recalled his connected mate's final minutes. "Fighting me with my own blades until she recognized me, and in that moment, I saw true revulsion. Every cell in her body despised me. For leaving or for returning, I'll never know. Perhaps both. She screamed a howl so encompassing it froze me in place until she turned my blade into her own heart."

He stopped, frowning. "I almost turned her. The break of the connection as her heart stopped was the most painful experience of my existence. It dropped me to my knees before her body hit the ground."

"Why didn't you sire her?"

Ignoring the watery blue eyes, he kept his focus on Bee's lips. "Seline believed suicide was a sin, believed it led to eternal damnation of her soul. She saw eternal damnation as the lesser of two evils. I was the other choice."

"Why would you tell me this?" she demanded, angrily wiping a tear from her cheek.

"You asked if I ever saw Seline again. I'm telling you," he gritted out. "The infant was locked to her bosom, cradled even in death. I carried them to a nearby cave I had inhabited and laid them to rest. I have perfect recall of over four centuries of my existence, but much of that time is lost to me. I may have sat there for days or for weeks. The screaming wouldn't stop. The longer I sat at Seline's side, the louder it became. I even began to hear the cry of the infant."

"And that's how you—"

"Stop interrupting, woman," he growled. "I can't hear you, but it's distracting, nonetheless. I had a small pack with me, abandoned when I first ran from Turgutlu. It contained a lot of useless gems, a few rusting blades, and a vial of mercury for Rhys. I can clearly recall holding the vial, how mesmerizing the flow of the liquid was as it moved along the glass.

"I can clearly recall my decision to end the cries in my memory. I can also clearly recall the moment the intense pain of the mercury in my ears lessened, and I realized I had successfully sealed the screams into my mind. So to answer your question from the Lincoln parking garage, yes, I did see Seline again. And I've heard her every moment of my existence since."

An awkward stillness fell between the pair. He monitored Bianca's eyes as they flickered between sadness and pity before settling into anger.

"You told me this to guilt me into staying with you."

His shoulder's slumped forward slightly, his hands working their way into his pockets. "No, Bianca. I told you this because I have four roads ahead of me. As do you. And since two of my paths intersect with two of yours, you need to know how I failed the only other woman I ever craved with every fiber of my core." He took a step back and straightened his back. "I've chosen my paths. Your decisions tonight may eliminate one of those roads, but at least the uncertainty will end."

****

Bianca toyed with the keys in her hand. Only one of the three was meant for the vehicle. She ran her finger along the jagged edges of the other two, halfheartedly contemplating the silliness of expecting tiny metal formations to keep danger at bay.

"Why do you hum?" she asked, hypnotized by the cool smoothness of the car key.

Jagger took another step back, increasing the distance between them. "It counters the screaming," he replied softly. "Being around you does the same thing. You silence it completely."

She nodded absently, watching the moonlight reflect off the key as she turned it over in her hands. "What did Anton's note say?"

Pulling it from his pocket, he passed the note over. She scanned through it quickly, the enormity of the contents slowly settling in her mind. "There are over two dozen signatures on this," she stated in disbelief. "Jagger. Between the haunt leaders on here and the proxy signatures, this paper pledges over three hundred vampires to you."

"I am well aware."

She shook the paper in his direction in an attempt to force him to comprehend the strength the single sheet held. "You," she repeated. "Not the Kaius haunt. You."

"And you," he added.

"And me," Bianca breathed. "What if I don't want this?"

He motioned toward the keys gripped in her hand.

"Do you want this?" she asked uncertainly.

"Want, no. Accept, yes," he replied tersely. "My decision has no weight on yours."

She nodded in acknowledgment. "If I say yes to this—"

"You are not saying yes to me," he finished for her, his hands returning to his pockets. "A clear business relationship. We could have Nichol draw up contracts if it makes you feel better."

Despite the seriousness of the discussion, she laughed. "Something with more backing than my pillow wall?"

"Substantially."

Holding the note out, she walked toward him. When he accepted the note and began to back up from her again, she stopped her advance and cocked her head. "Do you want me?"

He took another step back, as though the extra eighteen inches between them would shield him from her. "I thought I did," he began slowly. "Then I thought I needed you. But that isn't it, either."

Throwing her hands up in exasperation, she huffed. "Well then what the hell is it?"

His brow crinkled in contemplation, his hands fisting in his pockets. "Would it make sense if I said I think I've fallen in love with you?"

Chapter Thirty-three

The drive back to Bianca's Omaha condominium was a blurred race against the rising sun. The nape of Jagger's neck heated as he pulled into the safety of the underground parking garage, the sun unapologetically cresting.

Bianca's lips were moving a mile a minute as she bounced between chastising his time management and fretting over the sunlight breaching the weak barrier of his hoodie. They exited the vehicle, him stomping through the halls toward the apartment door and her scurrying alongside, scolding him for "inflicting his impatience on her neighbors."

Fuck the neighbors.

He paced the living room, watching her as she padded barefoot around the kitchen in search of food.

"You understand the implications of this, right?" he demanded as she opened a can of chemically preserved soup.

"Yes." She huffed. "Perhaps we should have Nichol draw up the agreement if you're so concerned. Make it nice and official."

"Maybe we should," he grumbled, resigning himself to sitting on the sofa while she ate the foul-scented food directly from the can.

She set the spoon down. "You realize that's essentially a marriage contract." She laughed, shaking her head. "I promise I understand what exclusivity is, dear. This isn't my first rodeo."

He pulled his sweatshirt off and stretched his arms over his head. "Yeah, well, this is the first time my rider will be living alongside all the other bulls she rode," he groused. When she flopped forward on the counter, her shoulders heaving with laughter, he glowered in her direction. "They've all seen your—" he gestured toward her. "Those degenerates can pull up the image any time they want to."

She strode over to him, failing miserably at schooling her face into seriousness. "You're getting all worked up over something decades old," she retorted, straddling his lap.

"Boy." he stated pointedly.

"A byproduct of a bygone era."

An unfamiliar contentment washed over him as she lowered her head to his shoulder, her tiny form shaking from the effort of holding back her laughter at his irrational jealousy. Even he knew he was being ridiculous, but the reassurance she was providing soothed the niggling reservations in the recesses of his mind.

"Say it again?" he grumbled into her hair as he rested his hands on her hips.

Small hands lifted to his temples, holding him still as she locked onto him. "I don't think I'm in love with you, you stubborn, emotionally stunted Kaius male. I know I am."

"That soup smells horrific," he replied, smiling as her lips brushed his and pulled away briefly.

"Love me, love my dinner."

Throughout the centuries, he had partaken in more than his share of debauchery. Between Rhys's trainees and the multitude of brothels the brothers had visited over the years, he was well versed in sex and the cravings that came with it. And as a connected mate, he had experienced core-driven fulfillment during his time with Seline.

Hell, he'd even been fucked senseless months ago by the woman currently grinding her hips against him.

So when her tongue leisurely dove into his mouth, chemical soup taste and all, he was thrown by the intensity of his desire to freeze the moment, to hold it in his memory indefinitely. Cataloguing every sensation, he relaxed against the sofa and fell into the tranquility of his first languid make-out session.

****

"Could you at least pretend to be breathless?" Bianca panted as she pulled away from Jagg's lips, gasping for air. "Maybe level the playing field a little?"

When his chest began to rise and fall, she smiled sweetly. "Much better. You breathe. I'm going to brush my teeth. You've proven your dedication enough."

She hopped off his lap and walked gingerly into the bathroom, her hips protesting the time spent splayed across him. When her teeth were scrubbed clean of the tomato soup taste, she reentered the living room to see him leaning forward on his elbows, studying her intently.

"You're injured," he stated, confusion tinging his voice.

She looked down at her dress and legs. "Where?"

Rising to his feet, Jagg circled her with a critical eye. "You're walking strangely."

"Oh!" She laughed, taking his hand and leading him into her bedroom. "I'm not injured. Just aging.

Which means I need sleep. Come on."

She selected a white negligee from her drawers and held it out for his approval.

"Aging how?" he demanded, ignoring the silk and lace garment. "Johan's blood should keep you from aging for at least another century or two. Mine as well."

Sighing at the obvious dampening of his libido, she stripped out of her evening wear and shimmied into the neglected lingerie. "Yours wore off quickly from being overworked in my healing. And it's been well over a decade since Johan," she explained in frustration. "Besides, it's very poor form to mention a lady's age."

He began pacing the bedroom as she climbed into bed. She watched the ice-blue of his eyes change from confusion to fear to resolve. "I can fix this," he said as he knelt beside her, scoring his wrist with a fang.

"You're being ridiculous and impetuous. Again." She huffed, pushing the bleeding arm away. "Now come to bed. We have better things we could be doing."

Jagger's lips drew tight against his fangs as he rose to his feet. "Fine."

She watched him storm past the dresser, wipe his bloodied wrist on the comforter, then flop onto the bed and toss his arm over his eyes.

Oh no. No, no, no, no.

She climbed onto him, her thighs holding him in place as she pried his arm away. "You are not seriously picking a fight over this," she admonished, giving her hips a swivel. "It's against the rules to go to bed angry."

"I'm not angry," Jagg replied, his tense jaw revealing his lie. "You need rest."

"You don't get to boss me around anymore," she murmured before she lowered her lips to his earlobe and ran her tongue along the shell. He let out a low groan, covering it unsuccessfully by clearing his throat. Pleased with the first reaction, she trailed her tongue down his neck, pausing to suck lightly at his jugular. His hands flew to her hips, stilling them.

"You really need to rest," he growled as his fingers dug into her skin.

She ignored him, snaking her hand up his singlet and grazing her nails along his rib cage. His grip grew tighter before he released her hips and grabbed the sheets instead. "That won't help you," she whispered into his neck, well aware he wouldn't hear her.

She adjusted her hips slightly, aligning her heated core with the hard bulge in his cargos. Resting her head on his silent chest, she rocked against him leisurely while she lightly dragged her nails down the muscled arm pressing into the mattress.

His complete refusal to mentally give in to her coaxing was offset by his traitorous body. Every twitch of his hips and flexing of his arms gave away her effect on him, and she reveled in the power rush each involuntary movement provided. She sat up slowly, smirking as she took in the ravenous gleam in his eyes.

"You REALLY need to rest," he insisted, his gaze locked on the white lace of her negligee bodice.

"I will." She panted as she placed her palms on his chest to support herself and ensured her lips were in full view. "You know, I really don't care if you come tonight," she moaned as she ground against him. "As long as I do."

A low chuckle rumbled through his body, sending delicious ripples through hers. "I'm very okay with that," he grunted, gritting his teeth as her speed increased. "Because until you take my blood and I'm...fuck...sure you're strong enough, we aren't hav...holy damn...having sex."

"Fine by me," she whimpered as her arms began to tremble from exertion, throwing her rhythm and pulling her back from the edge. He released the sheets, his palms rising to her waist to hold her steady as he dug his heels into the bed and gently thrust his hips against her panty-clad sex.

She dropped to her elbows, gripping Jagger's shoulders as her body tightened in anticipation of her release. With an unexpected speed increase, he pushed her over the edge and held her there, pulling her flush to his chest as her body convulsed and writhed atop him.

Breathing deeply to counter the dizziness in her head, she lifted herself onto her arms, grinning at the smug vamp below her. "I'm going to bed now," she teased, making show of stretching as she ground against his hardness.

"About time," he retorted, lifting her off him and tossing her gently onto mattress.

Eying him, she began to sit up. "I'm not leaving you li—"

He tossed the comforter on her, his long arms flipping her onto her side and pulling her up against him. "Now you can't talk to me anymore," he murmured into her hair, his arms caging her in place.

She fought his hold momentarily before she nestled against him, squirming until she found her comfort zone in the mattress.

"Not helping, Bee."

Chapter Thirty-four

"You're doing it again."

Jagger rolled his eyes and returned his attention to the road, focusing his attention on the warmth of Bianca's thigh where his hand had rested contentedly since they left Omaha. After a brief spat about who would drive, he won out by promising Bee he would stop at three fast food drive-thrus to secure her nightly feast.

While her meals had provided ample distraction for the first half of the trip, his mind had repeatedly sunk into a flood of disturbing images as his companion relaxed happily in the seat beside him throughout the second leg of the journey. Thoughts of the vivacious blonde becoming old and frail began trickling through his consciousness, punctuated by visions of her falling ill. Injured. Dying.

Fading on a hospital gurney while he stood helplessly outside.

"If it's such a big deal, send your wrist this way, big boy." Bee grinned, her eyes closing.

"You don't know what I'm thinking about," he groused, squeezing her leg.

"Of course I do," she replied. "Your lips get thin. You start assessing me like an antique appraiser. And you growl. If it'll make you feel better, toss your arm this way."

He grimaced. "We're not doing it going eighty on

the highway. But maybe when we get home—"

"I'll drain you dry."

Shifting in his seat, he smirked at the double entendre. "Is that it?" he asked, pointing toward a house shrouded among a ring of trees.

She nodded. "We'll turn around up ahead and circle the property before we head in," she said before reaching into the back seat to tidy her bags and collect the numerous empty food containers.

He slowed the car, looping back toward the house and turning onto the gravel driveway. The headlights illuminated the boarded structure, highlighting the abandoned haunt's years of neglect. The vehicle jostled as they crept around the back of the property, examining the area for any signs of inhabitants. She tucked her legs under her, lifting her higher in her seat and giving her a better view of the large home.

"There," she said, angling her face to him as she pointed at the boards of the lower windows. "Do you see movement?"

He scanned the darkness and began absently patting himself down to check for his blades. "Bottom right," he muttered, pulling a knife from his boot. "Wait here."

"Yeah, right," she whispered. Leaning forward to kiss him quickly, she grinned. "Let's go."

Slipping the keys into her back pocket, he held her back as he scented the air. The night's high winds diluted the peculiar odors he picked up, ripping them away before he could fully identify them. Leading Bee across the overgrown yard, he crouched against the boarded window and peered in.

Even in the blackness of the room, he could clearly

make out the figures of dozens of females, their feminine forms distinguishable despite the jerking movements of their damaged bodies. He adjusted his stance, leaning closer to confirm his suspicions before he stood, snatching Bianca's hand and dragging her across the yard.

"What the hell?" she hissed as they arrived at the car. "What's in there?"

"Deviants," he whispered, pulling the keys from Bianca's back pocket. "Dozens of them. Female Deviants."

She froze, her eyes widening. "Impossible," she said, glancing back at the house. "You obviously didn't get a good look."

He opened the driver's side door slowly, hoping it wasn't creaking. "Get in, start the engine, and be ready to rip out of here," he whispered, pulling blades from his cargos and placing them on the dashboard for easy reach. "I'll be right back."

"I don't think so, buddy," she mouthed as she collected the knives and handed them back to their owner. "If we're going to be the faces of the revolt, you better figure out I'm coming along."

He looked back at the house, his mind whirling through different scenarios convincing enough for her to wait safely in the car. Coming up empty, he ran a hand through his hair and adjusted his hood. "Fine."

They slunk back to the window, and he put himself in an offensive position as she took a moment to peer through the slatted boards. When her eyes grew wide and turned to him, he cocked his head toward the vehicle, glowering when she shook her head and glared at him. Creeping along the side of the haunt, he glanced in each window and quickly calculated the number of Deviants in the large basement room.

As they approached the front of the house, Bianca pointed toward the storm cellar entrance. "That leads to the underground bunker," she mouthed. He nodded and cupped his ear. She shook her head and stood back as he lifted the hatch a fraction and inspected the empty stairwell.

He closed the hatch and turned to Bianca. "We don't have to do this," he said quietly. "We can head toward Denver and report to Kaius when we arrive."

"And risk whoever this is being gone by the time we return? No." She gripped her butterfly stars in her fingers. "Lead the way, honey."

He knelt down, feeling the overgrown ground for a stone. He lifted the hatch and crept down the first steps, watching Bianca as she descended past him and setting the stone on the ledge of the hatch before he lowered the wooden cellar door. Slinking past Bee, he led their descent into the underbelly of the haunt.

He flattened a palm on one wall and skimmed his fingers along the other, hunting for movement in the unknown bunker. The stairwell curved at the bottom, a skiff of light peeking from under the closed door. Placing one hand on the frame and one on the wooden door, he noted little more than the heavy, jolted movements of the Deviants above them. He cracked the door open, flooding the stairwell with light. Bianca squinted at the sudden assault to her eyes, nodding once she adjusted to the change.

The bright hallway was a stark contrast to the darkness of the stairwell, but just as deserted. He led the way, staying tight to the wall and scenting the air. The vast number of Deviants on the premises compromised all other olfactory information, their base odor of decay overpowering the identifiable subtle scent of a vampire bloodline. He kept his eyes flickering between the closed doors leading off the hallway and Bianca, her safety clearly positioned in the forefront of his thoughts.

Her safety, and the realization he had not fed properly in two weeks.

Halting their progress, he pointed back up the stairs, gritting his teeth when Bianca shook her head. Checking to ensure the hallway remained secure, he lifted Bee's wrist to his fangs, hoping she would correctly read the apology in his eyes. Weakening Bianca was dangerous but continuing on with his own strength compromised was more so. Whatever vampire was creating female Deviants en masse would have to be at or above his physical strength at peak form. And he was currently far from peak form.

Her enthusiastic nod quashed the reservations he had at feeding at such an inopportune time. As his fangs sank into her vein, he ignored the blissful taste of her blood and focused his attention on her heart rate, assessing it for any change regardless of significance. His eyes continued to scour the hall, fingers pressed to the wall in search of vibration. When Bianca's pulse faltered slightly, he released her wrist and quickly scored his own.

He smirked as Bee rolled her eyes and latched on. Her tiny intake would do little more than provide a temporary rush of adrenaline, but it would be enough to counter the weakening effects of her blood loss.

For an instant, he could feel her more intensely.

The quiet hum in the back of his mind morphed and flashed through his head before disappearing entirely. When she released his arm, not even the weak link remained.

****

Bianca wasn't sure what she expected when Jagg opened the door to the dark room. Deviants, perhaps. A conglomeration of vampires plotting a world takeover. Even an orgy would have been more anticipated than the broken, silent ancient resting calmly on a dusty sofa. Jagger's large form filled the doorway, leaving little room for her to see into the dim room until she wedged herself under his arm, fighting for her place as he subtly pushed her back.

The injured vamp kept his eyes closed, his nostrils flaring as he identified his intruders. "I know you," the vampire rasped, his scorched lips barely moving. When Jagger didn't react, she elbowed him gently in the ribs, mouthing the ancient's words.

"Chen," Jagger growled, sending her brows up in surprise. Chen was so old, he held no bloodline name before him. Even Kaius, with rumors placing him at well over two millennia, held the Khthonios line.

The ancient's head turned slightly toward the pair, white irises unseeing.

"I know your blood," Chen repeated. "You. Diluted."

Jagg looked to her, confusion furrowing his brow. "Who else is here?" Jagger demanded, stepping into the room and positioning himself in such a way as to monitor the doorway and the ancient. "The Deviant sire. Who is it?"

She adjusted her hold on her butterfly stars,

prepared to launch them at the ancient until Jagger shook his head, his eyes locked on the vamp as he leaned into her ear. "His blood on our hands would be a death warrant," he whispered before straightening and addressing Chen again. "Who's siring the Deviants?"

Chen's head turned again, his blind eyes staring at the ceiling. "I know your blood."

"This is fucking useless," Jagger snarled quietly. "It has to be Dovidas. Chen hid him after we took out Kaspars's home in Memphis. And I can't feel your link with me. Dovidas is a Subduer, so his presence dampens or eliminates blood links. He has to be here."

"Chen's a long way from home," Bianca mused. "His injuries are so great, there's no way he's creating the Deviants. He can barely speak."

"He speaks just fine when he's hungry," a baritone voice interjected from the hall.

Chapter Thirty-five

Bianca intuitively crouched in position, her stars prepped to launch. Trusting in her aim, Jagger stepped back, ensuring he kept Chen in his peripheral as he studied the vampire leaning casually against the doorframe.

"It has the instincts of a hunter," Dovidas murmured, his steel gray eyes assessing Bee with cold appraisal. "How much?"

His question was met with silence as he and Bianca assessed Kaspars Dovidas's intent. The nonchalant crossing of his arms was unnerving, his ability to defend himself unnaturally hampered in the face of unknown intruders.

"No matter," Kaspars continued conversationally. "I have little interest in Kaius haunt cast-offs. They tend to leave a bad taste in the mouth."

Rage rose in him at the flippant reminder of Dovidas's abuse of Dominic's connected mate, Molly. The thinness of her body, the burns on her throat from his collars...all of it flashed through his head as he stared down the raven-haired vamp smirking at him.

Dovidas stepped into the room and strode calmly across his path on his way to Chen. They held their position, Bee glancing over at him in confusion before she refocused her attention on the vampire kneeling beside the ancient.

Kaspars completed a clinical assessment of the

injured ancient, appearing completely unconcerned by his uninvited guests. Apparently satisfied with his findings, Dovidas rose to his feet, motioning toward the door.

"Perhaps we should move this unexpected meeting into the hall," he offered cordially. "Chen requires rest, and even the slightest excitement can throw off his healing progression."

When neither moved, he led the way, his back exposed as he passed the duo.

"I can take him out," Bee mouthed to him, frowning when he gave a quick shake of his head and cautiously led her out of the room.

Dovidas stood at the base of the stairwell, blocking their only known exit. "Which one are you?" he asked, methodically scanning Jagg. When he remained silent, the vampire leaned against the wall and crossed his arms. "The Medico Della Peste? The Germanic Metallurgist? One of the impudent Russians, perhaps? Are there any other mutts I've forgotten?"

His fangs drew out long against his lower lip. "The female Deviants," he snarled. "Who are they tied to?"

Dovidas rolled out his shoulders. "Which one are you?"

They stared each other down. "Jagger," he finally growled, lowering his hood. "Of Saxony. The metallurgist. Who has sired the Deviants?"

"We're practically brothers," Dovidas sneered, his nose wrinkled in disgust as his eyes fixated on the tattoos.

"Don't presume to attach your filth to the Kaius line," Bianca spat back, stepping forward.

Dovidas chuckled low as he sized up the tiny

woman. "I presume nothing," he purred. "Jagger Kaius. Who is the defender of your good name?"

Before he could stop her, Bee responded, eliciting a laugh from Dovidas.

"The illustrious Bianca Schumann," Dovidas drawled, bowing in mockery. "Your reputation proceeds you. However, I must have missed the gossip about your penchant for slumming."

Jagger's hand shot out, tightening on Bee's shoulder and staying her advance. "The sire," he repeated, his patience with Dovidas's game thinning.

Kaspars reached up and tapped the ceiling, spurring a flurry of activity from the female Deviants in the room above. "Chen and I share the honor," he said, grinning as the vibrations of movements increased in intensity. "They belong to both of us, linked to both of us through our blood. It was a little experiment we decided to attempt a few months back. Quite successful, wouldn't you agree?"

His mind flashed through the logistics of what Dovidas was presenting. "A concurrent siring," he said in disbelief. "Impossible."

"Perfected," Dovidas corrected. "Others have tried with limited success. Chen and I merely tweaked the process. It does bastardize the bloodline, but I suspect you're proof corrupted bloodlines aren't always comprehensively inferior. The sun rises in five minutes." He stepped out of the doorway and gestured toward the stairs. "The closest town is twenty minutes away."

****

Bianca's hand trembled as she reached into the back seat and adjusted the yoga pants slipping off

Jagger's calf. The exposed skin was charring quickly despite the weak ultraviolet protection the window tint provided. Her eyes flickered rapidly over the horizon, searching desperately for any shelter from the sun she could find.

Minute nine.

"Your heart rate's becoming dangerously erratic," Jagger called to her from the back-seat floor. "We probably have another ten minutes before any serious damage is done," he attempted to reassure her.

She took a deep, shuddering breath and angled her arm to rest her fingers on the pile behind her. The air conditioner did little to battle the heat radiating off his body as the sunlight permeated the vehicle. Their meagre collection of clothing covering his body battled the rays valiantly but were inadequate to protect the entirety of his size. If any part of his body ignited, it would spread through his cells before she could even pull over.

Fumbling into her purse, she yanked out her cell phone and dialed the first name that came to mind.

"Bianca, baby," Rhys purred into the phone. "I've been waiting to hear from you. How's Canada?"

"I need help," she whimpered. "The sun's up, Jagger's in the back seat, and I don't know where to go."

The clomping of Rhys's boots echoed in the phone's earpiece. "NICHOL!" Rhys yelled, not bothering to cover the mic. "Bianca, I'm putting you on speaker. Tell us where you are."

"On the highway somewhere between Salina and Wilson," she replied, voice shaking. "I turned left when I should have turned right and now—"

"Why the fuck are you in Kansas?" Nichol snarled. "Open the settings on your phone. Enable the location tracker. I…there you are." Rhys's voice was muttering in the background, Nichol grunting in response. "Bianca, I have a bead on a house. Satellite shows an attached garage. Skip the next turn and make the right. Got it?"

She breathed out, her tension lessening slightly as Nichol took over. "Got it. How long until we're there? He's heating up so fast."

Rhys's curses muffled Nichol's reply until a loud thump was heard and only Nichol responded. "Three minutes at your current speed. The turn's coming up…there. Up ahead on the left you'll see what looks like a dirt driveway. Take it and follow it past the trees."

Checking Jagger's condition in the rearview mirror, she took the tight turn and sped up along the gravel. "What do I do once I'm there?" she asked, her mind focusing on the task at hand and not on the heated vampire in the back seat.

"We'll make that decision once we know if the house is inhabited," Nichol grumbled distractedly. "Our goal is to prevent ignition. Burns will heal, but if he lights up, both of you will be engulfed."

"You think I don't know that?" she hissed, slowing as she approached the large house.

"I wasn't sure, since somehow both of you decided driving around in daylight was acceptable." A small scuffle ensued on Nichol's end, the phone being jostled before another crash echoed in the speaker and Nichol returned. "Any signs of life?"

She squinted as she pulled in front of the home.

The curtains in an upstairs windows fluttered. A truck remained parked a distance away in the field. "Two. Maybe more," she reported as she glanced toward Jagger and adjusted the slipping yoga pants again. "Nichol, I can see his leg blackening."

"Fuck. Align the car's ass end with the garage door and gun it in reverse. We're going in dry," he responded, his voice tight. "Be prepared to slam on the brakes once you breach the door. After Jagg's out of the dircct sunlight, we can move from there."

She pulled up to the garage as directed, watching her mirrors for signs of the humans inhabiting the property. When she was certain she wouldn't run anyone over, she threw the car in reverse, slammed on the gas, and braced herself for the impact. A snarl of pain erupted from the back seat as they launched backward, increasing in volume as she hit the brakes to avoid crashing straight through the house.

Over the din of a woman's scream from inside the house and Jagger's snarling from behind her, she pulled the phone tight to her ear. "He's completely out of the direct light," she reported as Jagg's howl lessened. "Will he be okay while I deal with the humans?"

"Cover the windows with anything you can find in the garage first. Keep your phone on and in your pocket so Rhys and I can hear what's going on. You did good, Bianca," Nichol said.

She scrambled out of the car and frantically began pulling down the hunting tarps hanging neatly along the walls. The woman inside the house had gone silent, most likely contacting help if the sound of an approaching truck was any indication. Once the vehicle was covered, she slipped back in and uncovered

Jagger's head. His face was unmarred, ice eyes ovaled as he fought against the pain of his burns.

"Where are we?" he asked, voice graveled.

"Out of the sun. I'll be back," she whispered, running a hand quickly across his temples before she dodged his attempt to grip her wrist.

"Hey," he called after her. She held the door and turned. "I probably should have made love to you when I had the chance. Maybe this is karma." When he grinned, she slammed the door shut.

Locking the doors for an added layer of protection for him, she strode into the house on the hunt for the owner. The place was silent, her footsteps on the hardwood the only sound echoing in her ears. She patted her thighs quickly, ensuring her stars were easily accessible as she began to climb the stairs to the second level.

"Please," she called into the silence. "I need help. I'm not here to hurt you."

The engine of the truck was uncomfortably close and progressing at a speed which gave her little time to subdue the first human. She scanned each room as she passed, head cocked for the panicked breathing she was certain would reveal the woman's location.

"I don't want anything from you," she said. "Just a place to stay until sunset."

A soft shuffling.

Following the sound, she made her way into a large bedroom and shook her head. The only exit from the room was the doorway she was blocking.

"I know you're in here," she said softly. "And I know your husband is going to be walking in the door any moment." She listened in the quiet of the room, methodically walking toward the closet door. "My partner is injured," she continued as she placed her hand on the knob. "I'm sure you can understand the desperation I'm feeling right now. Your husband is on his way up the stairs. You and I are about to be in the same boat."

Wedging her boot against the door, she turned toward the exit with her stars in hand. A stocky man filled the doorway, his shotgun rising as he caught sight of her. The rifle fell to the ground as the butterfly star embedded itself in his bicep.

"That's a warning shot," she said calmly, placing more weight against the closet as the woman inside screamed. "Kick the gun this way. And don't dislodge the star. It'll rip your muscle straight from your body. I'll deal with it once we reach an agreement."

The man hesitated, his hand gripping the star tighter before he released it.

"Smart move. Now send the gun over here, or I demonstrate my skills on your wife's jugular." The rifle slid across the hardwood, just out of her reach. "You're being remarkably agreeable," she complimented, stretching her foot out to pull the weapon into her range. After a moment of awkwardly balancing her remaining throwing star, the closet door, and checking the barrel of the gun, she smiled at the man.

"I'm really not here to hurt anyone," she explained calmly. "My friend and I are in desperate need of shelter for the day, and your home is it. Now, honey," she called toward the closet, "I'm going to let you out, and you and pops are going to lead me downstairs. Just as an incentive to behave, I'll tell you now one wrong move from either of you and the other will be bleeding out."

A sob came from the closet as she moved her foot away and allowed the woman to step out. With the gun cocked, she motioned for the wife to join her husband.

"Down the stairs we go!" she called cheerily, hiding the increasing worry she felt for Jagger.

Hands held, the couple waited silently in the living room for her instructions. "That is absolutely adorable," she cooed, calculating the distance between the garage and the basement steps as she smiled at the couple clinging to each other. "How long have you been married?"

The woman looked to her husband quickly, answering once he nodded tersely. "Twenty-three years."

"Well, here's to another twenty-three." She laughed, tipping the rifle in their direction. A snort came from her back pocket. "Hush, Nicky. It's beautiful and romantic. Now here's what we're going to do. I'm going to secure this handsome beast and you," she said, looking at the woman, "are going to help me out with my friend. Yes?"

Despite the woman's frantic shake of her head, she motioned for the couple to move into the damaged garage where she could reassure herself Jagg was still safely cocooned. Pleased to find the car wasn't engulfed in flames, her mood lifted.

"This will be a little tricky," she muttered, fumbling with the tarp to allow access to the back seat. "Sweetie, I'm going to ask you to come here for a moment."

The woman stayed at her husband's side, her hand gripping his.

"I promise you nothing will happen to you. I just need a little assurance your husband will play nice. Now come here and wait in the back seat." She huffed, pulling the door open. "Wait there, Superman," she called to the man. "One wrong move and things will go very bad very quickly."

With a soft shove, she pushed the wife atop Jagger and scrambled onto the seat to remove his hood. His eyes snapped to the woman briefly before meeting hers. "Hold her tight," she instructed as the woman struggled in his grip. "Fangs off."

The scream from the back seat followed her out of the vehicle, launching the still bleeding man in her direction. Lifting the shotgun to his head, she cocked a brow. "As you can see, my friend is exhibiting excellent control on my orders," she warned, motioning to the exposed window. "He does so until I'm no longer happy. And right now, I'm tired, hungry, and prone to irritability. Now grab the twine over there and take a seat on the floor."

With one eye on Jagger to confirm his control, she trained the rifle on the man until he sat at her feet. "Scoot back, honey," she said, placing the weapon out of his reach and beginning the arduous process of knotting the twine around his arms and legs. Searching the area for something to secure his to, she came up short. "Well, darn." She sighed, turning to face Jagger. "I suppose if he rolls out of sight, you could just drain his wife. I'm going to head inside and grab a bite to eat. Be right back."

Slinging the rifle under her arm, she scoured the kitchen for food, returning to the garage with a heaping plate.

"This is fantastic," she moaned, climbing into the back seat and balancing her plate carefully on the leather. She lifted her sleeve and lowered her wrist to Jagg's mouth. As the fangs pierced her skin, the woman began sobbing. "Oh shush," she chastised as muffled laughter came from her phone. "This is awkward enough with you lying on top of my guy. The least you could do is avert your eyes."

Chapter Thirty-six

"If you keep flinching away from me, I'm going to shred your bicep," Bianca cautioned her captive. "Honey, tell him."

Jagger adjusted his position slightly, his recent switch to sitting against the passenger door infinitely more comfortable than his previous state. He relaxed his grip on the woman in his lap, allowing her to shift her own cramped legs. "Those beauties are designed for a smooth entry and rough removal," he explained. "If you relax the muscle as she pushes in, the release should be relatively easy."

The man grit his teeth and focused his stare on his wife as Bee set to work. Within seconds, the butterfly star was in her hand. "Perfect." She smiled at him. "I was a little worried the third hook wouldn't dislodge."

Eight hours into their stay, he was impressed with the relative calm settling over their captives. Once they accepted their compliance was rewarded with food and trips to the bathroom, both had become significantly more docile as they waited out the sunlight.

Bianca looked tired, her somber blue eyes betraying the forced smile she maintained as she periodically checked his healing. It would take more than she could spare to completely repair the most severe of the sun damage, but he was in far better shape than he was in earlier.

By his calculations, he had been two minutes from

ignition.

The intensity of the early morning rays had pierced the vehicle's protective tint, boring deep holes into his bones. Away from Dovidas's subduing power muting his link to Bianca, he now clung to the thread of her sanity weaving through his head unobstructed. It kept him focused, alert, and reassured she had suffered no lasting damage from his excessive feeding. Nothing a week of rest and unlimited food wouldn't repair.

"So what happens when the sun sets?" the man ventured, looking to him.

He chuckled as Bianca poked the man in the ribs. "I'm running the show, not him." She huffed. "While it isn't ideal, you'll both be secured in the house until we are far enough away to place a call to the police. Unless you'd like to leave me the number of a friend. No, of course not," she shook her head.

"I'm sure you'd prefer reporting this. Anyways, my associate has identified your names through land titles and is in the process of depositing a sum into your joint bank account to cover the damage to the garage, as well as a small compensation for your assistance today."

He grinned, knowing Nichol's temper. "Is your associate displeased with us?"

"Very."

The man eyed Bianca warily. "How much is a 'small compensation'?"

"Thirty thousand on top of the fifty for repairs. Should you decide to keep the authorities out of this, he will deposit a second sum of fifty thousand in appreciation of your discretion."

While he couldn't make out what the woman on his lap said, Bianca's sly smile was response enough.

****

"Why don't you let me drive the rest of the way?" Jagger asked quietly, running his hand through Bianca's hair and delicately massaging the knot from her shoulder blades.

"It's only two more hours," she replied, arching her back slightly to give his hand better access. "How are those burns doing?"

"Manageable. Fucking Dovidas," he growled, thinking back to their frantic dash to the car once they realized neither Kaspars nor Chen would halt their escape.

"Why on earth would he let us go?" Bianca mused, rolling her neck. "He had to know we'd feed his location to the others."

His brow knotted. "I would bet they hit the road tonight as well. There are no active haunts in the area, so the likelihood of fire power of any kind reaching them prior to their escape is minimal."

"But why not take us down?" she pressed.

"Maybe because our knowledge of the Deviants is inconsequential to their plan."

She shuddered. "What the hell would be worth the risk of dozens of female Deviants?" She blew out a breath. "Bastardized Deviants."

His jaw tensed. The knowing smile gracing Dovidas's face when he called the Kaius bloodline "corrupted" hung in the back of his head. It was an impossible insinuation, but one capable of tarnishing the reputation of the Kaius haunt if it was to spread through the wrong channels.

Vampires deemed to be sired from weak lines never attained status among their peers. The lines also died out within a few centuries, the lack of inherited strengths and skills making them easy targets for the mightier, more robust bloodlines.

Shortly after they began their trek home, Bianca had touched base with Nichol, talking him through the location of Dovidas and recalling every detail of their encounter she could remember. Every detail except the implication the Kaius bloodline was compromised. The insult bore no weight, she hissed angrily when Jagg noted the omission. Dovidas, she insisted, was likely compromised stock, given his age and lack of descendants.

He couldn't help but notice she didn't address the Kaius brethren's lack of proliferation.

"How is Rhys going to react when we arrive?" Bianca questioned, her shoulders tensing once again.

"He'll be fine."

The flat glare he received told him she believed his reply as much as he did.

****

Bianca set her hands on her hips and pursed her lips. "You're being ridiculous," she bit out as Jagg tried unsuccessfully to cover his limp. "Just put your arm around me and let me help."

The stubborn vamp straightened his back and placed his full weight on his most damaged leg, jaw clenching as he fought to appear unaffected. "I'm not walking in there leaning on a wo…" He paused a moment. "Leaning on anyone. It's fine, Bee."

Fine. If every step didn't bring an instinctive flinch of pain, the peculiar fall of his cargos over his hollowed shins definitely indicated the severity of his injuries. She watched him take his last step down the stairs, not buying the casual smile he gave her as he leaned against the wall.

"See? All good," he said as he extended his hand, pulling her into his arms and resting his chin on her head. "I could get used to this."

Such a common, normal action, she mused inwardly as she sank her weight into their first true embrace. She closed her eyes for a moment, exhaustion from the past few days settling over her.

"Your little experiment in self-actualization cost me a lot of favors," Rhys's voice called from behind her. "And wasted a shit ton of my time on paperwork."

She laughed as Jagger's grip tightened and a low growl rumbled through his chest.

"I assure you, I've reached peak actualization," she said, prying herself from Jagg and greeting her trainer with a quick hug. Jagger's finger remained hooked in the waistband of her pants, a direct message of his claim.

Rhys read the notice clearly, rolling his eyes. "Bianca, baby. I thought I taught you better than to feed the strays. Next thing you know, he'll be crawling all over your lap and spraying the furniture."

When Jagger stepped forward to take a playful swing at his older brother, all humor left Rhys's face.

"Let me see the damage. Bee, you remember where the com room is, right? Nichol is expecting you."

As she kissed Jagg's cheek and began walking toward the communication room, Rhys's muffled words drifted down the hall, his voice low with concern. Leaving Jagg in Rhys's capable hands, she trailed her fingers along the walls as she slowly bypassed the exit to the Tender quarters and continued on into the main haunt. Little had changed in the decades she was gone, the dark walls and scant lighting a stark contrast to what she knew lay beyond the Tender entry.

She took her time, deviating her path to wander through the vampire's bunks. She tapped lightly on each door as she passed, her mind flickering through memories of which brother inhabited each room, wondering which one belonged to the youngest hauntmate, which belonged to Jagger. She knew Rhys had a room in the wing as well, but in all her time training under him, he had never used it.

"You're sure taking your time," Nichol's voice called, drawing her out of her thoughts.

She hopped over to the surly vamp, hugging him tight and refusing to let go as he stood rigid and uncomfortable. "I know you're going to yell at me later, but I must say it is so good to see you," she muttered into his shirt as he attempted to step out of her hold.

Nichol grunted, untangling himself and placing a good distance between them. "Jagger and Rhys are heading down to the bloodslave quarters for a bit. I've been tasked with securing you a meal, ordering any necessities you require, and listening to you talk with as much feigned interest as I can muster."

Chapter Thirty-seven

Jagger watched as Nichol turned Anton's note over in his fingers, his eyes thoughtful. "This is Spiro's Former Tender, correct?"

Bianca nodded, brushing Jagg's wandering hands from her hips as she leaned over the table. "I can contact him if needed," she offered, tossing him a quick glare of warning when his fingers hooked into the hem of her shirt. "Maybe question him a little more on some of the lesser-known names on this list."

"Do it," Nichol instructed, passing the note back to her and leaning back in his chair. "I suppose we can discuss the stupidity of the past week tomorrow night. I've been able to secure a satellite feed to monitor the abandoned haunt Dovidas and Chen were in, but I believe you're right. There's no movement in the area. We likely missed them by a few hours."

Grabbing Bianca's hand, he led her from the com room before Nichol could change his mind about the tongue lashing they were due to receive.

"Did you manage to feed?" she inquired as they walked slowly down the hall.

He nodded. "Rhys hooked me up in the bloodslave quarters, and Boy bagged half a pint of his own for me, so I've got a bit of a drunk going on right now," he warned as he debated his next words. "Rhys has offered one of the empty rooms in the Tender quarters if you want."

When she didn't reply, he became nervous. He slowed to a stop, releasing her hand. "I won't be offended if you need some space here," he said, glancing around to ensure there was no one listening in. "It's probably weirder for you than it is for me."

Her brows knotted as she looked down the hall leading to the Tender quarters. She remained silent for a few minutes, refusing to look his way until she gathered her thoughts. "It scares me," she finally stated.

"The idea of staying in the Tender wing, regardless of whether the program is being shut down. It would be so easy to return to it, to fall back into what I've spent decades perfecting… Stop growling. You're being silly." She grabbed his hand and started walking toward the hauntmate quarters. "I'm not picking up after you. Or doing your laundry."

They entered his room, Bianca crossing her arms as she took in the mess he'd left behind.

"You shower. I'll clean it up now," he promised, picking up a pair of socks and tossing them into the corner. Apparently content with his offer, she kicked off her boots and disappeared into the bathroom.

He zipped around the room, shoving clothes into drawers, and placing his collection of blades into neat rows on the table. The opening of his door caught his eye, and he greeted Kaius as he entered.

"Nichol promised me I had a reprieve until dusk," he said, taking the bags Kai had retrieved from the car's hatch for him. Knocking on the bathroom door, he called out to Bianca. "Your stuff is here."

Kaius looked around the room and scented the air. "I was just checking on your healing before I retire for the day," he said, his eyes flicking to the bathroom door as Bianca opened it a crack and snatched her bag from Jagger's hand. "Good evening, Ms. Schumann," he called to the closing door before he returned his attention to Jagg and whispered his words. "What is her function in the haunt? I hesitate to offend."

He grinned at his awkward creator. "I offend her enough for both of us. I suppose she'll officially join me on weapons and training, given her strengths. I'm sure Nichol filled you in on Anton's note," he said, waiting until Kai confirmed with a nod. "We'll figure that out, too. And if any of you try to feed off her, I retain the right to stake you. Clear?"

With a smirk and a bow, Kai exited the room, leaving him to wait anxiously for Bianca. He paced the floor, taking his first moments of solitude to assess his link to the woman he was now bunking with. As he struggled to navigate through her swirling emotions of apprehension, excitement, and discontent, he debated texting Mickey for a brief lesson on reading links.

Logically, he had known their return to the haunt would be an adjustment for both of them, but the intensity of her negative feelings was quickly overpowering his rational thoughts.

He slumped onto the sofa, closing his eyes and leaning his head back in preparation for whatever state Bianca's emotions settled into as she opened the door. A burst of fear followed by resolution bounced through his head as her footsteps drew nearer, her soft floral scent overtaking the room. When her advance stopped short of joining him, he steeled himself and opened his eyes warily.

"I want to paint the bathroom lavender," she stated, hands on her hips and towel loosely knotted across her chest. "And we need a full-length mirror."

Fighting his natural instinct to stare at the half-naked beauty in his line of sight, he forced his gaze to remain on her lips. "You've decided to, uh, stay."

"Of course I have," she replied, straddling his lap and distracting him further from his concerns. "I'm not sure what shade of lavender I want, but nothing with a strong red undertone."

The gaping towel at the juncture of her thighs was calling to him. "Bianca," he growled, keeping his eyes away from temptation as he stammered through his words. "You can have anything you want, any way you want it. But I need to know if you have any reservations now that you're here."

She leaned back and narrowed her eyes. "I have reservations about your inability to decorate a space. I have reservations about the possibility of leading a resistance against a species outnumbering us a million to one. I have reservations about engaging Dovidas and Chen in whatever plan they are attempting to hatch. I also have reservations about how you're going to handle the green-eyed monster already rearing its head on our first night here."

She placed her small hands on his temples. "What I don't have reservations about is us. After all, we're forever linked through a shared laundry list of felonies I can use as blackmail should you ever tire of me."

****

Bianca stretched out against the muscled body lying motionless beneath her before she sat back on her haunches. Pushing the blanket off him, she took a moment to scan Jagger's body for any remnants of his burns, pleased when she noted even the bones of his legs had completely filled in.

Boy's blood was truly miraculous.

When she had finished her shower, accompanied by intense contemplation of the color scheme she would select, she had exited the bathroom to see him sagged against the back of the sofa, his eyes closed, and brows drawn tight. Visions of the faint trail of smoke rising from his leg as she blasted through the homestead's garage door flashed across her mind and sent a jolt of fear through her body.

His cautious gaze when he took in her approach eased her anxiety over his physical state. A quick glance down told her his legs were healing at a rapid rate, Boy's old blood working overtime to heal the most severe of the damage. Once she was assured he was on the mend, she found herself enthralled with his valiant attempts to hold a serious discussion despite her state of undress. His eyes flicked rapidly between her bare skin and her lips, his tongue tripping over his concerns about her commitment.

It was endearing. Unnecessary, but endearing.

She ran her fingers across the tattoos on his temples, tracing the intricate patterns.

"I'm not getting up," came a grunted response to her prodding. "I'm never getting up again. You drained me, and now I'm done forever."

When his ice-blue eyes opened a sliver, she grinned down at him. "I'm going to go eat," she told him, patting his chest.

"Don't hug anyone," he grumbled. "Or talk to anyone. Maybe text Rhys and get room service."

Shimmying down his body one last time, she hopped from the bed and set about making herself presentable. Once she was content with her appearance, she slipped from their bunk and wandered down the hall.

The Tender quarters were eerily similar to her memories from decades past, the pastel walls and decor smacking of femininity and tranquility. The kitchen, her favorite room during her training time, was updated with the newest appliances and stocked with a sumptuous array of fresh fruit, cheeses, breads, and sinfully salty ham. She was well into her third sandwich when a curly-haired brunette entered the kitchen, watching her with a mixture of curiosity and unease.

"You're welcome to join me," she offered, pushing a plate of snacks toward the reluctant Tender.

The woman shook her hair, the rainbow streaks in her curls dancing as she did. "Rhys told me there were no more Tenders joining the pool," she stated, crossing her arms. "I'm the last."

She leaned back in chair and watched the woman closely. "I was in your place eight decades ago," she said slowly. "Now I'm here of my own volition, alongside Jagger. What's your name, honey?"

The woman went silent, her eyes narrowing as she assessed her.

"Bianca," Rhys's voice purred from the entrance. "This is Simone, Simone, this is my greatest accomplishment and Jagger's ball and chain, Bianca."

At the sound of Rhys's voice, Simone's eyes became hard, the look of a predator momentarily flashing across her face until she schooled her reaction and smiled at her trainer.

Rhys leaned into the woman, whispered a quick instruction, and winked at her as she sashayed from the room. He pulled a chair up across from Bianca and straddled it, poking at her unfinished sandwiches.

"Add your requests to Nichol's delivery list," he grumbled, pulling the bread apart and wrinkling his nose at the ham inside. "Watch the salt intake. Jagg's not fond of the taste."

She yanked the ham away and shoved it into her mouth. "He's smart enough not to make requests," she stated. "How long has Simone been here?"

Rhys cocked his head to the side. "Why?"

Swallowing her final bite, she leaned forward and lowered her voice. "She will stake one of you. And soon. She's turned."

"She was never aligned," he replied, scratching his tattoos absently. "I pulled Simone up from the bloodslave quarters on a whim a few months back. She was an escort prior. I'm not sure if it's vamps she despises, or males in general."

He paused, glancing out the door Simone disappeared through. "She keeps her hostilities out of her work environment and performs on par with some of my best. Besides, as Audra would say, we've established a healthy outlet for her frustrations."

She pursed her lips. "You aren't concerned she'll attempt to end her buyer?"

He smirked.

Chapter Thirty-eight

"I told you that was too long," Bianca grumbled, crossing her arms and glaring at him, her foot tapping impatiently.

Jagger flipped the switch on the Deepfryer and waited for the enclosure's UV lights to completely fade before he pulled the protective wooden door open to assess the damage. The frozen pig had burnt to an unrecognizable charred lump within ten minutes, its remains still smoking as he prodded the blackened pile. "Something happens between minutes nine and ten," he muttered in curiosity, glancing over at Bee.

"Yeah," she snarked. "You burned my bacon."

He grinned and grabbed a garbage bag. "Nichol promised a bacon delivery within the next three days. If you're going to be this cranky until then, maybe you should go work with him for a bit."

A butterfly star whizzed past his shoulder and embedded in the wooden door of the protective Deepfryer box. Before she could reach for another weapon, she was lying flat across his workbench, a glimmer of mischief in her eye.

"Your speed doesn't impress me." She yawned as her legs wrapped around his hips. "You can't do your best work when you rush."

She was baiting him, pushing for attention.

He was more than willing to play along.

The past three nights were an exhausting exercise

317

in restraint, humility, and negotiation. At dusk on their first full evening in the haunt, Kaius had officially summoned the couple, sending Boy to Jagg's bunk with a written request for their presence in the com room. After a grumbled territorial warning he was grateful Bianca hadn't heard, he had showered quickly, waiting for Bee to return from her hunt for food.

Rhys, Kaius, and Nichol sat on one side of the meeting table, Boy standing to the side with his empty eyes focused on the floor. He felt Bianca's uncertainty, the strange formality of the situation leaving them both unnerved.

Rhys was first to speak as he pushed a stack of papers in Bee's direction. "Ms. Bianca Schumann, Former Tender and companion of Johan Holst of the Holst bloodline," he opened, holding out a pen. "You are hereby presented with documents amalgamating you with the Kaius bloodline. Once signed and filed, you will be recognized as one of us, a full-blood member of the Kaius haunt. Should you agree, you will carry the benefits and the detriments of affiliation with our line. Your wars will be ours. Ours yours." With uncustomary ritual, Rhys bowed to Bianca before he sat and watched her attentively.

Bee pulled the papers in slowly, reading the meticulous handwriting as Jagg scanned his brethren intently. The offering of a bloodline amalgamation was almost unheard of, the only instances in memory being the unification of two dying lines in times of unrest. Kaius was stoic, his face unreadable. Nichol was less schooled, his impatience at Bianca's reading pace evident in the twitching of his brows. Rhys's dark eyes glinted in anticipation.

Boy, having never been presented the option to affiliate with the Kaius line, studied the paint on the far wall. It didn't escape his notice Bianca had looked to the mute vampire often as she read the proclamation, her blue eyes melancholy.

Her hand grazed his, bringing his attention to her blue eyes. "I assume you knew nothing of this. What are your thoughts?" she asked quietly before turning to the others. "Has this been discussed with Mikhail and Dominic?"

With a nod, Kaius looked to him as well.

He pushed his hood off his head. The protections the amalgamation would provide Bianca were immense, her access to the Kaius haunt knowledge, finances, allies, and reputation a sizable benefit as they maneuvered their new roles. "As long as this doesn't interfere with you and me or have some stupid relationship clause," he stated, looking pointedly at Rhys, "welcome aboard."

As Bianca's pen completed the final stroke of her signature, Rhys snatched the papers away, decorum gone. He looked down at the signature, then up at him with a grin. "You disgust me, man," he said, shaking his head. "Sleeping with your fucking relative."

He nuzzled Bianca's neck and shook the thoughts from his head. The steady increase of her pulse as he licked along her clavicle brought his attention back to the moment. Her hands tangled in his hair as she arched against him, legs pulling him tight to her warm body. Determined to make the most of what little uninterrupted time they had, he made quick work of divesting Bianca of the slip dress she'd been teasing him with all evening.

"I wonder what it's like having morons for haunt elders," he grumbled as he and Bee trudged into their bunker. "It's probably pretty chill. No damage assessments, no contingency plans, no ramification spreadsheets. Just eating, fucking, and sleeping."

Bee swatted his chest half-heartedly, the heaviness of the evening's discussion showing in the circles under her eyes. "I'm going to shower. You think up a cool name for us. Something 'dynamic duo'-y, but without the cheese factor."

After she was officially deemed a Kaius hauntmate, the rest of the evening had quickly morphed into a discussion about the revolt and their place in the developing movement. Dawn had come and gone, with Jagg finally putting an end to the conference when he saw Bianca's head bob for the third time. He'd carried her to bed only to wake the next night alone, his lover already going head-to-head with Nichol over clothing orders while Rhys and Kaius observed, wisely silent.

The second night had gone much like the first, the dialogue morphing into Dovidas, Chen, and the female Deviants. Despite their repeated assurances the Deviants were indeed women, Kaius and Nichol held looks of reservation whenever he or Bianca reiterated the information.

No one, not even Dovidas, was foolish enough to believe he could rein in female Deviants for long. It was a death wish.

The shaking of her hair drew his eyes up from Bianca's breasts to her face.

"They stay on," she insisted, swatting his hand away from her panties. Black with red embroidery. He had memorized them earlier and had brought up the image hundreds of times over the past hour. "My butt will get cold on this counter."

He hesitated for a fraction before switching tactics. He unzipped his cargos, slipped the fabric barrier to the side of her thigh, and buried himself in her heat.

Even through the poor video quality, he could see the pure elation Mickey extolled as Nichol testily informed the hauntmate the missing women Mick was tracking were indeed a link to Dovidas. Although he couldn't read Mickey's lips when he turned away from the camera to speak to someone, Audra's appearance at Mickey's side filled in the blanks.

Nichol was unimpressed.

The first BRP mission was nearing its closure, the first small contingent of former bloodslaves scattered throughout Santa Fe and Albuquerque. Mick and the others would be arriving before dawn of the next evening, Louis having successfully erased all memories the humans held of their time in the quarters.

Despite the amicable discourse at the start of the third evening, the topic of discussion had eventually turned to Lincoln. Jagger was properly chastised by Kaius for his role, for his lack of forethought regarding the widespread implications his actions bore. However, it was Bianca who received the longest, severest admonishments. Rhys and Nichol ganged up on her, going so far as to physically silence him when he attempted to intervene on her behalf.

One harsh glare from Bee during the last of his valiant interjections was significantly more effective than a combined two millennia of strength holding his mouth shut.

Even Boy had made his displeasure with her

decisions known. As Bee attempted to rationalize her insistence on joining him in his inspection of the abandoned haunt outside Salina, Boy's gigantic boot made contact with the com room table, sending it skidding across the room.

His uncharacteristic outburst froze Nichol and Rhys in place, their uncertainty over Boy's next move evident in their refusal to react. Jagg had instinctively jumped up, placing himself between Bianca and the old vampire.

Of course, Bee had scurried around him and walked straight into the line of fire. As she reached up to pat Boy's cheek, cooing reassurances, he could see Nichol and Rhys rise slowly in preparation to attack.

At least he wouldn't die alone if Boy went off the deep end.

He stilled inside Bianca, looked toward the entranceway of the weapons room, and dropped his head to her neck.

"Fuck off."

Rhys's form remained in the doorway. "I can wait, man. No hurry. I've already burned fifteen minutes playing solitaire out here. I can spare another two."

His hauntmate disappeared from the doorframe, his shadow remaining on the hall floor.

He didn't have to see Bianca's expression to know she was laughing. And wholly out of the moment. Her tiny body shook against him for all the wrong reasons as she dislodged her hands from around his neck and pushed his weight off her. He reluctantly handed her dress over, watching wistfully as her perfect breasts disappeared under the fabric.

"I really fucking hate him," he grumbled as he

tucked his protesting erection back into his cargos and yanked the fly up.

Rhys sauntered back into the weapons room, fangy smile on his face.

****

Bianca wasn't the least bit fooled by Jagger's continual smoothing down of her dress as Rhys poked around the Deepfryer with interest. The poor guy had just been cockblocked moments from the finish line. She could toss him a bone or two.

When he finished his perusal of the light unit, Rhys turned to them and leaned against the wooden enclosure, absently scratching at his arm. "I'm not sure you two are legally allowed to be doing that anymore," he opened, grinning when Jagger flipped him off. "And yes, I will never let this whole blood-family thing go. It's too good to waste, and I intend to taunt you mercilessly with it until the end of time." He paused a moment, chuckled, and shook his head. "I'll file that one away for later. Anyways. Bianca."

She relaxed against the pillar of muscle behind her and crossed her arms.

"We've known each other a long time," Rhys continued slowly, all humor disappearing from his face. "You know I have immense respect for you, and I've always been proud of how you turned out. However, Jagger is my blood. Amalgamation or not, he is, and will always be, where my first priority lies."

Jagg's arms snaked around her waist, a low growl reverberating in his chest.

"Shut the fuck up, boy," Rhys barked, rolling his eyes. "Bee, every move you make from here on out affects Jagg and therefore affects me. Despite all your perfections, you and I both know you're up against decades of training to appease the vampires in your sphere. You're also reactionary with a pretty amped up vengeance streak. And none of that is good when living in a haunt or when working intimately with large numbers of vamps. Take it for what it's worth, but if any of these faults bring about the death of my hauntmate, I will personally make it my mission to end you."

She stepped back as Jagger launched himself around her and tackled Rhys to the floor. Kicking aside the few loose blades scattered on the ground, she ensured they remained out of reach while the hauntmates grappled, fists and fangs flying. Hopping back up on Jagg's workbench, she watched the scuffle, noting Rhys's controlled counter-reactions to Jagger's relentless assault.

"Rhys," she called. "Could you please get his attention for me?"

The elder vamp flipped Jagg onto his back, using his thighs to restrain him as he forced Jagger's head in her direction.

"Hey, honey." She smiled. "While he could have perhaps spoken with more finesse—" She paused to give Rhys a pursed disapproval. "—I believe he was merely giving me the standard 'mess with my best friend, mess with me' speech, as only an obtuse, inelegant Kaius male can. Am I right, Rhys?"

Rhys nodded, adding a quick elbow hit to Jagger's rib cage when his brother snapped his fangs.

She jumped down to the floor and knelt beside Jagg. "And this is where I assure Rhys I have no intention of placing you or myself in danger. I understand his concerns, and I'm so mindlessly devoted to you, so completely in love with you, he has nothing to worry about. Are we all on the same page now?"

****

Jagger was pretty certain Rhys had left the room.

And if he hadn't, oh-fucking-well.

Bianca's slip dress was currently pooled around her waist as she straddled him on the workroom floor, and the visual was erasing all rational thought from his mind. She reclined back against his bent legs, her fingers lightly pinching the firm peaks of her nipples as he thrust up into her slowly.

It was killing him.

A good death, for sure.

He released his grip on her thighs momentarily and pushed the dress up so he could watch as he pushed inside her heat.

"Damn," he muttered, adjusting his hips slightly to bring her more upright. When the change in angle sent a jolt through her, he clenched his teeth and increased his speed.

No way was he going to lose it first.

But the threat was definitely looming as one of her hands dropped to his calves and her nails dug into his skin.

He locked his gaze on her lips, mesmerized by the chanting of his name and the light sheen of sweat covering her body as her eyes closed. Her small hand wrapped around his and guided it toward her sweet spot, her head lolling back onto his knees when his skin made contact.

And when she held her hand over his, guiding his movements, he nearly came undone.

Although seduction and enticement were key teachings for Tenders, taking the lead during sex was definitely not. Her blatant commandeering of his actions was, in a word, reallyfuckinghot.

She gently adjusted his speed and pressure, the shudders rippling through her body the only encouragement he needed to follow her lead. As her breathing became faster, her thighs tightened around his waist.

"Faster," she demanded breathlessly, tapping his hand before she gripped his other and brought it to her throat.

Yes, ma'am.

He dug his booted heels into the cement floor, watching her intently as he hit vamp-speed. When his fingers felt the vibrations of her moans, he grew impossibly harder, his back arching off the ground.

"Fucking damn," he grunted, certain his back molars were cracking with his effort not to come before she did. When her body began tightening around him, he forced his eyes open to watch her.

So goddamn beautiful.

The first fluttering of her orgasm ricocheted through him, breaking his concentrated tempo for a beat. The unintended lull was just long enough for him to hold off his own moment as the sensation of her moans traveled along his fingers. But when her hands flew to his thighs, nails drawing blood as she came hard around him, he released inside her with a feral groan, his hips bucking against hers. He was vaguely aware of her bringing his hand to her face as he came, and acutely aware of it when her blunt teeth bit down on his wrist.

Fucking. Damn.

The unexpected bloodletting compounded the intensity of his orgasm as he fell into the sensation of her taking both his blood and his body. As the final tremors shook his limbs and hips, his vision returned, the fog of ecstasy slowly lifting.

She looked down at him with satisfaction, licking the red stain of his blood from her lips. "That's how I like it," she stated smugly. "Let's try again, shall we?"

Chapter Thirty-nine

Rhys rose to his feet and adjusted Simone's stance, bending her knees a fraction more and nudging at her lower back to correct the sway of her spine. Resuming his seat against the wall, he continued to toss small rubber balls her way, barking instructions as she sliced her knife through most, missing a few.

The sounds coming from the weapons room reassured him both his best friend and his greatest creation were, indeed, on the same page.

When the box of balls ran dry, he hoisted himself up and retrieved the blade from Simone. "Beautifully done," he complimented, motioning to the destruction surrounding them. "Get this cleaned up and shower before you check in on Kaius and Nichol. If they don't need anything, the rest of the evening is yours."

Simone nodded, her chest heaving with the exertion of her practice. "Will you be around later?" she asked, a gleam of calculated desire flickering in her eyes.

He shook his head and headed toward the door. "Sorry, cupcake. I have some shit to deal with before dawn. If I'm in the mood, I'll track you down later."

Bianca was right. Simone was going to ash a vampire in the near future. And he was currently in negotiations with her target.

He entered the com room and flopped onto a chair. "Lay it on me, Nicky," he said, scanning the computer monitor for clues.

Nichol flung a pen at his head, grunting when he dodged it. "All the major networks have picked up the interview," he stated, motioning toward the screen as it sprang to life. "Representation has been split pretty evenly down the middle so far, with half presenting her as a victim, the others portraying her as an accomplice. Social media shows a similar divisiveness among the human population. A classic hero/villain spin, depending on who's examining the info."

He watched the interview unfold on the screen. "What the fuck did she do to her hair?" he muttered. "It's the same color as your new phone."

"Pretty sure that's the biggest problem you're facing right now," Nichol replied drily, turning up the volume.

Returning his attention to the woman's statements, he rolled his shoulders and slapped quickly at the burning sensation crawling across his bicep. He should have insisted on her return months ago. It would have meant a little extra paperwork, but it would have been immensely less trouble than a full hour-long interview broadcasted across network television.

He and Nichol sat in silence as the questions and answers flowed, neither commenting on the public relations disaster unfolding before their eyes. With every revelation, he hunched further onto his knees. By the time Lis's face faded from the screen, he was flat across the com room table, his wrists extended toward Nichol.

"Wayward Tenders are going to be the fucking death of me."

A word about the author…

Katja Desjarlais is a music teacher by day and a paranormal romance writer by moonlight. She is an unapologetic music addict and has an obsession for bad Bach puns despite her irrational aversion to Baroque. Her favorite words include "plethora" and "dapper," and she is physically repulsed by the word "moist." Katja's interest in the paranormal can be traced to her early childhood film choices and to the revolving book collection on her phone.

Desjarlais lives in the Okanagan Valley with her husband, three children, and three cats. Her ideal summer vacation is spent traipsing through the United States with her family and attending heavy metal concerts.

Visit her at:

katjadesjarlais.wordpress.com

Thank you for purchasing
this publication of The Wild Rose Press, Inc.

For questions or more information
contact us at
info@thewildrosepress.com.

The Wild Rose Press, Inc.
www.thewildrosepress.com